CHRIST̶͟ ̶ ̶I̶O̶N̶)

ROTHERHAM L̶ ̶ ̶ ̶ ̶ ̶ ORMATION SERVICE

2 0 MAR 2013 *DINNINGTON* ''/16		
3 0 MAY 2013		
WICKERSLEY		
MALTBY ²⁰¹⁵ ''\15		
1 3 JAN 2016		

This book must be returned by the date specified at the time of issue as the DATE DUE FOR RETURN.
The loan may be extended (personally, by post, telephone or online) for a further period if the book is not required by another reader, by quoting the above number / author / title.

Enquiries: 01709 336774

www.rotherham.gov.uk/libraries

Published by Accent Press Ltd – 2003

ISBN 0 9544899 1 8

Copyright © The authors 2003

The rights of the listed authors to be identified as the authors of these works has been asserted by them in accordance with the Copyright, Designs and Patents Act 1988

The stories contained within this book are works of fiction. Names and characters are the product of the authors imaginations and any resemblance to actual persons, living or dead, is entirely coincidental.

All rights reserved. No part of this book may be reproduced, stored in a retrieval system, or transmitted in any form or by any means, electronic, electrostatic, magnetic tape, mechanical, photocopying, recording or otherwise, without the permission in writing from the publishers, Accent Press Ltd, Pembroke Dock, Wales.

After the Wink by Carolyn Steele Agosta, published at Conversely, July 2001, and at East of the Web, March 2003. Almost by Lynne Barrett-Lee published by QWF Magazine in January 1998. Make Me No Promises by Sue Dukes in Jade, Australian magazine in 1996. A Magazine Christmas by Katie Fforde, first published as The Secret of Roast Potatoes, in You Magazine for the Daily Mail, November 2002. Christmas Stockings by Christina Jones first published December 2000 in that's life! Comfort and Joy by Christina Jones first published in December 2001 in that's life! Santa's Little Helpers by Jan Jones, first published December 1994 in Loving Magazine. Forbidden Fruit by Caroline Praed first published in Bella magazine, 1996. Just Like Old Times by Pam Weaver first published January 2001 in Take A Break Fiction Feast. Carla's Gift by Jane Wenham-Jones first appeared in QWF in 1997

Printed and bound by Cox & Wyman Ltd, Reading
Cover design by Brian Cookman

This book is dedicated to the scientists who are striving to find a cure for breast cancer and the fundraisers who support their work.

We would like to thank the authors and Brian Cookman (cover designer) for generously donating their work.

ROTHERHAM LIBRARY SERVICE	
B53043071	
Bertrams	15/02/2013
AF	£6.99
MAL	

Contents

A Magazine Christmas	Katie Fforde	1
After the Wink	Carolyn Steele Agosta	9
Make Me No Promises	Sue Dukes	15
The Fragrance of Lemons	Jeanette Groark	29
Wedding Day	Lesley Cookman	41
Santa's Little Helpers	Jan Jones	47
Almost	Lynne Barrett-Lee	63
Peaches	Jo Mazelis	77
Birthday Special	Liz Young	93
May Day May Day	Liza Granville	107
Christmas Stockings	Christina Jones	111
Fantasy Lovers	Rosie Harris	119
I Saw Mummy Killing Santa Claus	Robert Barnard	125
Forbidden Fruit	Caroline Praed	145
Memory	Sara MacDonald	151
Edward Lewis Gambit	Sophie Weston	155
Christmas Wish	Tina Brown	175
Mixed Messages	Bernardine Kennedy	183
Just Like Old Times	Pam Weaver	189
Ten	Hazel Cushion	195
Nibbling at Nachos	Bill Harris	199
Stormy Weather	Sue Dukes	203
Crumbs of Affection	Biddy Nelson	215
Something in the Water	Sarah Salway	221
Comfort and Joy	Christina Jones	231
Are Diamonds Forever?	Sue Moorcroft	239
Wanting Wanted Wanton	Linda Mitchelmore	255
First In, Last Out	David Wass	265
Liberation	SophieWeston	269
Carla's Gift	Jane Wenham-Jones	277

A Magazine Christmas
By Katie Fforde

'As it's the first time they've come to us for Christmas, I really do want it right.'

Jess knew all this perfectly well. Even if she hadn't endured seven perfect Christmases at her in-laws' Georgian rectory, her husband had been telling her since October. And ever since October, she had been dreading it.

'You did make the puddings when I told you?' her husband went on.

Jess nodded, wondering if she should mention he had a fleck of shaving soap on his neck, or not bother.

'And you ordered the free range, corn-fed bronze turkey from that farm in Norfolk?'

'What?'

'Through the butcher? You did do that, darling, didn't you? The right bird is crucial.'

'Oh yes. Through the butcher.'

'You should really pick it up today.'

'It's only the twenty second. Where am I going to keep it?'

'I cleared a space in the shed. It should be fine in there. Oh, and the ham. I hope you ordered a big enough one. I'd better give you some money.'

Dominic, supremely elegant, except for the shaving

foam, took out his wallet and produced an alarmingly thick wodge of twenty pound notes. 'I know old Higgins doesn't take credit cards – lives in the dark ages - so you'll have to pay him in cash. Bloody good butcher, though.'

Jess reflected that 'bloody good' was the right sort of epithet for a butcher.

'Here.' Dominic handed her the money.

'Will it be all that?' Jess looked at it. Living in a mostly cashless society, she had not seen so much of it in one lump for ages, if ever.

'Oh yes, and the rest. Here, you'd better have a bit more.'

'Darling, that's over two hundred pounds! For a turkey and a ham!'

'It's not all for the turkey, Pumpkin, it's for the stuffing. Now don't let Higgins fob you off with ready made sausage meat, get him to do you some specially. Have you got a list of the other stuffing ingredients?'

'They're in the book, aren't they?'

'Yes, well make sure you don't forget anything, like pine nuts, or pecans. And we need two stuffings, one each end.'

'It's not considered good practice to cook the stuffing actually in the turkey,' said Jess.

'Rubbish! My mother's always cooked the turkey with the stuffing in. Never done anyone any harm.' He pecked her cheek, giving her a good whiff of exquisite after-shave. Sometimes Jess thought his after-shave was what she liked best about her husband, that and his beautiful suits.

When she had loaded the dishwasher with their two coffee cups, two plates, two saucers and two (brand name) knives, she washed the orange squeezer and the glasses by hand. Dominic didn't like her to put glasses in the dishwasher. As she smoothed on her hand cream afterwards, she wondered about all that money on the kitchen table.

Dominic was a kind husband, at least, he thought he was. He didn't expect her to work while they waited to start a family, and was happy for her to spend a couple of afternoons a week doing watercolours. He didn't even comment on the fact that after three years of trying, she hadn't yet become pregnant - at least, not often. He did make reference to his brother's huge and noisy progeny sometimes, implying that if his brother could father so many children, the problem couldn't possibly lie with him. His family, it was acknowledged, was perfect. And, with his family, so was Christmas.

The first Christmas she had spent with them, as a bride, she had been enchanted, if overwhelmed by the ritual, the perfection, the enormous quantity of food, the impression that this was the house on which every magazine Christmas special was based.

The decorations were traditional but perfect. Dominic's mother made her own Christmas wreath out of holly which obediently produced berries, every year. Swags of greenery decorated both huge fireplaces and even the downstairs loo had a jug of rosemary and box.

The tree, real, of course, and ten feet high was decorated with glass baubles from Bavaria, antique angels, real crystal snowflakes and hand carved cherubs. There was nothing on it that wasn't tasteful, no bells made out of egg boxes and tin foil, Santas made from lavatory rolls and crepe paper, no cotton wool snowmen. It didn't even have lights, but proper candles, in holders which had been in the family for aeons.

Jess had never asked Dominic to go to her parents at Christmas, not after that time when they were first engaged, and he was so stiflingly polite. Her parents were very understanding and never made a thing of it.

This year, because they were having the house re-wired and new central heating put in, Dominic had persuaded his parents to leave their beautiful house in the country, and have Christmas with them, in their terraced house in town.

'We've got to show them that we can do it right,' Dominic had said, so many times that Jess stopped listening. He didn't mean 'we' anyway, he meant 'her.'

It may have been her inability to produce children that made her unsatisfactory to her parents in law, but with so many grandchildren, Jess didn't think so. She was unsatisfactory because she wasn't enough of a homemaker, wasn't educated to the required high standard and wasn't connected to any ancient families. She just wasn't posh enough.

So there it was, a big pile of money on the table.

She should really have told Dominic that she hadn't made the puddings on Stir-Up Sunday, as requested. He'd been away, and she'd gone to see a film with a girlfriend, thinking she'd do it another day. Somehow the day when she felt willing to spend all day cutting special whole candied fruit into cubes, stoning raisins, and getting the grit out of Vostizza currents, and then to fill the kitchen with steam never came.

She also should have mentioned that when she went into Higgins, the 'bloody good butcher', who leered and leched and intimidated Jess, he had gleefully told her that she was too late to order a turkey, and that next year she'd have to be better organised.

So, all that money to spend on a turkey, (and a York ham) and neither turkey nor ham forthcoming. She picked up the money, stuffed it into her wallet, and got ready to go shopping.

She stood at the bus stop, wondering where to buy food of the appropriate quality, and decided on Selfridges. It was a pity that on the way she spotted a little boutique that had a sale on. She hopped off the bus at the next set of lights and went back to it.

She came out feeling light headed, wearing all her new clothes. She felt so light headed that she went into a café for coffee and ordered white wine instead.

'What is happening to me?' she wondered, looking at the much depleted amount of money in her purse. 'Why aren't I doing what I was told?'

It was the cash that did it, she realised. She and Dominic shared a credit card, but he went through the bill with a very sharp eye. She couldn't possibly have put the bright, slightly hippy clothes she was wearing on the card. There was a sort of blousy sexiness about the way the top fell of her shoulder slightly, showing far more cleavage than she usually did. Dominic would hate it; he liked her to shop at Aquascutum.

She sipped her wine and considered her plight. She was going to get into an awful lot of trouble. She even wondered if Dominic would instigate a divorce, his grounds being not taking Christmas seriously enough – an especially heinous crime when they were having his parents.

They'd already broken several taboos. They weren't having people in for drinks on Christmas morning, when real people were in their dressing gowns, opening presents, drinking sweet sherry. Dominic's parents, Sebastian and Margot, served Buck's fizz, hot sausage rolls and mince pies to women who wore court shoes and men who asked Jess every year if she was pregnant yet. When told that she wasn't they told her she was a career girl and that she shouldn't put it off too long. 'The old biological clock is ticking away!' they would say, as if they were the first, and then they would pat her bottom.

Jess had also refused to carve the potatoes into perfect ovals, as suggested by Gary Rhodes. Margot had been doing it for years, long before Gary Rhodes appeared on television and Dominic mentioned them when he was promising to help.

For once, Jess had been adamant. 'If your mother chooses to make sculptures out of her roast potatoes, that's fine, but I'm not doing it. I won't have time.'

'Mother always has time, and she had children to look after.'

'That's low, Dominic, and you know it is!' Using this as an excuse, she had disappeared into the spare room and slept there, glad to be spared his tedious lovemaking.

She'd also argued against having a starter, but lost that battle. She'd agreed on segmented oranges and grapefruit, in some sort of alcohol. When she'd have a moment to scrape pith off the fruit, which would be walnut sized by the time she'd finished peeling it with a knife, she didn't yet know. Dominic was going to prepare a time table for her, which would presumably tell her.

Jess was gloating over the beautiful, purple, jewel encrusted mules she had bought to go with her outfit, when a man asked if he could share her table. Guiltily, Jess thrust the shoe back in its box.

'You're not Cinderella, are you? If so, can I be your Prince Charming?' He was older than Dominic, more solid, with smiling eyes and a very attractive voice.

'I know this is the pantomime season, but no, I'm not Cinderella. I was just admiring the shoes I've just bought, and wondering if they were worth it.'

'Can I get you another glass of wine? Then you can show me your shoes.'

Jess may have denied being Cinderella, but he was definitely charming, if not actually a prince. He admired her shoes, he made her laugh, he made her feel attractive, and best of all, he was extremely impressed when she told him what she'd done with the turkey money. 'A woman of spirit, I see. How interesting.'

Dominic had never found her interesting.

Jess wore all her new clothes, including the purple mules for Christmas dinner. She had insisted on serving the meal in the evening, or according to the timetable Dominic created on his computer, she would have to get up at five am to start cooking the turkey.

Jess felt wonderful; accomplished, beautiful and in control. Aware of the change in her, Dominic gave her a glass of champagne before wrapping himself in blue stripes and heaving the turkey out of the oven to rest. When they all sat down to eat he raised his glass to her admiringly.

'This is splendid darling!'

The turkey was admired by everyone. 'So moist, well done Jess!' said Sebastian. 'We'll make a cook of you yet.'

'I always do say, buying the right bird is vital,' said Margot.

Jess offered a small prayer of thanks to Bernard

7

Matthews and helped herself to roast potatoes, which, she was pleased to note, were browner and crisper than ever her mother-in-laws had been.

Dominic laughed, sounding terribly like his father. 'I say choosing the right *bird* is what counts. Eh, darling? You're looking particularly lovely tonight.'

Jess inclined her head. Choosing definitely was important; what to wear, what to spend your money on and when to tell her husband that she was leaving him – for a man with smiling eyes, who appreciated fabulous shoes and who told her the secret of roast potatoes.

After The Wink
By Carolyn Steele Agosta

It starts out so harmlessly.

I don't really mean anything by it, I'm just in one of those moods. I mean, when you're fortytwo years old and have three kids and a husband and responsibilities, who figures on finding excitement, too? Other than bad excitement, like when you have to hit the brakes hard and all your blood vessels get a quick *yee-ha*.

It's true, I've been noticing men a lot lately. Their arms, in particular. Don't ask me why, but I've become fascinated with men's arms. Forearms, lightly furred, with those lines of tendons and the swell of muscle below the elbow that women just don't have. And men's hands, square and capable. I see them everywhere. In restaurants, at gas stations, in the middle of the aisle at the freakin'K-Mart, for god's sake. It's embarrassing to know I'm lusting in Lawn & Garden.

It's not just the young men either, mind you. I've been noticing older men, too. Men in their forties and fifties, men who maybe think no woman is looking at them that way any more. Mostly I like the ones who still have plenty of hair and rugged looking faces, who look like they still get some, you know? Ponytails too, on older men, catch my attention. Here's a guy who thinks young, I figure. I could be wrong. Maybe he's just a guy who hates going to the barber.

Anyway, I'm sitting there at the coffee shop, I'm reading a book by Robin Hemley and it makes me laugh out loud. I look around to see if anyone notices and there's a man smiling at me. He's good-looking too. He's sitting at one of the tables, reading a magazine, and it's not just any magazine, not about motorcycles or computers or entertainers, it's the *New Yorker*. The guy's literate, for crying in the sink.

I give him a little smile. Going back to my reading, I shift in my seat, cross my legs, straighten my back a little. Knockers up, my aunt used to say. I rest my chin on my hand, arching my neck a little. That's body language for "I'm interested". Or something like that. A customer near the front makes a huge mess by dropping her coffee, the tray clattering to the floor. I take a quick glance at Mr. Attractive and he's looking at me. So I smile. And then, God help me, I wink.

Now it's just a little wink, just an acknowledgement that he's there and I'm there and we both see the humour of the situation and that, perhaps, we're somehow both a little more in the know than the average joker and already have this little connection - and that's all it is. I swear.

But it's enough.

Because next thing I know, he's picking up his coffee and his *New Yorker* and he's coming over to me, doing that little raised eyebrow thing to ask if he can join me and I'm nodding, nodding, thinking I don't quite believe this. He asks me about my book and I ask him about his magazine and I mention, modestly, that I'm a writer and he mentions, modestly, that he's a musician, and even though we're really a bookkeeper and a systems analyst, we understand that we're not defined by our paying jobs. I tell him my name and he tells me his and it's one of those names I always admired. He has a little bit of curly black-grey-white hair coming out of the collar of his shirt. His eyes crinkle at the corners and his forearms flex as he leans forward on his elbows to talk to me in low tones that require that I lean forward too. I smile to show my dimples and hope that I don't have coffee breath and we keep talking. About books and music and the theatre. About the way that parking is getting impossible in this town and how traffic is ridiculous. He mentions that he lives near South Park and I mention that I'm over by the university and pretty soon our coffee is cold and it's somehow gotten to be an hour later.

It's really time for me to leave and he walks me to my car, which thank heavens is decently clean, with no McDonald's Happy Meal figures on the front seat. He mentions that he's going to the poetry slam next Friday because his friend is playing flute for some poet and I mention that I've never been to a poetry slam and he says I should try it. So I say maybe I will and I drive away with my hands perspiring on the steering wheel.

I have no complaints about my husband, that has to be understood. He's loving and thoughtful and sexy and he picks up his socks and puts down the toilet seat. But on Friday night I'm at the damn poetry slam, trying to look like I'm enjoying it but really keeping an eye out for Mr. Handsome only I don't see him and feel like a fool and I'm just getting ready to leave (I mean it, I'm only giving it five more minutes) when he walks in. And he winks at me.

The place is crowded and noisy, people are talking to

each other and completely ignoring the woman in purple tights and purple hair who is bellowing some poem about spaghetti, and when he takes my elbow and leads me away to a quieter corner, a little thrill runs right up my arm. He asks if I want to get out of there and I nod and suddenly my knees are way too loose and I'm afraid that if I walk, they'll bend backwards, the wrong way, which would not be attractive at all.

I manage to pull myself together and we get in our cars and I follow him to a bar, which is quiet and low-lit and has a nice band playing oldies. We talk and dance and his arms go around my waist, which has mostly been used to apron strings and babies' monkey legs and my husband's arms. Which are also nicely hairy and brown and have those good corded muscles. Which I'm trying not to think about just like I'm trying not to mention that both Mr. Gorgeous and I are wearing wedding rings. Because we are, and we're not kidding ourselves that this is anything but an exercise in visibility.

You see, it seems to me that after 40, you become invisible. Oh, you're still there and people see you but they don't really *see* you. They see this person whose daughter is now an adult and whose mother is now a child and who's supposed to hold everything together. A person who couldn't possibly have desires and doubts and unfulfilled longings. A person who is still, improbably, perhaps imperceptibly, a person.

I take a good look at Mr. Still-Has-It and I can see that he loves rock'n'roll and would look good behind the wheel of a Corvette and yet has a bit of anxiety about how he looks to a younger woman. Which I am, to him. So I smile and flirt and he flirts back and it feels real good. We dance and I think about how strange it is to be in the arms of someone else, another man, a man who is a bit taller and bulkier than my husband, with a different voice and different lips and different eyes. It feels so weird, and then it feels even weirder when he kisses me, which he does, right there in the middle of the dance floor. I haven't kissed another man on the lips in over 20 years and now his mouth is on mine, and it's different, a different touch and taste and style. More than that, it's real, I'm really here and I'm doing this thing.

I start to shake, start to vibrate like a goddamn tuning fork, until he probably thinks he's such a good kisser that I'm going into orgasm, but actually I'm about three counties away from an orgasm. I'm just shaking with fear because I realize that I'm thinking about a lot more than kissing and that scares the hell out of me.

He laughs a little, softly, in a pleased sort of way, and I blush all the way to my fingernails and we go back to the table. He's looking at me and I think, *yes, look at me.* I'm not ready to be old, to have all my fun behind me. I want to shimmy when I dance, and wiggle when I walk. I want a man to look at me and get a little *yee-ha* of his own.

Then I begin to think that maybe this is why people cheat in the first place. To have this warm glow that comes from someone else's eyes. To remember who they are and not to be the person that everyone thinks they are and, a little bit, not to be the person they know they are.

I look at him too. I see a man who's just as scared as I am of becoming invisible. Or being seen as past it, on the far side of manhood, as being old. So I reach across the table and take his hand (good hands, wide and blunt-fingered, the hands of a man who can fix things). I stroke his wrist, letting my fingers slide up that inner tendon and wonder whether it's his pulse that's thudding so hard under the skin, or mine. I think about all the things I've never done and all the things I'll never be, and I wonder if it's too late.

A rush goes through me, starting with my lips, making them feel warm and full, and I think, *damn, what a hell of a time for my first hot flash*. But it's not a hot flash. It's the realization that I'm not going to do a thing. Among all those things I wanted to do with my life, this wasn't on the list.

I give Mr. It-Might-Have-Been a quick kiss on the cheek. I'll have daydreams for a while about him, play with thoughts that should send me to confession, and keep the memory of his kiss for those days when I can't jump-start my own desires. I drive home and sit for a moment in the car, looking up at the light in the bedroom window.

You know, sometimes a wink is really just a nervous tic, a sudden twitch of muscles contracted in error by a mis-guided neuron, an accident of synapses gone awry. The muscles keep twitching until something clicks over and they smooth out, like a skip in an old 45 rpm record, and everything goes back to normal. The way it should be, I guess. The way it is. The way the music plays best.

Make Me No Promises
By Sue Dukes

Gloria pursed her lips towards the mirror and added a touch of gloss. There. She stood back and viewed herself. Was she overdressed for the occasion? She wasn't sure, yet for some reason she felt the need to impress.

She had only met Wade once before, and that had been at Julie's impassioned plea. 'It's only dinner,' she had cajoled, 'you can go on home afterwards, you know. No ties, no commitments. Pleeeease?'

'What do you need me for?'

'I've met this absolutely gorgeous guy,' her eyes had rolled suggestively. 'You have no idea. Anyway, we were all going out as a foursome, me and Darren, Christine and Wade, and now Christine has backed out, if you don't come Wade is going to play gooseberry all night, and it will be so embarrassing.'

'What is he? Some spotty teenager with greasy hair?'

'No, he's really quite nice, you know. Charming in fact,' she added as an afterthought.

'You've never met him,' Gloria had accused, reading the calculating glint in her eye.

'Well, no. But I know what Darren said. He's Darren's best friend. He's some sort of computer whiz who works too much, and doesn't have time to find lady friends.

That's why I told him Christine would come...'

She had thrown her eyes upwards. 'She'll come with anyone.'

'Glory! It's not like that. It's totally platonic. Believe me. And he'll pay for the dinner.'

'Platonic my ass. Man meets woman. Man buys woman a meal, man think woman owes him one.'

'OK, he is a one-night stand man, according to Darren, but he won't push himself. He doesn't need to. Apparently women fall over themselves to get into his bed, and if they don't well, he can afford to buy one.'

'Oh, my God. A damned Casanova!'

'Look, just because you've had one bad experience with a rich shit...'

'I don't expect to be taken for granted, that's all, and I've never slept with anyone I haven't been going out with, and never for money.'

'No-one's asking you to, believe me. Please?'

Afterwards Gloria couldn't think of a single good reason why she had accepted. Julie was doing her no favours, but was just looking after her own interests. Perhaps it had been the offer of a meal. Perhaps it was just because she was bored with her own company; whatever.

Strangely, it had been one of the nicest evenings she had ever had. And as to Wade, well, in spite of his computers, he was no square-eyed academic. And just as Julie had suggested, he was hot. He was older than she had expected, and was dressed kind of understated-expensive, and had that worldly-wise air of a man in charge of his life. He didn't even bat an eyelid when he paid the bill for the four of them. 'My treat,' he had said, his soft, cow-brown eyes melting her at a glance. In spite of her own assertions, she had felt a trickle of excitement fill her as those eyes wormed their way into her hardened heart, and she wondered, just fleetingly, whether it would be worth abandoning her unforgiving stance. But all that speculation went by the board, because in spite of his apparent reputation, he hadn't even asked to come back for coffee.

She had to admit she had felt vaguely disappointed at that moment. She had spent a lonely night imagining Julie and Darren sweating in the sack together, and trying to stop her vivid imagination from stripping the white polo-neck shirt from Wade to discover the hidden charms beneath. She'd bet her bottom dollar he was all muscle under that thin sheen of cotton.

But that had been days ago. Silence. No word, no acknowledgement, no thanks, no nothing. He was a one-night stand man, and she hadn't given him the goods. With a vague sense regret she told herself that perhaps it was just as well he wasn't as besotted by her as she had been by him.

And then he had phoned. Out of the blue. God, her toes had tingled at the deep and sexy tones of his voice. 'Hi, Gloria. It's Wade here, remember me....'

'I remember,' she had breathed.

There was laughter in his voice. 'How about doing it again, just you and me?' he asked. 'The candlelit dinner, the sizzling steaks and lashings of red wine. Are you game?'

My God, she thought, he was interested. She could feel it, even over the telephone. This was where she should say, with positive assertion: no thank you very much.

But had she? No, she had not.

And now the time had come for him to collect her, she

was almost afraid. Perhaps her imagination was fooling her. Perhaps in the light of day she would find her memory had been playing tricks. Maybe he was just ordinary, and didn't exude a sort of animal come-and-get-me appeal. Maybe he would just seem old, rather than sexy man-of-the-world. Maybe - long shot - they would truly find they liked each other....

She grinned at herself. Who was she fooling? That was surely the way to get damned-well hurt again.

There was a rapping on the door. She flinched, hesitated, then marched up and opened it determinedly. They stared at each other in silence for a moment. Then he smiled. A long, slow smile which reached right into her soul. 'I wondered if I could have been mistaken,'he said, his slow rich voice curling around the words. 'But I'm not. You're absolutely delicious and I could forgo the meal right now.'

My God, he was going to seduce her, she thought, and grabbed her bag hastily. 'Well, I could eat a whole cow,' she said. 'I'm starving.'

'Dinner it is, then.' He gallantly proffered an elbow, and she took it.

He made all the right moves, taking her coat, sliding her into her seat, and ordering the wine himself without embarrassing her with any overt displays of the connoisseur at work. 'You'll like this,' he said. 'Rich and mellow.'

'Like you,' she said, without thought.

He laughed, not offended, and his dark eyes undressed her slowly. 'It's just as well I didn't say rich and mature. That would have put me in my place.'

'Mature is supposed to be good in a man.'

'Maybe, if modern usage hadn't turned it into a euphemism for old. I hope I'm not past it, yet.'

She ignored the innuendo, and tasted the wine, startling a spontaneous laugh out of him. 'My, that's good!'

'You sound surprised.'

'I usually buy house red. I can see I have a lot to learn.'

'About wine?'

'Amongst other things,'she rejoined, casting him a sidelong glance.

'Perhaps I ought to take it upon myself to educate you further.'

She shivered as the words subtly betrayed another underlying meaning, but found herself fascinated by the thought rather than resentful.

'Tell me about yourself,' he said later, slicing through a rare and bloody steak with sensuous precision.

'Not a lot to tell,' she said, making a joke of a lifetime of disappointment. 'Failed school, failed marriage. No kids, thank God.'

'You don't want children?'

'Only if they've got a father.'

'I see.'

'Oh, don't be afraid,'she said bluntly. 'I'm not out fishing for a husband. I've just escaped from one unwholesome relationship, and I'm not about to enter into another. For now, I'm content to take things as they come. Enjoy the moment. And if it happens one day, well, it happens.'

'What, true love?'

'Do I detect sarcasm?'

'No. I think you detect a kindred spirit. Sex is sex, but for some, true love miraculously happens by.' His lips curled almost with sarcasm, suggesting that he never expected it to happen to him. 'Sleep with me, Gloria, if you will. Or not, if you prefer; but make me no promises, and I'll make you none.'

She gave a shout of laughter, then looking round guiltily, and gave a lop-sided grin. 'That is probably the most direct proposition I've ever had.'

'The most honest, perhaps. I fancy you. Later I would like to undress you in front of a roaring log fire, and make love to you. On an expensive Chinese rug worked in pastel shades; or brightly coloured Indonesian cushions, if you prefer,'he added diffidently. 'I can be versatile.'

Conscience warred against the stirring of lust, but she didn't have to answer. He could read the reply in her parted lips, her shortened breath, the high spots of colour in her cheek.

There was little said through that slow meal. They didn't rush. Beneath the red glow of the low lighting they savoured every bite, every morsel, and as flushed gazes lingered over the tops of empty glasses, each felt the warmth of anticipation slide and curl in secret places. There was no wondering 'if' this time, only 'when'; and somehow that foregone conclusion was even more erotic, spiced with a touch of devil-may-care bravado.

'Are you ready?' he asked eventually.

'Absolutely,' she replied softly, and when she arose his strong fingers brushed against her shaking arms as he helped her into her coat, sending a shiver of delight through her middle.

'My place?'

She stared at him. This was it, the time when she could say no, take me home. 'Yes,' she said.

He drove the plush car with quiet confidence.

Throughout the short journey they glanced at each other continually, each with a sort of surprised awareness at the depth of desire they felt, and deep inside Gloria knew she was not going to be disappointed. He was too sensitive, too absolutely overpoweringly astute not to be a good lover. And just this once she was going to be a one night stand. She was walking into it open-eyed, and would not regret her decision.

His house was in a quiet part of the town, secluded and select, though not overtly expensive, and as they walked in, the heat from a burning log fire reached out to welcome them.

She glanced at him with faintly accusing amusement.

He grinned back. 'Anticipation,' he told her without apology. 'I have a man who does odd jobs for me.'

'I see.' Warning bells jarred in her mind. Careful, she told herself. Very, very careful. You know exactly what this is about. Keep it firmly fixed in your pea-brain. Sex. No more, no less.

He settled her with a drink, and she melted into the embrace of a soft sofa, as the red glow of the flames to licked sensuously around white, split logs, driving away the damp autumn misery. She gazed around the room appreciatively. Everything was very tastefully decorated; a polished teak floor, plain walls, dark wood antique furniture, all of which complemented by brightly coloured fabrics and exotic ornaments. It was a room designed for wallowing in, for being comfortable in; for sex.

At the thought, her eyes flicked back to the broad shoulders of the man who had made this room what it was, designed it with meticulous attention to detail, perhaps subconsciously reflecting an integral warmth of character he was unwilling to betray to or share with his feminine partners.

She pursed her lips fractionally and smiled at the progression of her thoughts. No point being interested. No point thinking that this room was one she could get used to, that his taste was in perfect harmony with hers, and that she had never been so at ease with a man's presence. No point at all.

He had stated his terms categorically, and the only way to survive was to do as she had said: enjoy the moment. She had to bury the strange desire to unburden her deepest feelings to this man, and just allow herself to retain memories of a moment's pleasure which could be recalled over a lifetime, rather than a lifetime of disappointment through a single careless thought.

Heat pulsed from the fire's red heart to the outer edges of the room, almost too violent for comfort; but that was the intention. It was then that Wade knelt before her and took one of her feet in his hands. His eyes lifted, locked on hers, mesmerising her with the lust which spiralled from the hidden depths, and slowly he slid off the shoe to caress her stockinged foot. She shivered with strange delight, waves of sensual pleasure ripping through to her core.

No one had ever done that before.

He was in no hurry to reach in and grab what was clearly on offer. Now he was the connoisseur, sipping, tasting the wine, rolling it around in his mouth to savour the hidden bouquet. Only when both shoes had been removed, and every inch of her warm feet had trembled beneath his touch, did those strong, bewitching hands slide further up her calves, her knees, her thighs, tantalising her body into a frenzy of desire.

'You have no idea how much I've been wanting to do this,' he said huskily.

'I think I have,' she gasped.

A slow smile curved his lips, and he reached for hers. After that there were no more words; just the heat of the fire and the heat of their bodies glowing eventually in slow and rapturous unison.

And as they slowly kissed, gazing deep into the swirling depths of each other's eyes, their bodies became one. It was the magical melding of two individuals, as they moved slowly and sensuously to the age-long tune.

Finally heat drove them to frenzy, the most primitive of instincts taking over from conscious thought until they reached violent and necessary culmination. And later they sat naked and unashamed before the log fire, and talked, swirling rich, red wine into a riot of sparks in the light of the naked flames. What they talked of, Gloria did not recall, but what she did recall was the strange sense of belonging which wrapped her in a cosy, time-locked shell of happiness.

For a while, she forgot to guard her thoughts.

And then they made love again.

Wade continually surprised her with his sensitivity, with his unexpected consideration and concern that he was pleasing her as well as himself, and between spontaneous bouts of bodily pleasure they talked away the night. They talked, joked, laughed, and shared desires, dreams, and aspirations.

And then in the morning he went and spoiled it all.

She awoke draped in his strong limbs, and opened bemused blue eyes to meet brown eyes already shuttered with renewed lust.

'I love you, Gloria,'he whispered from the deep warmth of a huge bed, wrapped in the lingering scent of their loving. 'You are warm and passionate, and considerate, you have a lovely mind and a body which a man would kill for.'

And now he was moving, she could feel the urgency of his sex against her body; but no longer wrapped in the shielding cocoon of wine, his words chilled her.

'You don't have to use the word love for sex,' she said acidly. 'We both decided we wouldn't lie about it. It's sex. That's all. You are turned on by me, and have proved it a hundred times....'

'Slight exaggeration,' he murmured, lips twitching into the hint of a smile.

'Which is flattering in itself,' she carried on, heaving herself out of his arms and out of bed. 'So you don't need to lie about love. You don't want the commitment. You don't want a woman who tells you loving bedroom lies, and you promised you wouldn't do that to me. You promised.'

His smile died. He watched her dress, and she was aware of the anger she betrayed with every violent movement.

'I'm sorry,'he said. 'I shouldn't have said that.' He patted the rumpled sheets. 'Come back to bed. Erase those last foolish words from the memory.'

Now her hint of tears became obvious, and she tried to hide them. 'I'm not a damned computer. Word can't simply be erased. I want to leave. I should never have - but there was no point in wishing the night's work undone, any more than he could wish his words unsaid.

He pursed his lips, and began to rise.

She halted him with a raised hand. 'No. Please. I would like to walk. I think I need the air.'

'It's too far, you can't...'

'Then I will get a taxi! I don't want you to take me - '

'I think you're over-reacting. I wasn't thinking. I shouldn't have said that. I'm sorry.'

Strangely, his admission that he hadn't meant those few words fuelled her sense of betrayal into rage, and she was furious to the point of hot tears as she marched out of that house on her silly evening heels into a grim drizzle, without looking back.

Half way down the street she realised how silly she must look in her evening clothes, and strappy heeled sandals, and it was as she barged into a telephone box to call a taxi that she saw his car go by.

Was he looking for her, or just going about his business?

Strangely, she didn't allow herself to dwell on the hurts of that fateful encounter. That Wade was sorry, or interested in repeating the experience was made clear by the arrival of flowers, by messages of sincere apology on the answer- phone, but she replied to none of these. The kind of passion, the desperate physical awareness they had experienced was not love, and never would be. They had had a single night of unmitigated passion, no strings, no promises. That was all it was, and that was how she had to remember it.

In anything else lay heartache.

And yet every small nuance of his body, every warmly uttered phrase in that long night of loving echoed disturbingly around in her brain until she felt almost unable to carry on. Loving, she thought. Yes, that was what it had been. On her part, anyway. She berated herself for a fool - Julie had told her this man was a committed bachelor, a one-night stand man, and from his own mouth he had confirmed it. Fool, she told herself. Wake up to reality. Get on with your life.

So she got on with her life, and gradually the flowers stopped coming, the messages petered out. But far from providing her the satisfaction of having won, she felt inordinately sad, as though something was missing, as though life had lost its flavour.

Her previously vivacious and bubbling nature calmed to the mature and worldly-wise sadness of the newly bereaved. She saw life distantly with new eyes, and only occasionally wondered what Wade was doing with his own life. Was he still going on one-night stands, enjoying a woman whenever he could - without commitments or ties? Was he still using the same line: make me no promises, and I'll make you none?

It was a grey day in January, a dismal Christmas thankfully passed, when she stopped at the all-night shop on the way home. She had worked late, catching up with things left lurking on her desk during the madness of December, to realise belatedly that there was no food in the flat.

Tiredly, she loaded the bags into the car, and it was only when she stood up that she felt a strange sensation prickling between her shoulder blades. The sensation of being watched.

Slowly she turned.

She did not have to see his face clearly, she knew who it was by something more basic, more primitive. She would have known him in pitch dark; his presence a comforting shadow still in the darkness of her dreams.

And yet he was different. There was a hesitancy to his stance as he came towards her, and she realised he was unsure of his reception. Every cell in her body warned her to run, because she could not survive the hurt of lost love a second time. Eventually he stood there, a few feet away. She felt the unfair blossom of love swell her chest, she wanted to reach out to touch, to hold, but she didn't. She wrapped her arms around her chest, and hid her feelings behind the mask she had worn for those long three months.

'I've said a lot of silly things in my time,' he said finally. 'But saying I loved you wasn't one of them; apologising for saying it was. You see, I wasn't looking for true love, but that night it reached out and took me by the hand. I find I don't want to live without you.'

He held his hand out towards her.

Finally, of its own volition her own reached out to meet it.

The Fragrance of Lemons
By Jeanette Groark

Here I lie on the ground. I'm a fixture, a statue in the 'Garden of Fugitives'. I lie on my side, one arm tucked under my head, in a state of permanent sleep.

It wasn't always this way. Until the date of the explosion I'd lived all my life in Pompeii. As Julius Philippus, I resided with my wife, Livia and our two children, Marcus and Julia, on one of the city's main thoroughfares. Today it's known as the *Via dell'Abbondanza*; the men who came later named it thus. I was a magistrate, appointed by the Emperor Vespasian himself, and an amateur poet of some local renown. It would not be bragging to say that I was well respected among our citizens. Things were looking good and, on the face of it, I must have appeared satisfied and content with my life.

At least, I was until the day I saw Claudia. I did not mean to follow her but I couldn't resist. I acted on impulse, something that was normally anathema to me. I was crossing the Forum one afternoon in June when I glanced across to a nearby market stall and something caught my eye. A spark of gold glinted in the sun. But it was the gold of her hair that transfixed me; hair the colour of honey, which she wore piled high on her head, thick curls cascading to the nape of her neck. The reflection had come from one of the gilt pins which held it in place.

She was a slave, of course. With that dark yellow hair and her creamy complexion she could be nothing else. But, in her dress and adornments she appeared well cared for. I watched like a spy as she purchased some dates and figs, touching the fruit, feeling its texture and ripeness. Her fingers were tapering, careful. She joked with the stall-owner and I envied the pleasure of their intimate exchange. She said farewell then made her way towards the *Vicolo del Lupanare*, where she entered the house of Africanus and disappeared from view. *Vicolo del Lupanare*: the alley of the she-wolf. For those unfamiliar with my native tongue, *lupanar* was the name we used for a house of pleasure, a brothel, named after the howl of the she-wolf in heat. An irony, as I was the one who burned.

That day I entered the building for the first time, but I was to become a frequent guest. I knew what I wanted and I had the means to pay. Africanus gave a look of astonishment when he saw me, which he quickly masked.

'The girl with the golden hair?' He rubbed his stubble chin with his knuckles. 'Ah, yes,' he said, 'the new one. I named her Claudia, after the old Emperor's conquests.' He roared with laughter at his own wit. Everyone knew that Emperor Claudius had loved and married a whore and the double joke came from the fact that Claudius had conquered Britain. Claudia originated from that country.

'She's special,' he said, 'with that body and colouring. And she's a fresh one. It'll cost.' And so I paid, willingly.

I was led down a vestibule and upstairs to a cell-like room. It was stark but the upper level meant that it was one of the better rooms, for a better class of whore. The main piece of furniture, tucked into the far corner, was a masonry bed, covered with a palliasse, upon which was spread a worn quilt. Opposite, a rickety table bore an oil lamp from which spiralled a plume of smoke, leaving a shadow of soot curling up the corner. The whitewashed walls were decorated with suggestive frescoes as well as spattered with the graffiti of previous customers and inhabitants. My eyes alighted upon a daubing of a man with an enormous phallus being pleasured by a kneeling woman whose head he held towards his groin. I looked away, only to be assailed by another view of a woman straddling a reclining man. Their smiles were beatific. I swallowed and spun around, my courage gone. I had just decided to retrace my steps when the curtain was rustled aside and there she stood.

Claudia. She paused for a moment and put one finger to her lips, her gaze flickering up and down, appraising me, as if I were the one on approval. She gave a little shrug and flounced the skirt of her robe.

Her finger then pointed to a fresco. 'You like? This? Or this?' she asked in a lilting accent, turning to the lewd paintings one by one.

I had not thought that far and was feeling increasingly foolish. What was I doing in this dreadful place?

An awkward silence yawned between us. She must have decided that more direct tactics were required, because she slipped her robe from her shoulders and it dropped to the floor. Her skin was milky, appearing tender to the point of translucence, her body firm but shapely, the curls at the apex of her thighs a combination of dark honeys and golds. She raised her arms and began to let down her hair, the pins clattering onto the table. The movement caused her breasts to lift, the pink tips offered to me like a sacrificial gift. I exhaled sharply, suddenly realising that I'd forgotten to breathe.

She stepped closer and ran her fingers along my jaw, then closer still, her teeth nibbling softly, licking my ear, running her tongue down my neck. I grabbed handfuls of her hair and buried my face in it. Ah, Claudia. Even now I can smell her hair, the fragrance of lemons, mingled with the scents of wild thyme and rosemary which infused her chamber.

She quickly undressed me and we tumbled onto the bed. I took her face between my hands and rubbed a thumb over her mouth. The tip of her tongue darted out in response, sending a frisson of longing to my groin. I tried to kiss her lips but she turned her head and nipped my bicep. I rolled above her, my weight resting on my arms, the muscles taut as I readied myself. I was poised on a dilemma of longing. Part of me wanted to ram myself home while another was exhilarated by the anticipation of what was to come. Meanwhile Claudia lay beneath me, stretching sinuously like a cat, raising her pelvis to meet mine.

Before I knew what was happening, her hand was guiding me inside her, and my control shattered. Mindlessly, I thrust, my head in her hair which was spread across the pillow, my hands clutching at her flesh. I was desperate to touch her, to possess her. My senses meshed as I tried to postpone my release, to prolong the sensations, but it was futile. I raised my head and gasped for air, my chest heaving and sweating, while Claudia strained to lick the hollow of my neck.

'I'm sorry,' I said, looking at her through a glaze of

desire, and gave myself up to complete abandonment.

Afterwards, a boy attended upon us so that I could complete my ablutions. We lay on the bed, my arm underneath her neck, the other stroking her thigh. I was already beginning to want her again. My attention drifted around the room until one of the graffiti caught my eye and I twisted my head to read it. My body froze.

'Who wrote this?'

'I not know,' she replied, with a diffident shrug. 'What does it say?'

I contemplated lying then changed my mind. 'It says,' I looked down at her, an eyebrow arched, 'it says, 'Claudia has an arse like a peach'.'

'Oh,' she said, frowning, then, after a minute's silence, asked, 'What's a peach?'

My shoulders relaxed and I couldn't hide my smile. 'They come later in the summer,' I replied, kissing her temple. 'It's a succulent fruit, with a delicate skin which bruises easily. I'll bring one to you when they ripen. We have a peach tree in my courtyard.'

I went to kiss her lips and she turned her head. She evidently did not want this intimacy with a customer.

My head sank back into the pillow. I shouldn't have mentioned the graffiti or my home, which had caused reality to invade that tiny space. I shouldn't have tried to kiss her because then, when I knew I mustn't, it was the one thing I desired most in the world. I wanted to possess her lips more than her body. At once, the mood had been destroyed and my stomach began to churn with a myriad of feelings: jealousy, regret, guilt. Sensing this, Claudia shifted beside me and put her arms around my neck. She nuzzled my ear.

'You come again?'

'I don't think so,' I said. I got up and started to dress. Nothing more was said until I was ready to leave. As I pulled back the curtain she clutched my arm. 'Come back,' she said, her eyes large and mournful. 'I see you, yes? I give you gift, yes?'

'What can you possibly give to me?' I asked haughtily. I already had everything I could want and she, after all, had nothing.

She stood on tiptoe and kissed the corner of my mouth, then turned away. It felt like both a rebuke and a promise.

On the way out, Africanus was waiting for me.

'I thought you said she was new,' I said, feeling sourly antagonistic.

He smirked. 'I said she was new. I didn't say she was a virgin.' He scratched his neck. 'You can buy her outright if you like,' he said, naming an exorbitant price.

I knew my wife Livia to be both understanding and pragmatic but even she would baulk at such a transaction. Instead I feigned disinterest.

'I'll use the whore until I tire of her,' I said in an offhand manner. 'Here,' I added, throwing a purse onto the table, 'Take it or leave it.'

So, I bought the exclusive right to Claudia and, on the whole, I considered it a bargain.

I returned to an empty house. My family was visiting relatives on their estate near Herculaneum, which was both a blessing and a curse. Instead of having to focus my attention elsewhere I was able to indulge my own private thoughts. I feared I hardly knew myself, that I was discovering something that was at once both exciting and repugnant. More significantly, for the first time ever, I felt *alive*. Colours were brighter, objects in sharper focus, every sound distinguishable and magnified. And what of Claudia, the object of my obsession? Was she thinking of me? I scoffed at the notion but that didn't stop my daydreaming.

I couldn't settle. I paced the rooms, stared at the walls and wandered into the courtyard garden, which by then glowed as the sun dipped into the trees. I found myself before the peach tree, and plucked down a branch. The crop was green and hard, unripe but promising a good harvest. I put my nose to a cluster of tiny fruit and inhaled their acrid perfume.

The next day, after an interminable round of legal disputes and complaints, I found myself back at the archway of Priapus, leading to Claudia's room. The god leered at me as I crossed his threshold, his cock at attention. Claudia was waiting as I opened her curtain. She rose uncertainly from the bed and we stared at one another.

'Did Africanus tell you that you are mine?' I asked. My voice rang authoritatively in my ears but I was tingling with nerves. She gave a brief nod but did not move. 'Come here,' I said, and she came towards me, her hands locked by her sides. 'You said you'd give me something. Where is it?'

She raised her face and pressed her open mouth to mine, her soft lips moist and pouting. I sighed, sensations coursing through my body. I was like an untried youth enjoying his first embrace instead of a man in his late thirties. Claudia arched her back, pressing her breasts against me and I deepened the kiss, tonguing her mouth in mimicry of the sex that was to come. First, though, I enjoyed the gift of her kiss to the full.

Later, after a lengthy bout of lovemaking, I produced a small, kidskin pouch. 'This is my gift to you,' I said. 'Wear the contents for me but take care. If Africanus finds out he'll take them from you.'

She gave me a curious look, probably thinking me mad: an idea which wasn't far from my own thoughts. She fumbled open the strings and, peeping inside, her mouth and eyes turned into rounds of surprise and delight. She extracted a turquoise necklace and earrings which she then dangled from her fingers, turning and admiring them. She looked uncertain so I beckoned her closer and helped her to put them on, my fingertips brushing against her skin as I did so. She shivered and purred her pleasure, then lowered her chin in an attempt to look at the chain. She had no mirror so I offered to bring one on my next visit.

'I go with you, yes?' she asked, stroking my face.

I took her hands and kissed her palms, shaking my head. 'No, it's impossible, but I'll look after you. You are mine and no-one else's.'

'Yes,' she said, 'for now.'

'Forever,' I replied.

Before leaving that night, she removed the jewellery and returned it into my hands.

'You take home,' she said, 'and bring again. Then you bring this gift each time. You will come back, no?'

So that's what I did.

I had to find somewhere safe to secrete our cache. I felt like a thief, sneaking about my own house, looking for a suitable location to hide the jewellery. I discovered a nook at the back of the shrine where I prayed to Isis and used that as my hiding place. I covered the private recess with a plaque inscribed with a poem I'd composed in praise of the goddess.

The weeks passed and both the heat of summer and my passion for Claudia deepened.

'You smell sweet,' said Livia one evening when I returned, ostensibly from a trip to bathe and gamble with friends. She sniffed the air around my neck. 'Sort of sharp and herby. Like the countryside.'

I felt myself blush, my face a healthy glow. 'It must be those unguents they use at the bathhouse,' I lied.

Livia and I had married according to the wishes of our families. Ours had been a marriage of friendship, not of passion, but I knew she would feel betrayed by any hint of scandal which might sully her name or reputation. I also knew I should be less reckless, more careful in covering my tracks. I considered removing Claudia from the brothel and setting her up in her own house. It would be less dangerous, and was the custom of many men of my status and position.

Better still, though, I knew I should give up Claudia entirely. If such a liaison were to be discovered it would make our family the object of ridicule. I was treading dangerously and I knew it. I had already considered giving her up, a fleeting thought which I'd immediately quashed with a sense of panic. It was easier said than done. I couldn't imagine life without Claudia, but we couldn't go on in the same way. The lies, subterfuge and deceit were wearying. Next time I saw her I determined to do it. I had to finish the arrangement for all our sakes and, for once, I would act as nobly as my position dictated.

But I would see her just one more time.

On the day of my final visit I hurried to the *Vicolo del Lupanare*. I looked at the sky. It was late August and already the intense heat of morning had turned the day hot and sultry. The air was heavier than usual and black clouds were encroaching on the horizon as if in anticipation of a fierce storm. It suited my mood which was as dark and leaden as the atmosphere surrounding me. Claudia's jewellery was tucked inside its leather pouch which I carried in my hand together with a substantial sum of money to pay for her *manumitto*, her freedom. This was to be my parting gift.

The passing weeks had not dulled my desire for Claudia. We lay together all afternoon, the unspoken words forming a knot in my chest. Her exotic, citrus perfume invaded my senses until I could hardly breathe. Finally, as I opened my mouth to make my speech she slid from the bed, tossing me a look across her bare shoulder.

'Wait a moment, Yool' she said, pronouncing her nickname for me in an elongated way. 'You give me many presents, every day. I have gift for you.' The curtain shimmered and she was gone, a breeze travelling from the open window down the hallway of the bordello, escaping with her into the early evening.

I lay on the bed and waited, half in anticipation of what surprise she would bring, half in dread of her return when I would have to tell her that this would be the end of our affair. I turned onto my side and fingered the turquoise necklace, studying the simple, elegant setting in which it was crafted. After today, the turquoise pieces would be hers for good. I tucked my arm under the pillow, the necklace coiled in my fist and closed my eyes, remembering how the turquoise and silver droplets sat beneath her throat, like a mermaid's tears.

A bluebottle buzzed somewhere in the room and beyond,

through the open window, I heard the bustle of Pompeii. A fruit-seller was hawking his wares, offering peaches for sale. 'Juicy and sweet,' he called in a rasping voice, and then he made a lewd comment which was followed by the sound of Claudia's laugh. She was buying peaches and I looked forward to quenching my thirst. The air that day was especially dry. Peaches, I thought sleepily, she's found them for herself. Her backside was better than any peach, and I would tell her so when she returned.

I must have dozed off, for a sudden crack awoke me and I had hardly time enough to open my eyes before a cloud of dust, an impenetrable fog, overwhelmed my senses and I knew no more. That is, until the day when the light reclaimed me and I was momentarily freed, only to endure another form of imprisonment.

Here I now reside in the Garden of Fugitives, the links of Claudia's necklace still wrapped inside my stiffened fingers, the scent of lemons in my nostrils forever. People come to see me, to stare at what must have been, one remnant of the glory that was Rome, the memory of Pompeii's living death made real. They can't know that I wrote the graffito inscribed on the wall of my house so don't see the impact of the irony which was buried with me in the *Vicolo del Lupernare*. I wrote the words before I left to see my lover for that final time, more in resignation than in hope. How could I suspect that those stanzas would survive and be as fixed as the effigy I was destined to become?

Nihil durare potest tempore perpetuo;
Cum bene sol nituit redditur Oceano,
Decrescit Phoebe quae modo plena fuit.
Sic Venerum feritas saepe fit aura levis.

Nothing can last forever;
When the sun has run its course, it sinks into the Ocean.
The moon wanes where it was once full.
Thus wounds of love often disappear like a puff of wind.

Wedding Day
By Lesley Cookman

Somebody was thundering on the door. Janie's eyes opened slowly and met the extravagant pink froth of the dress hanging on the wardrobe and memory returned on a flood of alcoholic remorse.

'Janie?' A head encased in large foam rollers poked round the door, the very last person she wanted to see. 'Oh, good, you're awake. Here - I've brought you some tea.'

Janie closed her eyes again. 'Ah,'she said faintly. 'Tea.' A heavy weight descended on her legs and she winced.

'Come on, Janie. It's today. Aren't you excited?'

'Paula, get off my legs.' Janie sat up and took the mug held out to her.

'You've got a hangover,' Paula accused. 'that isn't allowed, you know. That's why I had the hen night last Saturday.'

'I know, I know.' Janie sighed. 'And it's why you shouldn't have had the rehearsal and the family dinner last night.'

'Well, when else are you supposed to have them?'asked Paula reasonably. 'Anyway, I had to make sure you and Mark were going to get on today.'She smiled a little tightly. 'I thought you seemed to be getting on rather well.'

Janie felt sick. 'For your sake, Paula. You know how I feel about him. You shouldn't have asked me to be a bridesmaid.'

'Janie, you had to be there. You're as much part of today as I am.'

'Rubbish.'Janie turned away to put her mug on the bed-side table. 'You're the blushing bride.'

'And you're my best friend.'

'Yes.' Janie's stomach revolved ominously. 'Your best friend.'

Paula's round face beamed again. 'That's better.' She leant forward and kissed Janie's cheek. 'Now, come on, the hairdresser'll be here in half an hour, and you haven't had your bath yet.'

The bath made Janie feel better - physically, at least. Mentally, she was feeling worse by the minute. Memory was returning in devastating chunks, making her squirm first with embarrassment and then remembered desire. She sank below the level of the water to try and blot out the scene that rose before her eyes in all its gory detail.

The dark hallway, the smell of beer and aftershave and the heartstopping realisation that Mark's lips were only a fraction away from her own, and...

'Janie? The hairdresser's here. And guess what?'

'What?' Janie shook foam out of her eyes.

'There's a bouquet arrived for you.'

'So I should hope. Where's yours, then?'

'No.' Paula giggled. 'I mean - a proper bouquet - you know - like a birthday.'

Janie went cold all over, despite the hot water.

'Is there a card?' she managed to croak.

'Yes, but I haven't opened it. Shall I?'

'No!' Janie shrieked.

'All right, all right.' Paula said huffily. 'I'll put it in the spare room. Hurry up.'

Janie sat frozen. Flowers? As if last night hadn't been bad enough, why did he have to remind her? There was no doubt in her mind that they were from Mark. Oh, why had he stayed after Paula had gone to bed? And why had he... And why had she...

And in Paula's parents'hallway, of all places. Although it hadn't stopped there. Out into the frosty garden they had staggered and into Paula's Dad's garage, which Mark knew was open. He would, wouldn't he? He also knew where the mattress for the sun lounger was. And he knew exactly how much she wanted him. She'd hardly hidden it. And she was left in no doubt how much he wanted her.

She climbed out of the bath and realised she was shaking. In two hours, she was going to have to walk down the aisle behind Paula and see Mark turn round from the front pew, to see him step forward, to stand behind him all through the ceremony .

The huge bouquet lay on the bed. With trembling hands, she opened the little envelope attached to the cellophane.

'I won't forget last night,' she read. No signature, of course.

Paula and her mother sat in front of Paula's dressing table, while the hairdresser stuck pearls into Paula's upswept and overcurled hair.

'You look pale, Janie.' Paula's mother frowned. 'I thought you were a bit heavy on the white wine last night.'

Janie tried a smile. 'Overdid it a bit. Nerves, I expect.'

'I don't see what you've got to be nervous about,'grumbled Paula. She stood up and gave her seat to Janie.

'Go and put the kettle on, lovey, while Janie's being done,'said Paula's mother. Paula left the room.

'So, did you enjoy yourself last night, then, Janie?'

'Yes, thank you, it was lovely.'Janie's voice came out in a strangled whisper.

'Mm. Mark's a lovely boy, isn't he?'

Here it comes, thought Janie. She knows. Oh, good.

'Of course, Paula's known him for so long. They've always been close, even before they grew up.'

I know, I know, Janie wanted to scream. I've had Mark shoved down my throat for as long as I can remember. I've always hated him. How can I have done this?

'You know what you've got to do, don't you Janie?'

Janie's eyes flew to the other woman's face. 'What?'she croaked.

The sharply pencilled eyebrows rose. 'Your duties, of course. And you've got to pretend that you really like Mark. Just for today. For Paula's sake.'

'Oh - oh, yes, I see.' Janie's eyes returned to the bird-snest that was being created from her normally smooth hair. 'Erm - excuse me, but I don't really like my hair like this.'

'Oh, never mind, dear. It's Paula's day after all.'Paula's mother stood up and patted her firmly on the shoulder. 'Not yours.'

'Doesn't want you to outshine her little darling, that's what it is,' commented the hairdresser when they were alone. Janie nodded, feeling worse than ever.

The next hour and a half passed in a blur, but at last, Paula arrived at the church on her father's arm, an ivory waterfall of a bride, her round face glowing with happiness, and then they were walking up the aisle, and there, just as Janie had imagined, was Mark, stepping forward.

He smiled at her over his shoulder. 'Eating your words, now are you?'he whispered. That'll teach you not to judge people before you know them. Told you best man were best.'

Santa's Little Helpers

By Jan Jones

'A reindeer costume? With Jez?' I stared aghast at the supervisor. 'With Jez?' I repeated. 'In a flaming reindeer costume?'

Miss Walmsley stretched her lips in what passes for a smile. 'I have warned you time and again, Camilla, to behave in a more responsible manner in this store. You and Mr Masters have wrecked Santa's grotto with your infantile behaviour. So, since the actors we hired to be Rudolf tomorrow can't make it, you can take their place.'

'But it wasn't my fault,'I argued furiously. 'Jez was the one who started throwing snowballs...'

'Wasn't me who decapitated that gnome with the Visa machine though, was it?' put in Jez.

I turned on him. 'Yes, but if you hadn't been flicking me with the sleigh bells...'

'*Enough*!' said Miss Walmsley. 'If it was up to me you wouldn't have been back here at all this year. As it is...'

As it is, Jez's family own the store. Which puts him, you might say, at something of an advantage.

Jez and I have known each other for ever. Mum joined Masters straight from school (she's head of Soft Furnishings now) and I've worked for them since I was old enough for a Saturday job.

Jez had a Saturday job here too. Seems funny, doesn't it,

the youngest son of the owners queuing up to be paid with the rest of us? When I was little we used to play together. I really envied him his brothers and sister. There's only me and Mum at home.

Now that I'm at College, I only work at Masters during the holidays. The trouble is, they still treat me as if I'm sixteen. It's the same with Jez. He's doing a business management degree, but where did they put us last year? Humping boxes in the warehouse! And this Christmas it's worse; we're on crowd control in the Toy department dressed in his-and-hers elf suits.

'What about the Grotto, then?' I asked Miss Walmsley. 'How's Santa going to manage if his little helpers are off being a reindeer?'

Miss Walmsley's thin lips stretched in triumph. 'It is Christmas Eve tomorrow, Camilla. Santa won't be in his Grotto. Santa will be on walkabout, and Rudolf the Reindeer will be on walkabout with him.'

'All day?' I screeched, appalled.

'All day.'

I kicked Jez smartly on the ankle. 'Come on, brain-dead. Say something.'

Jez narrowed his eyes thoughtfully. 'The management won't like Santa not handing out pressies to the kids.'

Miss Walmsley's eyes shone in revenge. 'On the contrary, Mr Masters. We are hoping that he will hand out more presents than ever before. To anyone, in fact, who buys a Christmas ticket and can track him down somewhere in this store. His sack is going to be bulging.'

'How's old Joe supposed to carry around a bulging sack?' I asked indignantly.

'Old Joe isn't,' said Miss Walmsley, 'Rudolf is.' Then

she clasped her hands together and walked off, leaving me and Jez to wonder if perhaps we'd gone a bit too far this time.

I ought to say right now that there's never been anything between Jez and me. Never. Not even five years ago when we had a bet as to who could ride up and down in the customer lifts most times without getting caught and we ended up fusing the control board and being stuck in there all night.

Wild, they call Jez, but he isn't really. He's just been given this reputation and people expect him to live up to it. If he doesn't do anything crazy for a couple of days, they ask if he's ill. Mind you, I still fall about laughing every time I remember the warehouse foreman's face when he opened up the goods lift last New Year to find Jez's GTi Convertible crammed inside...

Right now, Jez was climbing into Santa's sleigh and flicking an imaginary whip at the flock reindeer.

'Cheer up, Mil,'he said. 'It could be worse.'

'That's true,'I agreed, picking up the gnome's head and squirting superglue over the base, 'I could have had to be a reindeer with you for two days.'

Jez lobbed one of Santa's fake parcels at me.

I ducked. 'Naff off, air-head, we're supposed to be clearing up, not making even more mess.'

He jumped down. 'You're doing that all wrong,'he said and grabbed the tube from me.

'Oh, give over,' I yelled, shouldering him out of the way. A couple of minutes later, the gnome was armless as well as headless. Jez moodily flung one of the gnome's arms into the main hall. With pinpoint accuracy it hit the star on top of the Christmas tree and five hundred fairy lights went out.

'*Mr Masters*!'bellowed Miss Walmsley, but by the time she'd stormed into Toys, we'd bundled the defunct gnome into the outside skip and Jez was innocently handing me the last parcel to add to the display around Santa's sleigh.

A flicker of surprise crossed her face. 'You've done that very nicely, Camilla.'

I grinned at her. 'I *am* on a design course,' I said. 'Not that it would occur to anyone in this store to actually use the skills I've been acquiring...'

Miss Walmsley snorted in what could even have been agreement. 'Oh, go home, both of you,' she said. 'Get out before you do any more damage.'

'Gosh, Mil, a whole twenty minutes off,' drawled Jez. 'What shall we do with it?'

Honestly, I could have kicked him.

Miss Walmsley's face closed up. 'Perhaps you should practise walking like a reindeer, Mr Masters...'

We changed out of our elf-suits and left. Passing the sleigh, Jez cocked his head at me. 'She's right, though, Mil. It is a good display.'

'That's nothing,' I said darkly. 'I could do a window that'd knock their socks off if they'd only let me.'

Jez was silent all the way down to the coffee bar. Yes, all right, so it's not actually a coffee bar these days, it's a wine bar, but it used to be a coffee bar and old habits die hard in this town.

In his own clothes, Jez looked older.

'What are you staring at?' he asked rudely.

'You,' I retorted. 'What's up?'

'Nothing.'

'Yes there is.'

He glowered at me, then shrugged as if he didn't care one way or another. 'Store's in trouble. Takings are way down.'

The weirdest sensation plummeted through my stomach. Mum's job, I thought. What would happen to Mum if Masters...

'That's ridiculous,'I scoffed. 'Masters is an institution.'

'Right,' said Jez, tossing back his drink. 'It is. "Good old Masters," people say, "the town wouldn't be the same without it." But they don't come in, Mil. They don't come in and spend money. We've got good stuff, but the place is too damned old-fashioned, and Dad's too scared to invest. Department stores all over the country are folding on their feet, and still my bloody family won't paint the crumbling facade or change the dreary window displays...'

He broke off suddenly and stared at me. 'You're on!'

'Pardon?' I said.

He grabbed the menu pad from the counter and pushed it across to me. 'It's Christmas Eve tomorrow. If we can't pull it off then, we can't do it ever. Come on, Mil, what do you need?'

'Jez, what are you talking about?'

Jez's eyes pulverised their way into my brain. 'The family won't listen to me. To them I'm still the kid who drew beards and glasses on all the window dummies. Christ, I'm doing my Finals in the summer! I could really help them! And where do they put me? Santa's flaming Grotto! Is it any wonder I go crazy?'

I opened my mouth to speak and then shut it again. Because he was right. We were in a time warp at Masters. The way we'd fought and fooled around after the store had closed tonight - well, I didn't behave like that normally, any more than I supposed he did.

'So?' I asked. 'What's Santa's little helper going to do about it?'

For answer he grabbed my wrist and pressed a pencil into my hand. 'What are *we* going to do about it, you mean.'

I looked at him levelly.

He lost patience. 'For Christ's sake, get drawing, Mil! Don't you understand? I want to see a window display that'll knock this town's socks off.'

A bottle of wine and two pizzas later, my courage was leaking away faster than bath water in a drought. Partly, I told myself, it was because it was so damn creepy in the service alley leading to the back of Masters.

'This is stupid, Jez.'

'Still think you're not good enough, eh?'

I chopped crossly at his neck with the side of my hand. 'Of course I'm bloody good enough! But it'll take us hours. And there're alarms. And...'

'And you call me brain-dead,' jeered Jez, 'You think I can't turn the alarms off?'

'But...'

'Okay,' said Jez in a bored voice, 'I've got your drawings, I'll do the windows myself.'

He caught my fist just as I was about to slam it furiously into his face. We stood there, locked in an angry tableau.

'Okay,' I said through gritted teeth, 'Break and enter, damn you. Let's get this stupid idea over with.'

Within minutes we,d pulled down the blinds and got to work. I knew exactly what I wanted for the main window, huge bolts of Mum's red and green material, red and green clothes from Ladies, and Gents, Fashions, and red and green toys from Santa's Grotto. We did the second window in blue and silver, and the third in shades of orange. Then we scavenged all the silver stars the store possessed and tacked them around in wild abandon. The only window we didn,t touch was the tiny side one which always held the Nativity. Some things shouldn't ever change.

Eventually we hauled the blinds up again, reset the alarms, and went outside to look at our handiwork.

'Christ, Mil,' said Jez after a long silence. 'This town won't know what's hit it.' He draped his arm round my shoulders and gave me a squeeze.

'It's not bad, is it?' I said shakily. I was damn near having an orgasm at the sight of my very first, drop-dead-gorgeous windows.

I shivered suddenly. 'What's the time? Oh, my God, Mum'll kill me!'

Jez tilted his watch to the yellow street-lamp. 'What?' he mocked wickedly. 'You're not going to tell her you were with me until four in the morning?'

'Damn right I'm not,' I said. I shook off his arm and pelted for home.

I overslept, of course, and just pulled on the first clothes I found, a big, sloppy sweatshirt and some faded leggings. Mum kept up a steady catechism all the way to work about what time I'd got in, where I'd been, who I'd been with, what the hell I'd been doing. All of which came to an abrupt stop as soon as we reached Masters and joined the early-morning crowd gawping at my stunning windows.

'Forget it,' said Mum in a peculiar voice, 'Tell me, daughter, have you left me anything to sell today?'

'Oh, Mum,' I said, blushing. 'What d'you think of

them?'

She gave me a brisk kiss. 'They're smashing, love, but if I were you I'd get into that reindeer suit and out on to the floor pretty damn pronto. If I'm asked, I haven't seen you.'

Jez had the same idea. He was already in his set of legs and he hustled me into mine so flaming fast I didn't realise until we were velcroing ourselves together that he'd snitched the front half.

'Pig,' I said, slapping the back of his head.

'Don't start,' he snapped back. 'There isn't time. We'll swap later.'

'If you live that long,' I growled. I didn't trust Jez further than I could throw him. I certainly wouldn't put it past him to walk his half of Rudolf into the lift and leave me outside.

The costume was dreadful. It must have been designed for a couple of Sumo wrestlers! After a disastrous first circuit of the main hall, we nicked a bag of safety pins from Haberdashery and headed for the canteen. Old Joe, who'd been the Masters Department Store Father Christmas for the past fifteen years, was supping a cup of tea and waiting for us.

'Got a neat hand with folds of material, hasn't she?' said Jez, as they both watched me roll up a foot or so of excess reindeer tummy.

I shot him a filthy look.

Downstairs we were loaded up with Santa's sack.

'My God, what are they giving away this year,' I muttered. 'Pet rocks?'

It was awful! I couldn't see where on earth we were going and all the weight of the sack seemed to be on my shoulders. Plus, I had to keep Rudolf's back legs in time with the front ones...

'You're doing this on purpose,'I hissed, as Jez changed step for the fourth time in as many minutes.

'You think this is easy?'he snarled. 'I've got to operate the eyes, turn the head, get a crick in my neck peering through this stupid slot *and* not run over any customers as well.'

'You two think you could keep the noise down in there?' murmured old Joe. 'Whoops, up the steps, Rudolf, lad!'

'Mind you,' said Jez smugly, a fraught few minutes later. 'There *are* a lot of customers.'

It was true. Old Joe said there were more than he'd seen for years. It was only ten o'clock in the morning, yet all around us, people were laden with stuff and buzzing excitedly to each other that they couldn't believe how it was they'd forgotten how good the store was!

And the kids! They were following us all over the place! We emptied the first sackful of pressies in record time, loaded up a second one, and still they kept coming. By the end of the first hour my back was breaking.

'Come on, Rudolf, time for a bowl of water,'announced Santa. 'Back in a few minutes, folks.'

Heading towards the staff exit I stumbled and grabbed at Jez. Caught off-balance, he head-butted a customer.

'Oi!' said an annoyed voice.

'Sorry, sir,' said Santa smoothly. 'Rudolf's a bit tired. Needs a rest.'

Rudolf didn't say anything. Rudolf was having a revelation. When I'd grabbed hold of Jez like that, there had been an incredible shockwave between us. His hips stiffened under my hands and he whipped his head round, drawing his breath in sharply. I let go, rather dazed.

The canteen was awash with reindeer jokes, and although Jez and I gave back as good as we got, our hearts weren't really in it. We'd grown up, I suppose, that was what it came down to. When I looked up from stirring my coffee, his eyes met mine. There was - recognition - in them.

We were just finishing when we heard Miss Walmsley's voice outside the offices at the top of the stairs. And with her was -

'Oh, Christ, that's Dad,' said Jez. Mischief gleamed briefly in his face. 'Not that I regret making the windows a million times better - but I'd rather not have a conversation about it just yet.' He hefted up Rudolf's head. 'Ready, Joe?' he called.

'Not so fast,' I interrupted quickly, catching sight of the sack of presents. 'It's your turn to be crippled for life, remember?'

'For Christ's sake, Mil - '

I narrowed my eyes implacably.

'Oh, come on then,' muttered Jez, 'But hurry up.'

Under the amused scrutiny of the whole canteen, we scrambled into each other's half of the costume.

Jez was still giving me a earful of instructions on which bits of string pulled which facial features as we cannoned into the door frame.

'Shut it,' I said, elbowing him in the ribs, 'I'm concentrating.'

Willing hands piled us with Santa's sack and with a genial Ho ho ho, we were out on the floor again.

It was far better in the front. Being shorter than Jez, I could see very nicely out of Rudolf's mouth slot, and hearing him curse behind me whenever I changed step added considerably to the fun.

Until, that is, I quickstepped once too often and felt his hands fasten furiously around my waist and jerk me to a standstill.

'Ooof,' I said.

'Whoa there, Rudolf, careful with the presents!'

Jez moved his hands deliberately and firmly underneath my sweatshirt. I gasped and tried to kick him, but only succeeded in pawing the ground, much to the amusement of the crowd.

'Can't go yet, Rudolf lad, we've got visitors!'

'Can we pat him?' I heard the children whisper.

I stood absolutely stock still. What the children were doing to the reindeer suit was nothing to what Jez was doing to me.

'Wake up, Rudolf,'said Santa jovially.

Feverishly I manhandled the strings to make Rudolf smile and wink at everybody.

Jez's hands slipped away from my body to balance the sack of presents again.

We stopped again a few minutes later and I found I was hardly breathing with expectation. After what seemed like an eternity, Jez chuckled. Furious with him for keeping me in suspense, I grabbed his wrist and hauled it firmly up under my top. Under cover of the noise around us, he blew me a kiss and then deftly unhooked my bra. I don't think anyone heard me shriek.

The next time we paused, in Ladies, Fashions as it happens, Jez's hands found my breasts and started flicking my nipples into peaks of unbearable excitement. And in Gents, Fashions. And in Household Goods. By the time

Santa decided we needed another tea break, I was a phys-ical wreck.

'Haven't had to Ho ho ho so much for years,' Joe com-mented. 'It's going rather well, don't you think?'

'Stunning,' I agreed raggedly.

Jez gave the wickedest chuckle I had ever heard and curled strong fingers round his mug. I watched them in fascination, my breasts aching and trembling under my baggy sweatshirt. (The bra had come off in Babywear and was now stuffed into the top of my leggings.)

'You two going to do your quick change act again, are you?' asked Joe.

I jumped nervously. 'What?'

'Swapping halves, like?'

'Oh - oh, yes. I - I suppose it is my turn.'

Jez grinned and mopped up my spilt coffee.

I swear, right up to the point at which we velcroed our-selves back into that fiendish costume, the only thing in my mind was getting a breathing space from those teasing hands. But as Joe adjusted the sack and I bent my neck, my eyes were caught by the sight of Jez's tight blue jeans just a couple of foot in front of me.

At the first pause for presents I took a deep breath, inched delicately forward, and started on revenge.

Rudolf gave out a strange, strangled moan as I discov-ered that I could fit my hands quite comfortably into Jez's pockets. And another as I found that the right pocket had a hole in it. And a third as I...

By our next break, Jez was looking decidedly pop-eyed. He excused himself, saying he had to go for a pee - I could well believe it!

We changed places with cautious determination. I wasn't sure what to expect this time, but whatever it was I got the feeling I deserved it.

He left me alone the first time we stopped to give out presents, prolonging the agony, the pig. But at the second stop, just as I was breathing more easily, his hand gently inserted itself into the waistband of my leggings...

Masters doesn't shut until eight pm on Christmas Eve. By four in the afternoon I wasn't sure how much more I could take. We reeled into the canteen, I lifted Rudolf's head with shaking hands - and found myself face to face with Miss Walmsley.

'Bring your coffee up to the office,' she snapped.

We did.

By Christ, that was a bad half hour. Part way through, Jez asked ingenuously if Rudolf shouldn't be rejoining Santa, only to be told curtly that Santa was having a sit-down in his sleigh and giving out presents there. Honestly, between them Jez's parents itemised every single thing we'd done wrong at Masters since we were out of the cradle. I didn't even realise they knew about some of them!

Jez grew grimmer and grimmer. When they'd finished, he stood up, his eyes stony, and my heart leapt with longing for him. 'How much are takings up by today?' he asked.

'That's not the point,' said his father.

'It's the whole point,' said Jez. 'Camilla's windows have done that. Camilla's windows brought the customers in. Camilla's flair and my know-how. If you'd started using us properly two years ago, Masters wouldn't be in the state it's in now. By the way, is it okay if Mil comes to Christmas dinner tomorrow?'

Jez's mother stood up and kissed me on the cheek. 'Of

course it is, darling. How about your mother, Camilla? Would she like to join us?'

'I'm sure she would,' I stammered. 'Thanks, Mrs Masters.'

Outside in the corridor, I balled my fists and looked Jez straight in the eyes. 'What's this Christmas dinner lark?'

For answer, he wound his hand in my hair and jerked my mouth up to his. One breathless, bruising kiss later and, 'Come on, woman,'he said. He pulled me, not downstairs to where we'd left Rudolf, but upstairs towards the store rooms.

'Jez - ' I said warningly.

He turned back. Every strong, vibrant inch of him challenged me. 'Are you telling me you don't want this as much as I do?'

I drew level with him, grinned, and kneed him in the stomach. 'Course I do, brain-dead. Catch me if you can!'

We reached the farthest store room neck and neck. Both of us wrestled with the other's clothes while wedging boxes in front of the door. Then we had an intensely enjoyable bout of hand-to-hand combat to decide who was going to unwedge the door and sneak back to the loos for a Durex. By the time we were finally meshed together it felt as if we'd been waiting for this exhilarating union all our lives.

'Christ, Mil,' Jez said, when we'd finished and were lying on our backs side by side amidst the wreckage of the store room. 'How come we never did this before?'

'They never thought to shut us into a reindeer suit before,' I answered flippantly. I pushed the hair out of my eyes and turned to him. 'Is this a one-off, Jez?'

I knew, or at least I think I knew, that it wasn't - I just

wanted to hear him say it. Huh! I should have known better.

His eyes glinted. 'Tell you at six.'

'Why six?'

He hauled me to my feet. 'Because six o,clock,' he said wickedly, 'is when Santa's little helpers get their next break...'

(That's what he thought. As soon as we were back inside Rudolf and posing with Santa and a couple of dozen kids for the local press, I put his masculine pride into a handlock twist and asked him again. This time he said it.)

Almost

By Lynne Barrett-Lee

'Diet Coke, Diet Sprite, Diet Fanta, Diet Lilt....' Robert grunted as he hoisted the boxes. 'What exactly do you have against sugar, Sal?'

'Calories, mainly,' I answered. 'That, and the fact that I'm quite sweet enough. Hold on, here's the chorizo.' I flung it across to him and continued to lean over and delve blindly in the car boot. The garage, a dank shack some way from the Villa, offered cobwebs and winged things but very little light.

'We should,' I continued, 'have unpacked *before* parking. It's senseless to be rummaging around here all hot and bothered in the dark.'

Robert's tall frame blocked the last shard of sunlight and the scent of his aftershave eddied around.

'Not from this viewpoint, darling.' He moved closer. 'The kids are exploring, Mel's whipping up lunch.... It makes a great deal of sense to me. Here, try a can up your back...'

I shrieked as cold metal connected with flesh, then squirmed as he smoothed it across both my shoulders. It bumped down my spine to the top of my sundress.

'Thighs feeling sweaty? This is just the thing...'

Sweaty I was, but what Robert had in mind wasn't going

to cool me down. I wheeled around.

'Hey! Look, my thighs are just fine, thanks...'

'I know, but hot, I'll bet. Let me roll a Lilt up them and.... Ah! Here's your husband. Adam, you're lucky. Five minutes more and I would have had to beat her off with a stick. Here, grab the sausage - it needs a firm hand.'

Adam and I had been going on holiday with Robert and Melanie every summer since our first babies were born. We'd met at one of those post-natal re-unions, where the men exchange shell-shock in packs in the kitchen and the women feed their newborns upstairs all evening, wincing and fumbling among the carrycots and change-bags. Despite its horrors, this must have proved cathartic, because we quickly realised that parental sanity on holiday was best achieved by having other grown ups around. It meant someone else to get drunk with in the evenings, and extended the scope of the childcare dynamics. It also meant that we could go out for romantic dinners for two, but we never actually did. We could be on our own at home, after all.

The shopping unpacked and the children's swimming things having been wrestled from cases, we stood and took stock of our new *hacienda*. The Villa was situated just above cloud base, beyond farmsteads and fields as well as the scope of our map. A crescent of coastline sprawled far below it with a sliver of indigo sea beyond. It had been described in the brochure as having 'lashings of character' and furnished in a style that would be particularly appreciated by its British Visitors. We, of course, read this as a peeling heap with lots of cheap, hastily installed MFI cupboards and scratchy wicker conservatory furniture, and a few Moorish knick-knacks scattered around. We were right, but we loved it all the same.

Adam soon went for his traditional sortie with the poly-pocket of domestic instructions, and the children went in to get changed. I lingered outside, enjoying the solitude and pushing my nose into the hibiscus blooms. From above I could hear snatches of terse conversation; Melanie, no doubt, dispensing unpacking directions to Robert. I smiled to myself as I moved away from the Villa. At the far end of the garden stood a small lemon tree, now barren and spent, bar one small fruit. I'd have that, I thought, to take home at the end. I hoped no one else would see it.

'There's a tree like that out front. Heaving with lemons.' It was Robert, escaped, and already stripped down to his old neon bermudas. His brown arms were folded across his white chest.

'Come on, I'll show you.' He took my cool hand in his warm one and led me along the hot string of concrete slabs that edged the pool. Once we were halfway he stopped and pointed.

'Look. There!'he said, and pushed me in, with a ringing slap on my buttock.

I came up, spluttering, my dress ballooned round my waist like pondweed. I scraped at my hair to see Robert doubled up with mirth at the poolside. I paddled over and made a grab for his leg. He hopped back quickly and col-lapsed on the grass. Adam was now on the balcony.

'Nice one, mate,' he said to Robert. 'Alright, my love?' to me.

That was the trouble. Robert was a terrible flirt. It was all quite harmless, of course, and Adam didn't care; he liked, I suspect, his proprietary role. Melanie, on the other hand, had no time for larks. Push Mel into a pool, Adam had said, and the water would jump out in terror. And she'd be very, very, *very* cross, possibly forever. Mel was okay, though, just lacking in humour. We'd never be mates like Adam and Robert, who shared matey banter and sat up late dissecting team selections for important international football fixtures. Mel and I had no such rapport, but we co-existed peacefully and swapped bonk-buster novels. I wondered if they made her feel randy too. I would never dream of asking.

It was Tuesday. A still afternoon, the air heavy with insects. We had fallen into a pattern of obscenely large lunches washed down with *Rioja,* and near-manic sessions of horseplay on lilos. The children, fed up with the adults being stupid, had gone to make camps for their Action Men and Barbies. Robert was reading, flopped over a sun lounger while I floated on a lilo wired carefully to my Walkman. Adam, not given to inactivity, was tinkering happily with the rusting barbecue, the better to scorch the sardines on later. I watched the intense concentration in his face, the flop of blonde fringe and smiling mouth. Comforting, familiar Adam, who would make love to me later in his gentle practised way, before the ritual slaughter of our mosquito audience. He looked up and grinned and I blew him a kiss. I smiled to myself, in the way that you do when the children are occupied, the sun is shining and somebody else has done the washing up.

'Robert, I *need* you!' Melanie's voice. It cut through the air like a rounders bat, and I paused in my tuneless humming. She'd clearly been calling for a while.

Robert didn't move so I sculled across the pool and stretched out a toe to poke him.

'Hey!' I bellowed (I was still wearing headphones).
'Melanie needs you!' He grunted and puffed and pulled
himself up.

'Now!' I added. Consciousness surfaced.

'Let's hope my luck's in.' He rose and stretched. Adam
and I shared a confirmatory look. We'd suspected as much
that morning.

'Not much happening there.' He'd guessed. Things
clearly hadn't improved.

'Robert, for God's sake!'

Melanie had an upset stomach. It hadn't been alluded to
but discussion was unnecessary. She'd darted off at inter-
vals all day. Perhaps she'd had a crisis. Robert shrugged
and strode inside. We didn't ponder further.

A blockage in the toilet, he explained on his return, had
caused a flood all over their bedroom floor. Adam's ears
pricked up.

'Tools!' he announced, dashing off. But he was back
within minutes, shaking his head.

'Not even a spanner,'he said, with his usual bafflement.
He was always aghast at peoples' DIY deficiencies.

'Couldn't she just use our loo?' I asked. 'Till the Rep
comes?'I could see Adam working himself up into one of
his repair and maintenance frenzies and was anxious to
head him off before he stripped out all the plumbing.

Robert spoke.

'No chance. You know what she's like. What about the
cars? They'd have tool kits.'

'You're right, 'agreed Adam. So I left them to it.

An hour or so later, the cursing stopped. The men
emerged, blinking, and dipped their feet in the pool.

'Hrrumph,' said Adam. 'The pan's off, at least. But the

water's off too, for a while, I'm afraid.'

Robert wiped an arm across his forehead. I could see he wasn't altogether confident about sanitary equipment.

'Shouldn't we drive to a phone and call the company?' I said. Adam shook his head. All he needed, apparently, was to root out the blockage, and if we could buy a wrench and a tub of something gunky, he'd pop it back on in no time. I recalled a hardware shop in Javea and offered to drive down and get what he needed. And call the Tour Company, I thought, but of course didn't say so.

'*You* can't go,' said Adam, predictably.

'Why not?' I rather fancied the idea.

'I can't have you galumphing all over the Costa Blanca in a rental car.'

'Why not?' I repeated.

'Because you're a woman driver,' Robert said smoothly, logic and reason both writ plain on his face.

I wanted to say 'bollocks' but made do with a snarl. Adam tried another tack.

'The gearbox. You'll never get it into reverse.'

'Don't be ridiculous!'

'I'd better come then. Rob can clear the loo.'

'Can I? Oh.'

'Or...no. *You* go with Sally.' Which solution seemed to suit them both nicely. Adam could get back to his grungy maintenance, and Rob didn't have to put his hands in the sewage again.

'But you're still hooched, so I'm driving.' I said.

The children were marshalled for mopping and nursing; boys for the former and girls for the latter. A job that Adam wouldn't relish. Adam didn't fancy Melanie at all. He lusted after my old school friend, Sue, who came twice a year and brought him out in a rash. Rob and I headed off to the car.

So there we were, Robert and I, bouncing along in an old dusty Renault under a still strong afternoon sun. Like two adolescents let out of school early, we giggled as we headed south down the track, over couch grass and pine cones and crackling needles. Predictably, soon, we began to get lost.

'Which way here?'

'It's left. No! Right! We eyed the junction and couldn't recall. A small peeling villa huddled at its axis, geraniums in tubs by its ancient door.

'It all looks the same,' said Robert, squinting. 'Left, do you think?'

'You should know. You've driven it enough.'

'But we always follow Adam!' he protested. I grinned. This admission touched me. Adam knew how to get absolutely everywhere and if he didn't, he simply pretended that he was just trying out a different route. Robert seemed suddenly very much younger.

'We'll try left,' I decided, full of reckless abandon, and the tyres churned the gravel as I wheeled down the lane.

Within minutes the scenery was foreign and new. Where our previous sorties had skirted fields, we were now heading into more dense vegetation and seemed to be headed uphill as well.

'It can't be up,' I reasoned. 'Let's turn back.'

'No, let's go a bit further. We can cut across country. It'll be fun.'

Conscious now that there was a recreational element involved, we drove a little further and reached another junction. I stopped the car. Crickets trilled in the silence.

A lizard skittered across the dust up ahead. Robert pulled himself out of the car.

'Christ, my backside's sore!'he exclaimed, rubbing. He was still in nothing but the neon shorts. The seat had carved stripes down the back of his thighs. I watched him stroll around the corner and then reached for the now tepid Evian water that had sat in the glove space since we'd first arrived. I was feeling sticky now in my swimsuit and dress. Gulping some water, I pulled up the skirt and splashed some of the liquid onto my knees. I was sitting, eyes closed, wafting the fabric up and down, when Robert returned.

'You want to stop that.' he remarked, climbing in. 'You'll have me jumping on you.'

I said 'tush' and pulled down the dress.

'It is a point though,' he said suddenly. I think it had only just occurred to him that he actually meant what he said.

'Right or left?' I asked. Flash points of anxiety were exploding in my head. I had never, I realised, been alone with Robert. Not really, not out of reach of our spouses. We were lost, remote and in very few clothes. My temples throbbed.

'Did you ever wonder,' he said 'what you'd do, if, say, Mel Gibson turned up and said, how about it?' He shifted in his seat so that he was facing me. His knee was hard up against the gear stick, so I couldn't drive off without touching it.

'No.' I said. It was a lie. Adam and I had discussed it often. Mel Gibson, Sean Connery, the guy on Blue Peter. Madonna, my friend Sue. Apart from Sue, who we agreed was an absolute no-no, we'd never reached a definitive stance. It didn't matter, because it was only a fantasy. We would have to decide when it happened, which it would-n't. Robert of course, would be in the no-no category. But I hadn't told Adam about Robert. Why not?

'You must have,' he snorted. 'Everyone does. I do.'

'So what? And You're not Mel Gibson anyway.'

'Ah! Where did I come into it? It was a hypothetical question.'

'Don't wind me up. You were trying it on. It's the heat. Have some water.' I felt safer with this tetchy banter. I took the bottle from between my thighs, and passed it to him. He watched.

'Right or left?' I said again.

' I'll take both. And you do fancy me. Don't pretend oth-erwise.'

'So?'

'So admit it. And it's left.' He didn't move his leg.

'Okay, I do.'I said this slowly, a warmth in my stomach radiating. Perhaps I should get out of the car.

'Good,' he said. ' Because the feeling's mutual.'

'Come on....'

'It is.' This was plaintive. I was struck again by the attractive boyishness in him.

'I know. But I wish you hadn't told me.'

'You love it.'

'I Don't.' I did. And the knowledge was scary. I was feeling aroused.

'Liar.' His arm snaked across the seat back and flopped onto my shoulder. It was damp and warm. His fingers felt hot. As if they were fusing with my skin.

I glanced at the hand, then turned back to face him, my lips parting, ever so slightly, to speak. It was all the invitation he needed, and he lunged across and pinioned me to the seat, while he kissed me, quite voraciously, for a good half minute. The inside of his mouth tasted sweet, yet strange. As it would; for eleven years I had kissed no one but Adam. The thought inflamed me further. Rob was squirming and urgent, and his knee began thrusting. I think he would have liked to bring it into play, like teenage boys always do on dance floors, but it was still wedged quite firmly in the gear assembly, and the kiss came to it's natural conclusion while we both stopped to breathe and gather our thoughts.

'Uh-oh!' said Robert, then, 'Phew!' He glanced across at the back seat, a swift, assessing sweep. It was strewn with ice cream and sweet wrappers and the odd smashed crisp. I thought, I bet the back seat of their car doesn't look like this. Melanie just wouldn't have it.

'I bet the back of your car doesn't look like this,' I said.

'Dunno.' And he freed his knee from the gear stick.

'I don't think...'

'Come on. We can't stop now.' He loomed before me once again, with that heavy-lidded, floppy mouthed look men have when their bodies are being driven by their reproductive organs. His mouth came down and his knee came up. One hand was now darting about too. It paused briefly to pull free the tie-neck on my dress, and then plunged down the side of the car. The seat back suddenly fell from behind me and my head crashed down soon after.

'Robert!' I spluttered, through the side of my mouth. 'We mustn't do this! Stop!'

'God!' was all he said in response. I wondered if he was one of those men who enjoyed a bit of thespian resistance. My words had only increased his fumblings.

'I mean it!' I added, and pulled at his hair.

'Sally, we must. You want to. You do.' He had started a rhythmic stroking of my midriff with short forays to my breasts. My enthusiastic nipples were quivering beneath the lycra. I took his chin in my hand and jerked it firmly towards me.

'Look at me,'I said sternly, 'And stop that!'He stopped, his hand dead on my breast. I could feel my heart beneath it. Thump, thump, thump.

'We can't do this,'I said again. His eyes, I noticed, were moist with sweat, his lashes clumping together.

'Can't,'he said. 'Not 'Don't want to'.'The hand started again. This time it made a bold sweep that took in a swimsuit strap *en route* and whipped it quickly down. My arm was pinioned by it now, so he capitalised by putting his face on my breast.

'Oh, Rob..' I gurgled. My voice sounded distant. It had a feeble warbling quality about it. The timbre, I knew, of an army in retreat. My nipples, it seemed, had won the day. Had Adam told him about them?

We spent an earnest few minutes in unrestrained groping, going over ground at once familiar and strange, and, in my case, examining the nature of conscience. A flighty fair-weather soul, I decided. Not something to be relied upon in a crisis.

'Are you..... have you.......?' I said, at length. My powers of word production seemed to have disappeared. *Poof!* along with my conscience.

'Vasectomy last year. You remember. And, hey - we're mates, aren't we?' He sat up, breathless, to pull off his shorts. His head bumped the ceiling and his leg scraped the handbrake, but his eyes were fixed on mine.

'Come on,' he panted, now huge and naked in the small airless box. 'I can't bear to wait any longer!' He bundled the material of my dress in his hands and reached over my head to remove it. His bits and bobs dangled on my stomach. They felt damp and alien, but the part of me that should have been operating on a strictly cost/benefit basis and reaching the conclusion that this was madness, had got stuck in a time warp and clearly thought I was eighteen. And sex, on a biological level, was obviously the preferred option.

'The sexual imperative,' I said, as he began carefully rolling down my costume 'The selfish gene.'

'What? Lift your bottom up..that's better...What was that garbage you were saying?'

'Science,' I said. 'We can't help it. Can we?' Somehow, it made it feel easier, safer. We could do it, get it over with, end all the games. A flicker of gossamer regret touched me briefly, but floated away again as our gazes fused. He cast his eyes over me. It was the same look He'd give to a menu in a restaurant. Thoughtful, lascivious, tinged with eager anticipation.

'There's very little here you haven't seen already,' I said.

'And seeing is not what I've got in mind now. It's .... Good God! Get your dress! Quick!'

'*Que es esto! Que es esto!*'

'What going on?' From my supine position I could hear but not see. Robert obviously could. He was struggling back into his shorts, bits of him banging into metal as he did so.

'It's an old woman!' he said. 'With a bucket!'

'A bucket?' My feet wouldn't go into my costume. It

had rolled into a swizzled sausage. 'Oh, damn! What's she yelling?' It was loud and largely incomprehensible, but I thought I could pick up *La Policia* in there. I said so.

'That's all we need! There's a law against sex in cars in Spain.' He groaned. How did he know? The woman was looming large in the window, fierce and malevolent in a chalk-smeared black shift. In one hand she did indeed have a bucket, the other was raised and fisted.

'Should I get out?' asked Robert. I had still not unravelled my swimsuit and was fumbling instead with my inside out dress.

'Yes! Anything. Just get her away from the car!'

He staggered out backwards and raised his hands in submission. The woman responded with another stream of incomprehensible Spanish and rattled the handle on her bucket. It was full, I could see, with small wizened melons. The debris, no doubt, of the recent harvest.

'*Ola!*' said Robert. '*Ola, Senora! Cual es la carretera de Javea, por favor?*'

We found our way, having fielded the harpy, and clattered back up to the villa. Robert, still randy, wanted to try for extra time.

'This is nil-nil England-Brazil,' he said. I refused, my wits back in place. It was one thing to turn a 'what if...' into fact, quite another to plan a clandestine affair. We were happily married to other people. It was just heat and circumstance and Mel's poor stomach.

Adam was splashing in the pool when we returned, the toilet crisis apparently over. He climbed out and waved as he saw us pull up.

'Where did you get to? Benidorm?' he asked. He didn't look perturbed.

'Almost,' said Robert. 'We got ourselves lost, didn't we, Sal. Some local oldie had to show us the way. No wrench, I'm afraid. Sorry.'

'No matter. It's fixed, just Mel's Oil of Ulay bottle stuck in the U-bend. And she's feeling better. Come and get a drink.' He put an arm around my shoulder and gave it a friendly squeeze. We ambled back to the villa's cool interior. Adam glanced at the clock.

'Look at the time!' he said. ' You've been gone ages. See, I'm glad I didn't let you go on your own.'

'Mmm,' I said. What else could I say?

'Rob'll always take care of a damsel in a crisis, eh, mate?' they exchanged one of their laddish titters. Robert made a familiar gesture with his forearm.

'Any chance I get, mate. Too right I will!'

'Ha, ha, ha!' They laughed their blokey laugh. So that was alright then.

A lucky escape? I guess I'll never know. On days when I'm feeling kind to myself, I like to think that I would not, ultimately, have succumbed to Robert's charms. On others, well, I'm more pragmatic. We could have, we didn't, it no longer matters. And Robert and Mel? Well, fingers crossed for their golden wedding, but everything's still okay at the moment. Nothing has changed. Except that, for safety, I've told Adam now that I fancy Rob, that he's on my no-no list, like Sue. Adam thinks it's terrifically funny. I even think he rather likes the idea. And now Robert's back to courting me in my bedroom. In my head, where he belongs, but now the picture's clearer.

Peaches

By Jo Mazelis

I don't know why my mother told me our true family history at the particular time she chose. There seemed no reason for it. I'd suspected nothing and hadn't been asking questions. I suppose she'd been turning it around in her head for all those years, letting it grow ripe until it was full and plump and soft and close to the point of bursting.

The day she told me was hot - a real scorcher, and I was out in the back garden lying on a scratchy old tartan blanket. I had the top-twenty on the radio, so it must have been a Sunday. I'd shouted for her to come out and bring me a drink and to put some more sun oil on my back. She came, carrying a tray laden with the lemonade I'd asked for, a gin and tonic for herself and a plate of sandwiches made just how I liked them; cut into triangles with the crusts off and a little sprig of parsley crowning them. There were also some nice fresh peaches, which I reached for first. I picked the fattest, juiciest-looking one and turned it over in my hand, occasionally bringing it to my nose so that I could breathe in the sweet promise of its flesh while enjoying the tactile sensation of its furred skin. I glanced at my mother. She was watching me and grimacing. For her the surface of a peach was like the scratch of a fingernail on a blackboard. Her look, I must admit, made me caress the peach all the more.

'Ai! How can you do that!' she shuddered. In reply I bit in.

I was wearing my first bikini which was made of black shiny nylon. The garden must have been the one which belonged to the house in Ealing. The one that overlooked the common. Because I remember that after my mother unburdened her dreadful secrets, I sat unmoving in the twilight listening to the distant and joyous screams and the rattle of machinery and the hum of generators and the thumping distorted bass of the music from the fair. So it must have been August of 1978; the summer when I turned 15 and had my first boyfriend, first bra and first cigarette.

I was at that age when I'd begun to call my mother by her Christian name - a thing she resented by the looks she flashed me when I said it, but as she never actually forbade it I carried on in my own sweet way. I was, I suppose, at that most difficult of ages, desperate to shed myself of childhood, to shake myself free, but yet filled with the arrogance and ennui of barely tarnished innocence.

Maybe my mother could sense my transformation approaching, could smell it in the air or see it glittering darkly in my eyes. Perhaps that was why she acted when she did, catching me on the brink of change and holding me there with her secrets.

So, there I was in the garden, fifteen years old. Small breasted and skinny in a bikini built for a woman. Thinking I knew it all and about to discover that I actually knew nothing. About to learn that truth was a variable; a mere surface, like the flawless skin of a ripe fruit which hides a maggot.

'Eleanor,' said my mother, 'there's something I have to tell you.'

I sighed distractedly and undid my bikini top so that she could rub the oil in my back. I folded my arms in front of my chest in order to keep my breasts securely hidden, though there was no one to see them besides her.

'It's something you have to know. It will make you understand. It's about me and your grandmother really.'

All I had said to this was, 'Is this going to take a long time? Because I was going to go around Patrick's later to do some work on our project ...'

'Oh, that boy,' said my mother with agony in her voice and I thought she was going to give me her usual lecture about Patrick and 'nice boys' and my reputation and getting into trouble, but instead she'd said, 'I'll be as brief as I can.' So I resigned myself to listening, at least for a short while.

She began, 'My father was ...' then stopped herself. 'Oh! How to tell it? Your grandfather he was ... No, no, no. Now listen, you know that I was born in France in 1944? About the time of the liberation?'

'Yes,' I'd said, putting all the boredom and sarcasm I could muster into my voice, but she chose to ignore this and carried on. Unstoppable like she'd sometimes be.

'The war years were very hard - it wasn't like it seems in the history books. It wasn't just soldiers and leaders. It was surviving day after day, getting by any way you could. There's nothing neat about it. War is a mess. It was not knowing what's going to happen. Imagine growing up in all that, being a young girl, wanting all those things that young girls want, wanting love.'

'So?' I said archly. 'You didn't live through that, you

79

were just a baby.'

In reply my mother merely gave a long drawn out sigh and took her hands from my back and tapped my shoulder twice to signal she'd done with the sun oil.

'I'm telling you how it was, just like my mother told me.'

I reached around to do up my bikini again, sliding my fingers over the hot slippery surface of my back, then I turned to face her. She was rhythmically wiping the fingers of one hand on the edge of the rug and her head was bent down with her left hand clasped over her mouth as if she wanted to silence herself. I thought I'd better shut up and listen or I'd never get to Patrick's and it was important I get to Patrick's that day as his family were away for the weekend.

So I said, to placate her, 'Please, tell me, Mum. Please.'

My mother lifted her head and I saw that her eyes were swimming in tears. Maybe it was me calling her 'Mum' again that softened her, went straight to her heart like a knife. Maybe that's how it was with mothers, you only had to say 'Mum' or 'please' and they melted into the old clinging memories of hope.

'I wish,' she began then, 'I wish I didn't have to tell you, but you must know.'

I nodded sympathetically.

'Your grandfather was a soldier ...'

Well, this I knew. Wasn't that why we'd ended up in England? Hadn't there been the liberation and D-day and the soldiers, both American and British, swarming over France? All of them lonely khaki heroes finding grateful love in the arms of pretty French women? Wasn't that what liberation was all about? Bottles of champagne and

Pernod and dark red Claret uncovered from secret cellars to bless the lips and tongues of these laughing and hungry men? And everyone drunk on freedom and the sky an endless blue and laughter easy and language among the Babel of races reduced to signs and kisses and beckoning fingers; the gestures of pleasure in food and wine and love.

I had always thought that it was quite romantic the way my grandmother and grandfather had met, the way he'd brought her back to England like a trophy of war. Despite the big difference in their ages; the gulf between her youth and beauty, and his lack of any discernable charms. Although I must admit that into certain dark shadows of untold detail I'd always painted my own bright colours. There was also the problem of dates, of birth and marriage. I suspected that my mother might be illegitimate, but what did it matter? It made everything all the more interesting. 'Now,' I had thought, 'Now she's going to admit it.'

'Your grandfather's name was Holger Herzog …'

I stared dumbly at my mother. At first only taking in the information that this was not the name of the man I always called 'Grandpa'. This was not the blunt Yorkshireman called Archibald Bratley who masqueraded in the role of grandfather to this day; sitting in his armchair by the fire, chafing his hands together and saying, 'Make another brew, pet. I'm parched.'

I imagined this was exactly what he was doing at that very moment. While my grandmother, accent still so thick you could cut it with a good French kitchen knife, would be scuttling off to the kitchen and obediently rattling the kettle, teapot and cups into service.

But then, the name. The name! Holger Herzog! This was

no French name. This name was surely German.

The sun disappeared behind a small single cloud and no sooner had our eyes adjusted to the shadowless world than it appeared again, blinding and dazzling us. I blinked at mother and shaded my eyes. My breath came in shallow gasps.

'Oh God,' I had said, 'oh *god*.'

Mother watched me. She looked ashamed, like a child caught out in a lie. 'I am *so* sorry,' she whispered.

I wanted to get away from her. I wanted at that instant to be transported to Patrick's house. I wanted to be in his arms in the big hammock on the patio that overlooked his parents' garden; to tell him this thing, this terrible thing and cry and be comforted. Even then I imagined it more as my mother's delusion than anything like truth.

Instead, I listened to my mother's words - what else could I do? And let her distractedly stroke the soles of my feet and ankles like she used to when I was little.

Later she called a taxi for me to go to Patrick's and stood on the pavement under the trees waving sadly as the cab drew away. I sat there watching as she shrank into the distance and the shadows and rehearsed my first words to Patrick. I imagined myself falling into his arms, sobbing and faint as his concern and love washed over me.

I imagined many things during that short journey as I held myself hunched up in the corner of the cab, my head pressed hard against the dirty cool glass of its window. Most of them to do with Patrick.

Patrick's family seemed to me to be very rich, though Patrick, echoing his parents, said they were merely 'comfortable'. They lived in a large 1930's mock-Tudor mansion in a quiet leafy avenue near Walpole Park. His father did something for the BBC and his mother played the cello and both were, consequently, often away on business or tours. Their house was like something out of Ideal Home magazine. I couldn't imagine how anyone could live in such spotless perfection. It was as if their lives glided over the surface of everything without substance, as if their glands sent forth polish instead of sweat.

Patrick, their only child, was the sole blemish under their roof. His hair was cropped on top so that it stood up on end and reminded me of a hedgehog's back, except that when you touched it, it was soft. He wore old men's home-knitted sweaters that were always about three or four sizes too big and whose sleeves and necks ended in ragged loose ends of trailing wool. He spoke with a lazy cockney accent and his voice was husky from too many cigarettes.

When he came to the door he was wearing dark glasses with mirror lenses so that when I looked for his eyes all I saw was my face, pig-like, reflected back at me. Somehow in the taxi I'd imagined that my tears and the telling of my misery would just happen, but once there in the cool hall with him, I felt numb and dry; shrivelled somehow.

As soon as Patrick had shut the front door he put his arms around me and I, in return, wrapped my arms around his waist and put my head against his chest and shut my eyes. I could feel the plastic of his sunglasses digging into my head as he rested his head on mine. We stood like that for a long time swaying from side to side, almost, but not quite, dancing. It dawned on me as I stood there that this thing I wanted to tell him, this miserable truth that weighed on me was all wrong. I wanted his comfort and pity but I was on the wrong side. I wasn't on the side of the victims, or even the heroes, I was now the aggressor. Either that or I was the daughter of a mad woman.

I kept remembering the figure of my mother under the trees outside our house - her small head and tiny body and raven black hair which she wore in tight, Shirley Temple curls which gave her the appearance of a shrunken doll. She embarrassed me. She'd embarrassed me for as long as I could remember but until now I didn't know why. I thought it was those insignificant things like her stupid hairstyle, her continual fussing over me, the way she could never keep a man, the frown marks between her eyes, her slow and hesitant way of speaking.

I considered this as I stood rocking gently, but this other image of my mother kept clouding my resentment. Well, not an image so much as a smell and that smell was eau de Cologne on warm skin. But it wasn't just a smell either it was also a feeling; a feeling of security. And a place I'd been once. I felt tired suddenly; mesmerized by the black and white checkerboard of tiles swaying at my feet. Against my hip I could feel some hard part of Patrick pressed and his breath was hot on my neck. With some awkwardness I lifted my face towards his and pecked at his cheek leaving the imprint of my lipstick there. He responded by finding my mouth and holding me tighter.

I always shut my eyes when we kissed and I assumed that he had also removed himself to some blind place where sensation depended on touch and taste and sound and smell alone. Patrick and I were quite expert at kissing; that liquid drilling of our mouths and the tight press of our bodies. We could do it for hour after hour and frequently did. Standing up or sitting side by side with our bodies twisted at the waist towards each other or lying stretched full length. I had been waiting for the next stage which, I assumed, would be set in motion by Patrick, as he was the male and the elder and more experienced. This next stage would be the opening of my blouse, the unclasping of my bra, the coldness of his hand on the hot swell of my breast. Whenever I thought about this I would shiver deliciously and butterflies would leap and claw at the pit of my belly. But after six months all I had known of Patrick was the swirling tongue and the mysterious press of his body. I was beginning to doubt him, to not trust the looks and kisses. Yet when he put his arm around my neck it felt right, cool like water, part of me but not part of me.

I entertained myself as we stood there endlessly kissing by wondering whether kissing felt the same for everyone? Whether another boy would be completely different? How it felt for Patrick to kiss me? And, disturbingly, whether it had felt like this when my grandmother had kissed her German soldier? It was just as that last question rose in my mind that Patrick gathered all the courage and passion he'd been storing up for six months and without warning clamped his hand clumsily on my right breast.

My reaction was electric. It was as if the German, my supposed grandfather (bearer, upholder and celebrant of the ugliest episode in recent history possible) had lifted his claw in France and brought it down upon my breast over thirty years later. I leapt back gasping and opened my eyes to see poor Patrick - a look of absolute horror on his face. My own face, I reasoned, must have worn a mirror image of his expression. Or worse, exposed this terrible heritage of mine, the inherited cruelty and destruction, the love of marching and killing, the blue of my eyes, the grey of my heart.

I turned and made for the stairs, walking at first then running, taking the steps two or three at a time. Finally I plunged into the bathroom, slamming and bolting the door behind me. It was quiet up there. Quiet and cool as all sanctuaries should be. The bathroom, like the rest of the house, was immaculate, everything seemed to have been carefully arranged. From the colour co-ordinated towels on the rail to the orderly ranks of expensive bath oil and perfume, to the trailing stems and leaves of palms and ivy and spider plants which seemed to curl or fall or stab the air in artful shapes which belied nature.

I lay down on the carpet studying the ceiling while tears ran down the sides of my face and gathered in pools around my ears, trying to stifle my louder sobs. I knew that sooner or later Patrick would come to find me.

Eventually, the door handle was gently turned. I heard a soft, hesitant tapping at the door, then Patrick's voice, 'Ellie? Are you OK? I'm sorry. El? Can you hear me? I'm sorry.'

Back in the garden at home my mother had told me that the man who fathered her wasn't all bad. That not all Germans had been bad. Not even all the German soldiers. She said that maybe, somehow the fact that love could still happen even in circumstances like that meant that life was worthwhile. I was disgusted by her using the word 'love' like that. I thought she used it just to soften the truth. Or even, God forbid, to romanticize this thing.

Then she told me, and by then I was trying not to listen, trying not to hear or care or remember any of it, what had happened to Holger Herzog.

Though, first she said, 'Do you know how old this soldier was? He was just seventeen years old. The same age as that Patrick boy.'I was surprised by that, but somehow I couldn't quite erase the dreadful image I'd created of a brutish man snarling his thick-necked guttural language into the vulnerable world and trailing destruction in his black-booted wake.

The villagers had caught him and my grandma hiding in a barn, 'clinging to each other like Hansel and Gretel', mother said. They'd been wrenched apart and he had been dragged through the peach orchard by the leaders of the resistance and, helped by a small group of drunken Allied soldiers, he'd been strung from the highest tree.

As she spoke, I could not help (and perhaps this was a form of self-protection, a process by which all became a fiction as unreal as a comic strip) but imagine the rope around Patrick's throat, his neck fine and soft and delicate as a girl's, twisted and pinched by the noose. And his eyes wet with tears, fearful, tortured, knowing the end of his life was only minutes away. And beneath their feet, the wind-fallen fruits were crushed, their broken flesh giving off a sickly sweet perfume.

Then she had told me what had been done to my grandmother; the clumsy shaving of her head, the threats, the way they had marched her around the town and spat at her. But worst of all they'd made her watch him die. She felt as if she had killed him.

My mother and I had sat quietly after all those words, both of us exhausted. Then she'd said, 'How many wrongs, do you think, it takes to make a right?'

I stood up and turned on the cold tap and splashed my face with water. I picked up one of the bottles of scent from the glass shelf and unscrewed the cap and tipped the bottle against one wrist, then rubbed my wrist against my neck. I felt better then, ready to face Patrick again.

I unlocked the bathroom door and there he was. The dark glasses were gone and his eyes looked red, as if he had been crying. He said, 'I'm really sorry, El.' I put my arms around him and said, 'It wasn't that,'and to prove it I took his hand and guided it under my t-shirt and placed it on my breast and he let out a little sigh that could have been pleasure and could have been relief. 'Come on,'said Patrick, taking hold of my hand, before leading me out of the bathroom and down the stairs, 'let's listen to some music.' We walked together towards the back of the house to a room I hadn't been in before. At the door Patrick stopped and said, 'The best stereo is in here, this is the old girl's music room,' before kneeling down at my feet and unfastening my sandals, 'so you have to take your shoes off.'He smiled up at me as I stood there barefoot, my eyes still stinging from all the crying I'd done, as he gently ran his fingers over my calves and an inch or so up my thighs. Then he stood and opened the door and ushered me in with a sweeping gesture.

I entered a room that was almost entirely white. The carpet was white, the walls were white, the fireplace a high snowy marble one whose streaks of silver and black merely emphasized the whiteness of the rest. The end of the room was dominated by a huge window hung with curtains of white muslin, in front of which was a white grand piano.

The only things which had any colour were the records - shelf after shelf - and the sheet music and the framed concert posters and photographs. A cello was propped by the grand like a squat, brown-skinned soprano waiting for the appearance of the pianist. It balanced its bulk on one impossibly slim leg.

I would have liked to touch it, to have drawn some noise from it, no doubt in my hands, a screaming violence on the untarnished air. Or better, I would have liked to have sat straddling its hourglass figure and to take up the bow and find, by some curious magic, that music, low and throbbing, swept from my sawing fingers. But I dared not. Instead, while Patrick ran upstairs to get some albums from his bedroom, I strolled around the room, studying everything. There were piles of sheet music, some of it clearly very old. I opened one at random and ran my eye along rows of an alien language; the crotchets and quavers and semi-quavers whose connection and translation into the sounds of horn or violin or cello seemed, to me, an impossible miracle. I felt like an intruder in this room - everything about it was too pure and I half understood the destruction wreaked by burglars in rooms like this. Yet I also felt a part of it all as if my relationship with Patrick gave me licence, made me valid, made me more than myself.

One wall of the room was almost entirely filled from floor to ceiling with posters, photographs, programmes, and news cuttings. Each had its own frame and while these were of different shapes, styles and colours, the cacophony of their patchwork arrangement made a whole. I began to look more carefully, reading names, dates, details.

At one end, nearest the window, I found a face of the woman I knew as Patrick's mother. Her hair was that colour which played it safe, occupying the territory that existed between a young sensual platinum blond and a more staid and sensible white. It was long and she wore it drawn back, either, as on the day that I met her, in a silvery ponytail, or for more formal occasions, in an upswept bun or chignon. In the most recent photograph she was accepting an award of some sort and smiling a Mona Lisa smile at a man in evening dress as he handed her some shiny metal thing on a small plinth. Above that was a brightly coloured poster which advertised 'Summer in the City; a series of lunchtime recitals in the Barbican Centre'. Patrick's mother was listed to play on Saturday the 5th of May of that year.

As I progressed down the wall the clippings from newspapers became more yellowed and the style of the posters more staid, and his mother's face shed the years; growing smoother skin and more clearly defined bones, shaking her hair loose and letting its golden highlights shine more brightly. Halfway down the wall she even shed her name. Now, no longer did she call herself Rachel Murphy. Instead she went by the name of Rachel Greenberg and there she was, a tiny slip of a girl posing with a nervous smile (gone was the knowing Mona Lisa), her hair in two long plaits, on the gangplank of a ship with the unmistakable bulk of a cello case beside her. Beneath, the caption read, 'Child protégé flees Nazi Europe.'

That afternoon in the garden with my mother seemed a long time ago. I sensed that from that moment on my life would always be divided between knowing and not knowing, innocence (intoxicating, blind sweet innocence) and knowledge. I remembered that last glimpse of my mother under the trees and her secret seemed like a black hole that sucked everything in upon itself. I remembered too, her raised hand; the palm offered, in not so much a wave of farewell, as a gesture that meant stop.

Patrick, on finding Eleanor standing quietly looking at the picture collection, crept up behind her and gently put one arm around her waist. He felt her stomach contract beneath his fingers and her hands moved to rest on his. With his free hand he drew the hair from her neck. She smelt sweet and her skin was warm; the nape of her neck softly furred with fine pale hair. He put his mouth there and licked, but his tongue found a bitter chemical taint and he was disappointed. He'd imagined she'd taste like she smelled - of peaches.

Birthday Special

By Liz Young

I was very rude to him when we first met, but it was partly down to shock. There I was, watering my F1 petunias
and thinking I was getting the hang of not killing plants at
last, when he hopped out from between the tub and the
wall.

I jumped. Anyone would have. Loose, warty skin, bulgy
eyes – he was not a pretty sight. 'Do you mind?' I told
him. 'I just got shot of my resident toad – I don't need
another.'

He just sat there, giving me an unblinking stare. 'I'm
sorry, but I'm really more of a furry-thing person,' I
added.

And off he went. He hoppity-waddled round the corner,
out of sight.

I felt a bit mean, actually. Toadist, if you like.

I told my colleagues the next morning. 'I hope I didn't
hurt his feelings, but he did give me a fright. I nearly
dropped my watering can.'

There was general mirth. 'He'll be eating the slugs,'said
Angela, who was forty-three and had a thing about Alan
Titchmarsh. 'That's why your petunias haven't died on
you. Slugs love petunias. You should encourage him.'

Feeling bad, I looked for Toad when I got home, and found him lurking in the damp shade between the tub and the wall. 'OK, you can stay,' I told him. 'But just don't eat any slugs in front of me, all right? I'm a little bit squeamish.'

After that I saw him on and off for weeks, and my petunias flourished. I became quite fond of Toad. I even bought him a terracotta Toad Hole out of one of Angela's garden catalogues. I wasn't sure he'd find it a des sort of res, but I put some nice damp potting compost in the bottom and left it in the nearest shady corner. And blow me, he moved in. I was tickled pink, as it had cost nearly thirty pounds and I'd have been a bit miffed if he'd scorned it. He'd hoppity-waddle over while I was watering and dead-heading. While he hoovered up the odd passing woodlouse we'd have a little chat. I apologised for likening him to Dave, who was actually more of a reptile than a toad, and had dumped me for the new IT girl at his office.

'She's called Tabitha,' I told him. 'I said the only Tabitha I'd ever heard of was a cat, which was pretty appropriate when I thought about it. I also said that every time we'd made so-called love for the past few months I'd been staring at the ceiling, wishing he'd just get on with it. Which wasn't quite true, I have to say. At least once I was thinking, oh, shit, I forgot to take the washing out of the drier.'

Toad listened very politely, which was more than you could ever say for Dave. 'We were together for four and a half years,' I told him. 'And I really did love him at first. He had this way of sneaking up behind me, tweaking my waist very lightly, and blowing on the back of my neck at the same time. I know it sounds daft, but it really used to turn me on. Of course, I hadn't realised it was a trick he'd picked up from *Lads' Monthly*. Once I started ironing his shirts – and I'm never going to be that stupid again, I can tell you – he couldn't be bothered any more.'

Of course I had to lower my voice when anyone passed the gate, or the woman next door was putting her milk bottles out, and once the Parcel Express man caught me out, but I just smiled sweetly. I said it was amazing how a cosy natter with your plants encouraged lots of side shoots.

It turned into a joke at work. Angela would say, 'Any nice little chats with Toad lately?' and I'd say, 'Yes, as a matter of fact I'm thinking of hiring him out as a counsellor.'

Mike from Accounts said he was getting worried about me. He was afraid I might be wanting to settle down with him and have tadpoles.

Susie from Admin said, 'How d'you know it's a he? What if she's been chatting up a lesbian toad all these weeks?'

They all fell about, but I didn't care. The way I see it, if you can spread a little innocent mirth your day's not entirely wasted.

Toad appeared again that evening, and I told him what Susie had said. 'She can be very slightly coarse, I'm afraid. She told me I ought to check before this relationship goes any further, but I'm not sure I'd know one set of toad bits from the other.'

'Who are you talking to?'

I jumped. 'What are you doing here?'

It was Dave, looking semi-drunk. He eyes were pink-rimmed, as if he hadn't slept. He had a fair growth of un-designer stubble. His hair was scruffy, as if he'd just got out of bed, and his suit looked as if he'd been wearing it since yesterday. He'd put weight on, too. He really did look unbelievably unappetising.

'I'm back,' he said.

'*Back*? What d'you mean, back?'

'It didn't work out. I told her I was coming back to you – I was mad to leave you in the first place.' He looked around. 'Who were you talking to?'

'Toad.' I nodded down at him. 'Toad, this is Dave, who I told you about. Tabitha's thrown him out and he thinks I'm going to be mug enough to take him back.'

'Oh, come on, Rosie…' He lunged towards me, as if a beery clinch would change my mind.

'Get – off!' I pushed him away, hard. And suddenly, as I looked at the stubble and blooming gut, I wondered what I'd ever seen in him. Quite apart from anything else, Tabitha hadn't been the first. There had been that fling at a Bournemouth conference, for starters. I'd smelt Other Woman all over his clothes. 'If you think I'd have you back in a million years, you're way out. Believe it or not, I'm a lot happier without you.'

'Yeah, right. I can see you're doing just great – talking to toads.' He actually kicked at Toad with his left foot.

'Leave him alone!' I pushed him away, hard. 'And clear off! Go and find another mug!'

Dave smirked. It was that, 'Come on, you know you love me really,' smirk I knew all too well. Only this was the first time I'd seen it as such, not as a lovable, naughty-boy smile. 'You can't do without me, Rosie,' he said. 'Talking to toads, for God's sake - you're going to pieces.'

'Don't you understand English? Shove –*off*!' To underline it, I threw the contents of the watering can at him. It wasn't much, but it made my point.

Dave only smirked more. 'You know what they say violence is a substitute for, don't you? But not tonight, Rosie. I'll let you work up a bit more steam first.'

As he turned and went down the path, I gaped after him. 'If you dare come back, it'll be a bloody sight worse than water!'

Glancing back over his shoulder, he smirked again. 'Promises, promises....' He got into his car and drove away.

Dammit. Why had I said that? Now I'd have to have something really disgusting ready, but Waitrose had yet to do cat pee in tetrapaks. Sour milk, maybe? Yes, that would be good. The vilest stink on the planet.

Bastard. Belatedly I remembered poor, kicked Toad, who'd hidden behind the pot. I lifted him out, inspecting him for damage. 'Told you he was horrible, didn't I? Are you all right?'

Toad didn't look right at all. He sat limp on my palm, looking so miserable I was worried. What if his little internal toady bits were damaged? I felt so bad, I kissed a fingertip and touched it to his head. 'Please, don't die on me.' I carried him to his Toad Hole and told him to get a good night's sleep.

At work next day there was general approval that I'd told Dave where to get off. There was also much hilarity about Toad, which I appreciated not at all. 'I was worried about him! It was only a little kiss-it-better kiss!'

They cracked up, which I thought very unfeeling, especially when there was no sign of Toad that night. I was very upset, thinking he'd crawled away to die.

The next day was Saturday, which happened to be my thirty-fourth birthday. I was going with some of the work crowd to the *Trattoria Firenze* that night, and looking forward to it with mixed feelings. Two years previously they'd arranged a white and wimpy Tarzan, who'd burst into the *Peking Duck* just as we were getting stuck in. He'd tried to throw me over his shoulder, said, 'Christ, what a weight,' and asked if I'd like to peel his banana. While I was cringing at the memory, the doorbell rang.

I opened the door and bit my lips.

Might have known. Still, he was a vast improvement on that Tarzan. He wore a vaguely Robin Hood-ish costume, in sludgy greens with a leather jerkin. His hair was wavy golden brown to his chin, and he had a real beard. I wasn't into beards, but this could almost have changed my mind. It looked as silky and strokeable as next door's Angora bunny. 'Yes?' I said, deadpan.

Stepping forward, he took my hand and kissed it. 'My lady, I am forever in your debt. I'd been waiting for someone to kiss me for seven hundred years.'

Well, I'd asked for it. They wouldn't worry about minor details, like the fact that it was a toad. 'All right, so you're a prince.'

'Alas, no.' He made a courtly bow. 'Sir Guy de Montfort, at your service, though you would not perhaps take me for a baronet, the way I'm dressed. The fact is, I had only just come back from hunting when I was cruelly bewitched.'

I had a job not to crack up. He was doing it beautifully, but now I came to think of it Admin Susie shared a flat with a couple of 'resting' actors. 'If you don't mind my saying so, you sound remarkably modern for someone who's been a toad for seven hundred years.'

'My dear lady Rose, I've had nothing else to do but listen to other people's conversations. It helped to take my mind off what I was obliged to eat. And talking of food, I suppose you haven't got a morsel of roasted ox in the kitchen?'

Well, it was lunchtime. Resting actors were always broke and Susie had probably told him I'd be a soft touch. 'I'm right out of ox, but I might be able to manage a sandwich.'

He followed me to the kitchen, where I produced farmhouse cheddar, butter and pitta bread, which was all I had.

He ate ravenously, just as if he really had been surviving on horrible wiggly things for centuries. I was a bit hacked off, to tell you the truth. He was supposed to be throwing me over his shoulder or across his white charger or something. Still, at least he'd be able to manage it better than that Tarzan. Under that leather jerkin it looked as if there were some pretty hefty muscles.

'It took rather a long time for you to resume your human form.' I remarked. 'I thought it was supposed to happen on the spot.'

'Forsooth, so did I. It was slow and extremely uncomfortable. I bethought myself that I was going to explode.'

I bethought myself that I was going to explode, too. Maybe it'd be worth the wait. He had lovely, greeny-blue eyes, and a remarkably kissable mouth, when he wasn't stuffing it with farmhouse cheddar.

'I'm sure it would have been quicker if you were a frog,' I said.

'No, 'twas not that.' He looked almost awkward. 'I do gather that a *maiden* does the business more quickly, if

99

you'll forgive me for mentioning such an indelicate matter.'

'I'm sure. Still, beggars can't be choosers.' I watched him devour more bread. 'I bet you never had pitta bread in Merrie Olde England,' I said, just to see what he'd come up with.

'Not in England, my lady. But when I was in the East, I often ate unleavened bread.'

'Whereabouts in the east? Anywhere near Saffron Walden? I've got a sister in Saffron Walden.'

'The Holy Land,' he replied. 'The Crusades, you know. Unleavened bread was about all you could get in wartime, but there was a little place just outside Jerusalem where they did an excellent roasted goat.'

Well, he certainly beat the Archers. 'Who changed you into a toad anyway? Had you done some dire deed to a witch's daughter?'

'It was my wife.'

'Dear me. What on earth had you done?'

He sighed. 'It was because of the Crusades. I was away too long, and neglected to put her in a chastity belt.'

'I should think so! They were positively barbaric!'

'My dear lady, all the best people did it. My own brother swore by Fitzalan's Patent Love-Lock. But I trusted her, and lived to rue the day. While I was enduring battle, plagues and sunstroke, not to mention a spell of atrocious cooking in a Saracen jail, my Lady Elinor was disporting herself with my kinsman, Roger de Courtney-Montfort.' He paused. 'You've heard the term "rogering" I suppose? Well, that's where it came from.'

I bit my lips. 'So you were a bit put out?'

'Put *out*?' He looked positively scandalised. 'I should

just think I was put out, cuckolded by a lily-livered young pup like Roger. I vowed to string the varlet from the nearest meat-hook, and throw his guts to the hounds.'

Although I was dying to laugh, I wanted to see how long he could keep it up. 'So your Lady Elinor thought she'd cook your goose, so to speak?

'Indeed.' He gave a heavy sigh. 'She went to some old hag in the village and paid three gold pieces for a spell. She told me she was going to do it, but I laughed like Friar Tuck after a barrel of ale. And talking of ale, I suppose you haven't got any?'

This was bordering on the seriously cheeky. Also, it made me wonder whether he needed Dutch courage. Had he taken one look and thought, Christ, I should have charged more for snogging that? What if Susie had told him to watch out, after three man-less months I'd probably eat him alive?

Already making mental notes to 'field' any kiss on my cheek, and just look mildly amused, I found a bottle of lager in the fridge.

He tasted, and nearly choked. 'Forsooth, 'tis weaker than mother's milk. Not a patch on what I used to sup in the *Crusader's Return*.'

If this was a Real Ale man making a point, he was pushing his luck. Acidly I said, 'I'm very sorry, but it's all I've got.'

He looked instantly crestfallen. 'Pray, forgive me. I fear my manners have suffered appallingly. Centuries of social isolation, you know.'

He smiled, and I found myself trying not to laugh again, not to mention melting. He really was rather gorgeous. If he was 'resting' it was a crying shame. They should write him into *EastEnders*, as a tasty newcomer for the Slater girls to cat-fight over. He could be a long-lost illegitimate son of Pat. Having come to find her, he'd then have a complete fit over her taste in earrings and decide not to bother, after all. But of course he'd end up in the Vic for a quick one, and Kat would be flashing her cleavage before you could say 'leave it aht.'

'You were telling me all about your faithless Elinor,' I reminded him.

'Ah, yes.' He took another sip and sighed. 'She came to me in my bedchamber and threw some evil-smelling powder at me. "By all the saints!" I said. "What the fuck are you doing?" Of course, I wouldn't normally speak to my wife like that, but believe me, it stank worse than anything in that Saracen jail.'

'I can believe it. So what did she say?'

'She laughed. She said, "'Tis powdered newt, so put that in your quiver and shoot it. You'll be laughing on the other side of your visage in a minute.'

'Bitch.'

'Indeed.' He gave a melancholy sigh. 'I laughed, of course. I said, "If you paid three gold pieces for that, I'm cutting down your castle-keeping." I was still laughing even as she chanted her spell. Alas, the poor sceptic. Her laughter haunted me for at least three centuries. Still, all water under the drawbridge now.'

Sitting back, he poured the rest of his lager into his glass. 'Perchance I could get a taste for this, after all. "Tis growing on me.'

What kind of kissogram was this? Scrounging lunch, slurping beer, and not so much as a peck?

Suddenly I was no longer amused. 'If you've quite finished, I'll clear away.'

I picked up the plates and dumped them in the sink. Crossly I squeezed Lemon Morning Fresh over them and turned the tap on.

I heard him come to stand behind me. 'My lady Rose, that was the best repast I've had since twelve-ninety-two. Is there any little service I can perform for you in return?'

God, why didn't he just *do* it? Was I supposed to beg? 'If you really want a job, my car's overdue for a wash.'

'It would be my pleasure. But first...'

Unbelievably, light as egghells, his hands were on my waist. Like a warm whisper, he blew on the back of my neck.

My legs didn't know what had hit them. They didn't know whether to turn to jelly or wet cotton wool.

I turned around.

He was looking down at me, his eyes all glinty-warm. 'I would fain snog the knickers off you,' he said, 'but I fear to offend you.'

Gulp. 'Oh, no, honestly...'

And that was it. I don't know whether he'd been told that ancient baronets kissed differently, but boy, this was a snog and a half. Sort of Coeur de Lion, with fire and passion and steel. It was so deliciously overwhelming, my own furnace was soon blazing as it hadn't for years. I felt like Moll Flanders, Kat Slater, and every other trollop since Eve, rolled into one. It was me who yanked my top off, and tossed my bra after it. I'm sure he'd have helped, but he was too busy with his doublet and hose. And I can tell you, he had a weapon any lusty knight would have been proud of.

I've never been much into kitchen tables, though. Vastly

overrated, in my opinion. So with the final garments being tossed aside en route, still glued together at the mouths, I steered him towards my John Lewis duvet.

'Rogering' wasn't quite the word for the next few minutes. Think 'practised seducer' crossed with 'mediaeval battering ram' and you'd just about have it. All I can say is, every girl should have one on her birthday.

After a lovely, post-coital snooze in his arms, I awoke to find him already nearly dressed.

Come-down time. Still, what had I expected? 'Are you off?'

He looked positively shocked. 'My lady, that would be churlish in the extreme! Did you not wish me to wash your car?'

Bless him. 'Have a cup of tea first.'

So we were back in the kitchen, waiting for the kettle to boil, when the doorbell rang. 'Would you get that?' I asked, busy with PG.

He opened the door.

'Who the fuck are you?'

Oh, my God. Dave. And not a drop of sour milk to be had.

The next thing I knew, he was decorating my Magnet kitchen, glowering, 'What's going on?' He looked from me to my Birthday Special, who'd just followed him through. 'Who's this prat in fancy dress?'

'Sir Guy de Montfort,' I said, deadpan. 'His wife changed him into a toad, but I just kissed him better.'

'Yeah, right.'

Birthday Special's lip curled with wonderful, aristocratic disdain. 'Fie, what an ill-bred cur. The lowliest peasant on my estates had better manners.'

While I tried not to crack up, Dave turned an interesting shade of puce. 'Shut it, you!'

Before I'd blinked, Birthday Special had grabbed a knife from the draining board and pinned him up against the fridge, the tip at his throat. 'Ugsome, worthless brute - one more word and I'll have your miserable entrails round your neck.'

'That'll do, Sir Guy,' I said hastily. 'I only washed the floor this morning.'

Birthday Special lowered the knife. It was only an ordinary one anyway. 'As you wish. I wouldn't waste good steel on such a skulking knave.'

Dave, meanwhile, was looking shaken, and serve him right.

'This is Dave, my ex,' I told Birthday Special. 'And you're dead right, he is an ugsome brute. I suppose you couldn't remember that spell? He looks a bit like a toad anyway, now I come to think of it.'

Playing along beautifully, Birthday Special gave me an apologetic look. 'I fear it was tailored for me. It might perchance not fit this bladder of lard.'

'No harm trying,' I said gaily.

Dave's expression, meanwhile, had reverted to something between a sneering smirk and nervousness. I knew he wanted to leg it, but didn't want to look as if Birthday Special had scared him off. 'I knew you were cracking up,' he said to me. 'And I want my Barry Manilow CDs back.'

I ignored him. 'Do proceed, Sir Guy.'

Birthday Special cleared his throat. In a loud, dramatic voice he declaimed:

'*Scab of pox and dung of hog,*

Denizens of muddy bog
Take this man so proud and tall
Make him foul and make him small
Wrap him in a warty coat
Put vile insects in his throat.
Let him live in loathsome slime
Till the very end of time!'

I was nearly wetting myself. 'That was brilliant! Did you make it up just like that, off the cuff?'

But he didn't seem to hear. His eyes were fixed on Dave.

'By Our Lady,' swore Sir Guy de Montfort softly. 'I never thought it would work without the powdered newt.'

May Day, May Day
By Liza Granville

She hadn't wanted to come. When it came to anything natural, she never did.

'Someone has to go,'Nigel said, 'her father's an important client.'

Because she was ambitious, Jane agreed, even though it meant leaving at dawn. After all, it was only a wedding. And May the First was a Saturday.

The church was ancient, only half-heartedly Christian. Its carved doorway writhed with serpents devouring each other's tails. Shela-na-gig, the Celtic fertility goddess, crouched over the entrance exposing herself. The nave was massed with flowers flaunting their reproductive organs. Jane averted her eyes. Disgusting, all of it.

She sat at the back, on the end of a pew. Smoothing down her chic suit, she forced a tight smile for the old man on her left. He mumbled something to her chest. Jane yawned. Her eyes drifted upwards to focus on the roof bosses.

Nature again. Each was carved to represent foliage. Then she saw the face, half-hidden, leering. It was the Green Man, master of May Day ceremonies. Fertility ceremonies, she recalled, shuddering. Unbridled goings-on in the greenwood.

A couple of hairpins sprang from the sleek chignon. A

few wisps of hair escaped.

The congregation stirred. Heads turned. The organ choked on Mendelssohn as the bride sailed past.

A dark figure hesitated by Jane's pew. Her eyes flicked sideways and a quiver ran up her spine. He was huge. A beast in an expensive suit, with a tight, icy white rosebud in his buttonhole. She frowned. Surely he didn't think he could sit here. There was no room...

But already he was moving in on her, pushing his body into that tiny space, forcing her to slide further along, pressing her up against the old man's spindly frame. Jane squeezed her thighs together, to avoid touching him. Her arms crossed over her chest to escape the pressure of his shoulder. When they stood, his big hands rested on the pew in front. Thick hair erupted from his sleeves, lay like a pelt on his hands, coiled across his finger joints. Slowly but surely the flower fragrance was overlaid by a dense musky smell.

More pins erupted. She could feel the chignon slowly unwinding, lying heavy on her nape.

She began to sweat. Jane *never* sweated.

They sat down. Suddenly he was there again, jammed tight against her. She noticed the rosebud had changed colour. Its petals were flushed a delicate pink. And they were opening.

'Do you...'

He caught her looking. His eyes held hers. They were dark brown. Passionate. Full of secrets. His mouth was full too. The sensuous lips, curved in a smile, suggested he knew more than she wanted him to. Her own lips parted. Her breaths became quick and shallow. Her skin tingled.

'Take this woman...'

Furious, she tore her eyes away. This time, when they knelt, she prayed.

Impossible not to sneak another look at the rose. The pink had deepened. A space opened in its heart. Bud had become chalice.

'And do you....'

Against her will, her body began responding to his male energy. An electrical charge passed between them. A wordless conversation. Her mind was invaded by fleeting images that were nothing and everything to do with the ceremony. The remaining pins slid to the floor. Her hair cascaded round her shoulders. Buttons shot from the prim jacket. Her nipples erected. An ache began deep in the pit of her stomach: an old memory, reawakened, brought fierce waves of desire.

'Take this man....'

She pulled herself together. Ignore these feelings and they went away. Concentrate on thinking about something loathsome: bluebottles on liver; dog turd on shoes; a stone on the hips. It always worked.

It didn't.

The rose blushed deep red. A flower in full bloom, the moist petals turned back. Open. Waiting.

His hand brushed hers. Jane's body swayed towards him. But he'd only reached into his pocket. The panpipes lay on his palm like a silver toy. He left as silently as he'd come. From beyond the door, sweet notes soared above the death march groan of the hymn. They beckoned. She resisted.

But the sound was irresistible: a Pied Piper's tune, it drew her on, across meadows, into the roaring boiling green of the woods. The trees shivered with anticipation.

Twigs tugged at her jacket. Ivy uncurled to finger her buttons. Ferns unzipped her skirt with tiny green teeth. Moss tugged at her shoes. Brambles shredded her tights. When he stopped, she sank down, catching her breath; music curled round her dark as enchanter's nightshade.

She didn't pull away when his lips touched her cheek, her neck, her shoulders, soft as butterfly wings. Nor when his tongue probed with the insistence of a humming-bird reaching deep between the petals for nectar. His big hands moved over her body, rough and gentle as a cat's tongue, playing her as expertly he played the pipes.

She was lost in another place. The only way out was to go further in. A swarm of bees erupted from her navel. Rain forests tingled symphonies on her thighs. A rainbow arched her back. Flowers blossomed from her perineum. The trees absorbed her primeval wail. Nothing mattered. An explosion of triumph from the organ announced that the deed was done. The knot was tied. Jane sat up damp and disorientated. The old man snored. On her right was an empty space. She hugged herself, hoping nobody had noticed.

It was a dream. Just a bizarre dream. Of course it was.

Even so, something had happened. In those brief minutes of... sleep... a shell had been cracked, an iceberg melted, a door opened. The tune lingered. She'd go back to her old life, but nothing would ever be the same again.

Above her head the Green Man grinned. Jane hadn't noticed her ruined tights. Nor the fern fronds in her shoes. Not even the may blossom in her hair.

But when she opened her clenched fist, her hand was full of red rose petals.

Christmas Stockings
By Christina Jones

'That's it. Time's up.' Wriggling away from Barry, Deb pulled up her stockings, pulled down her mini skirt, and looked at her watch. 'I've got to go. My husband will be home soon.'

'Lucky sod,' Barry grinned, emitting an eye-watering waft of bad breath. 'He should keep a better eye on you, love. I wouldn't let you out of my sight if you were mine. Phwoar - them stockings do it for me every time. Does your old man know what you get up to while he's at work?'

'What do you think?'Deb frowned, tugging her coat on and rummaging through the pocket for her car keys. The wodge of notes under her fingers made the last twenty minutes spent in Barry's halitosis-ridden company almost worthwhile. 'Yeah, well - I'm off. Er - thanks.'

'Thank *you*,'Barry leered. 'Maybe I'll see you again?'

'Maybe,'Deb tried hard not to shudder. 'Who knows...'

Outside, the streets were gaudily bedecked with swaying fairy lights, lopsided Christmas trees and neon Santa Clauses, but Deb didn't even see them. She drove home quickly through the dark, icy rain, cursing every red traffic signal. She had to get indoors, wipe off the make-up, shower away the remaining stale aroma of Barry, change out of the tarty clothes, and be bustling round the kitchen by the time Tim put his key in the door.

She'd been living a double life for ages now, and there'd been some narrow squeaks, but so far she'd managed it every time.

'Mmmm, nice and warm in here and - hey, something smells good,' Tim walked into the kitchen about ten minutes after she'd got home and took her in his arms. 'And not just the food, either. Is that a new perfume?'

'Just a tester from work.'Deb kissed him. 'They gave us some free samples.'

'It's gorgeous. Maybe I'll buy you a bottle of the real thing for Christmas - if there's enough money...'

Deb shook her head. The scent cost a fortune and there was never enough money even for the basics. Tim's factory was on short time again, her job in the cosmetics department of Brown and Talbot hardly paid enough to cover the bills, and Christmas was only a month away.

Of course, this was where men like Barry came in so handy...

'Don't worry about buying me a present this year,' she pulled away from him and stirred the rice, feeling guilty like she always did. 'As long as we're together and got enough to eat and drink we'll be fine.'

Tim kissed her again. 'Sweetheart, however broke we are I'll buy you a present because I love you so much. I'd like to buy you diamonds or designer clothes or a luxury holiday but I can't - but whatever I give you will be given with all the love in the world. You know that, Deb, don't you?'

Deb stifled a groan. She knew. It would break Tim's heart if he knew that this year everything they had for Christmas would be because of men like Barry and Joe and Alan and... and - oh God, this was awful - she couldn't even remember all their names...

Two weeks before Christmas Tim's factory got a sudden rush order so not only was he back to full-time working but overtime too.

'I know it'll mean we won't see much of each other,' Tim called cheerfully up the stairs as he set off on his first late shift, 'but it'll take the pressure off and mean we'll have money for Christmas.'

In the bedroom, Deb smoothed up her black stockings and fastened the suspenders beneath her tight leather skirt. 'Yeah. Great. Er - will this mean you'll be working nights?'

'Not all night I hope,' Tim's voice laughed as he pulled open the front door. 'But late I guess. I hope I'll get to sleep with you sometime. Bye, then, darling...'

'Bye...' Deb called, parading in front of the mirror in a red satin basque. 'Don't work too hard. See you later.'

She listened for the closing of the door and pulled a tight black lacy top over the bra. With Tim working every evening she'd be able to make even more money. She slipped into her four-inch stilettos. This could be their best Christmas yet...

'You're so beautiful,' Jack murmured into her hair. 'I could eat you.'

'No emotional involvement,' Deb said sharply, turning her face away. 'And no tongues. You know that.'

Jack let his hands trail over the tiny leather skirt, his fingers outlining the mound of the suspenders. 'Spoilsport... Mind you, you certainly give value for money, don't you? It's worth it for the stockings alone. Sheer black stockings... What a turn on.'

Deb smiled to herself as she pocketed Jack's money. All the men went crazy over the stockings. It didn't matter what else she wore, they all got excited over the stockings. She thought they were ugly and uncomfortable but her men couldn't get enough of them.

And tonight had been a good one. She'd had three clients: Jack was the last, before him there had been a pimply embarrassed boy who she didn't even know the name of, and her first of the evening had been Alfie who was as old as her dad and went purple in the face the moment she'd curled her arms around him.

She tried not to think about any of them. All she thought about as she drove home through the freezing night was the wad of ten and twenty pound notes growing in the shoe box in her wardrobe. This year she'd be able to give Tim everything he'd ever wanted.

Every night Tim was working late Deb took the opportunity to fit in more and more clients. She still felt guilty when he came home after midnight, exhausted, and fell into bed beside her, cuddling her with love. She tried not to think about the other men whose arms had held her that night.

'Do you like me wearing stockings?' she whispered to Tim.

'Yeah,' he muttered sleepily. 'Stockings are dead sexy. I wish you'd wear them... All men love stockings...'

'Why?' Deb frowned in the darkness.

'Dunno,' Tim yawned. 'Probably because they're sort of dark and forbidden and authoritarian... Jeeze Deb, don't turn me on now. I'm knackered...'

She grinned into the pillow, curling against him, loving him with all her heart, as he snored gently. Once

Christmas was over she'd never wear stockings for other men again. She'd wear them for Tim. Just for Tim...

By Christmas Eve Tim's factory had completed their order, full-time work was assured for the future, and his late shifts had ended. Deb had one more man to entertain and then her sexy wardrobe would be dumped in the bin and that part of her life would be over forever - except for the stockings, of course. She'd keep the stockings for Tim.

'We're having a bit of a do at the pub tonight,' Tim said. 'The bosses are paying for it - a sort of Christmas box, a celebration that we're back on proper money, and a thank you for getting the work done on time. It'll be great to go out together for once and not worry about the cost, won't it?'

Deb sucked in her breath. Tonight she was supposed to be meeting some man called John. He'd ordered black leather, spike heeled boots, and - naturally - sheer black stockings. 'Er - well I might be working late... There'll be a lot of last minute present shoppers tonight... If you go with the blokes from the factory I'll come along later when I've finished.'

'Okay,' Tim kissed her. 'I can't wait to show you off to the rest of the guys.'

Deb could have cried. She wished she could ring John and cancel, but like all her clients, he hadn't made his appointment direct. Still, this was the last time. Tonight she'd see John, take his money, and then she'd never ever have to do this again...

Her men had provided some great presents for Tim. After paying the bills, she'd spent every penny on him. Everything he'd ever wanted was wrapped and hidden in the wardrobe. And she knew he'd spent a vast amount of his overtime money on the largest bottle of the expensive scent she loved. One of the girls from work had let it slip that he'd been into the department store, making sure he'd got it right.

This should be their best Christmas ever. And it would be, of course, if only she didn't feel so sickeningly guilty...

At eight o'clock she stopped the car outside The Jolly Postman, the biggest pub in town. John, she'd been told, would be waiting for her in one of the private rooms. The night was dark and bitterly cold, with black clouds chasing across an even blacker sky and the threat of snow on the keening north-east wind. Deb pulled her coat more closely round her and shivered her way across the car park.

The pub was packed, ablaze with Christmas lights and decorations and Slade were, as always, bawling out "Merry Christmas Everybody" from the jukebox. Deb elbowed her way across to the bar and yelled at the girl serving drinks that she was supposed to be meeting someone called John. For business.

The girl looked her up and down with mockery in her eyes. 'You called Star?'

Deb nodded. They all had to have stupid false names to safeguard their privacy.

The girl curled her lips in a knowing smile while her eyes shouted "TART!" . 'He's through there - out of this bar - along the corridor - second door down...'

Teetering on the spiky heels, Deb fought her way through the merrymakers and mistletoe into the relative peace of the corridor. This would be the quickest one ever, then she'd rush out to the car, get changed and join Tim at his party and - she stopped. Bloody hell! Where exactly was Tim's party? The pub he'd said. Which pub? There were dozens of them in the town. Damn... so, would it be The Swan, closest to the factory, or The Red Lion on the High Street, or - ?

She looked at her watch. Five to eight. John could wait. She pulled her mobile from her pocket and dialled Tim's number.

'Hi, sweetheart,'his voice echoed in her ear. 'Have you finished work?'

'Er, not quite... Won't be long though. I just wondered where we were supposed to meet up? Was it the Swan?'

'No,' Tim said. 'Too posh for us... We've booked a function room at The Jolly Postman...'

Shit. Deb swallowed. 'Oh - er - right... Okay I'll be there in about half an hour or so.'

'Liar.'

'What?' She frowned. 'What's that supposed to mean.'

'It means sweetheart that I know you're already at the Jolly Postman, dressed in black leather, wearing stockings - and all for the benefit of some guy called John...'

She almost dropped the phone in panic. How could he know? How? She'd been so careful... 'I don't know what the hell you're talking about.'

'Oh, yes you do - turn round.'

Feeling sick, Deb turned her head. 'Oh, God!'

Tim was standing in the doorway of the room behind her. She clutched her coat more closely round her. What the hell was going on? Her brain whirled. She had to think of a reasonable explanation. Had to!

'Er - um....'

Tim stepped towards her and ripped the coat open. Neither of them spoke. His fingers tightened round her wrist and he pulled her across the corridor and into the room. 'I think we'd better do this in private don't you?'

Deb bit her lip, willing herself not to cry. She'd done it all for Tim. All of it. She loved him. He'd understand - wouldn't he?

'Okay,' he stared at her. 'Do your stuff then, Star.'

'What?'

'That's what you call yourself, isn't it? That's what I booked. Star, eight o' clock tonight at The Jolly Postman, private corridor, second door down...'

Deb blinked. 'You're *John* ?'

'Yeah, well, you don't have the monopoly on name changing...' Tim pulled her closer and ran his hands down her thighs, his fingers lingering on the stocking tops. 'So am I going to get my money's worth?'

'I can explain... Look, it was only because we were so short of money. I wanted to help out. I wanted - '

'Shut up,' Tim said sharply. 'Shut up and do your stuff.'

'I can't... I can't... Oh!' Deb met his eyes. She punched him. 'You bastard! You *knew!* '

Tim laughed. 'Yeah, I knew. And I'm dead proud of you, sweetheart. And I can't wait for my mates to see you - but before they do I don't think we should waste the opportunity do you?'

Giggling, Deb entwined herself around him as he stroked the white flesh above the black stocking tops and pushed her down on to the sofa. This time there'd be no restrictions at all. And Star, the sexiest kissogram in town, would be giving the final performance of her life.

Fantasy Lovers

By Rosie Harris

Sue gave a blissful sigh as she lay back in the hot scented water. Sensuously, she stretched out one of her shapely legs lifting her foot until her red painted toenails pierced the white bubbles. Then she reached out for the glass of white wine balanced on the side of the bath.

She manoeuvred a foam pillow under the back of her head and resting against its softness, her blonde hair floating around her pretty oval face, sipped her wine appreciatively,

Steam rose in wispy swirls, she closed her eyes as soft music from the portable radio balanced on the window ledge drifted into the room.

Thoughts of Michael and their love-making began to infiltrate her mind. He was in his forties, almost twice her age but she loved everything physical about him.

His hard muscled body, his shock of dark hair, his firm chin and his piercing green eyes all excited her and set her pulses racing. He was breathtakingly handsome in his expensive sharply tailored business suits (and out of them).

He had charm as well as sex-appeal. She admired his ability to sum up a situation ahead of everyone else, and to decide on a solution to a problem almost before most people realised there was one.

She sat up abruptly. She'd promised herself she wouldn't do this. When he wasn't with her she must banish him to the back of her mind where he couldn't intrude on her thoughts. From her first day as Michael's PA, she'd resolved to keep her working life and private life quite separate.

There's a time and place for everything, her father had always drummed into her and after she left University and entered the business world she could see the wisdom of that.

When colleagues related heartbreaking experiences of office love affairs, she vowed that nothing like that would ever happen to her. She would neither jeopardise her reputation, or her chances of promotion, nor would she exploit her sexuality to gain advancement of any kind.

Yet it had happened.

Within weeks of starting to work for Michael as his Personal Assistant they'd been eating dinner together.

They'd had a gruelling day explaining a new system to a major company. The eventual outcome had been a triumph of diplomacy and skill. They had both felt so elated by their success that they agreed it called for a celebratory drink. After a second round of drinks Michael had picked up the menu and asked her to join him for a meal.

The ambience of their surroundings had been so relaxing that they lost all track of passing time. Michael insisted on giving her a lift home because it was so late; courtesy demanded she should invite him in for a coffee.

She didn't try to explain that her flat was so bare because the deposit had taken all her savings and she'd had only enough money left to buy curtains and a sofa. Unable to afford carpets or even rugs she'd polished all the wood floors. The walls throughout were a pale peach because it had been more economical to buy one large tin of emulsion rather than several smaller ones. As she drew the sumptuous ivory velvet drapes at the window and sat at the other end of the cream leather settee, the only item of seating in the flat, he enthused about the wonderful minimalism she had achieved.

'I abhor cluttered rooms. I hate it when flowers, plants, ornaments and mementoes fill every available space, and patterned wallpapers and carpets fight with flowered curtains, and piles of cushions,'he told her. 'It's all so claustrophobic. So much unnecessary dusting and cleaning. Such wasted effort. 'It's the same in a home as in business, one has to be ruthless and regularly clear out the clutter.'

In the ensuing months Sue had added very little to her flat, even though her salary had more than doubled. Michael found it a haven, one that he approved of, and one he was happy to visit regularly. After all, it was what they did there together that mattered.

As a lover, he was terrific. Hot as Hades. Tender, bold, ardent, exciting, innovative. She'd never experienced such passionate lovemaking. When he stripped to his boxer shorts he was a changed personality. Big Daddy and his Little Princess; Goldilocks and the Wicked Daddy Bear were two of the flights of fancies they indulged in. It never failed to amaze her how someone so cool and businesslike could be so turned on by fantasy.

At times like this, however, when she was alone in her flat she found herself wondering more and more about his home life. What did he do when he wasn't with her? He was exasperatingly withdrawn when it came to talking about himself. He never mentioned either his background or his family. His private life and his business life were in two completely separate compartments, so where did that leave her, Sue wondered.

Sometimes she felt as if she was living in a vacuum. She wanted Michael, needed him with every fibre of her being. She wanted to be able to look ahead, to plan their future together. Her time clock was beginning to tick and soon, very soon, she would have to take a stand about their relationship if she was to ever experience the satisfaction of having his child. The temptation to see for herself where he lived gnawed at her constantly. She didn't have a car and she was afraid to walk down his road in case he saw her and knew she was prying.

It became such an obsession that the next time he was away on business she left the office in mid-afternoon and armed with a folder of papers as an excuse went to see for herself.

She'd expected to find that it was a smart block of flats but the houses in the wide tree-lined road were detached with open-plan gardens. She saw his BMW in the driveway and for a moment her heart thundered in case he was there even though she knew he'd flown out from Heathrow that morning.

The woman who answered the door was middle-aged, and had a plump motherly figure. Sue assumed she was Michael's landlady.

'Mr Turner asked me to deliver these and collect some other papers that he said he would leave ready for me.'

The woman frowned and shook her head. 'He never said

a word to me. He goes around with his head in the clouds half the time. You'd better come in. He may have left something on his desk in his study.'

Sue felt uneasy. It was a cosy, muddled, but comfortable family home, studded with pictures, photographs and children's possessions and she wondered why Michael chose to live there. There was a big tabby cat sitting on top of one of the radiators in the hall and from somewhere at the back of the house she could hear a dog yapping.

Michael's study was a startling contrast to the rest of the house, like stumbling on a nude in a supermarket. It was starkly bare, not a single picture or memento. There were no papers lying on the huge walnut desk, only a blotter with a fountain pen and calculator positioned in the middle of it.

The woman looked puzzled, her eyes full of concern. 'I'm sorry, there doesn't appear to be anything here for you to collect. My husband has gone to New York on business. He won't be back until late tomorrow. Can I ask him to phone you?'

Sue shook her head. 'No, it doesn't matter,'She tried to smile politely, but her lips felt frozen and she wondered if she had heard correctly, or even if she had the right house.

As two children came into the hallway she had the answer. She knew instinctively who they were. The boy was about ten and darkly handsome like Michael. It was the girl though who made Sue feel she was walking on a thin tightrope of sanity. Trembling, and shocked, she even wondered if she had been astro-projected back in time. Slim, blue-eyed and with long blonde hair it was like looking into a mirror.

I Saw Mummy Killing Santa Claus
By Robert Barnard

'I can't think where food for seven is going to come from,'
complained Henry Threakleston-Bing.

'Nine,' corrected his wife Veronica. 'Susan and Gareth
have to have Christmas dinner too.'Her husband groaned.

'Yes, well.... They won't expect more than a small bird,
will they? About all we'll have.'

'Nonsense! The Christmas pudding is made - not quite
pre-war standard, but quite palatable. We have two ducks,
a very good-sized chicken - I've always thought turkey is
vulgar and tasteless - and a good sirloin of beef. We shall
all do very well.'

'We'll have to give the guests first choice. We'll get left
with what nobody else wants.'

Henry was selfish and a congenital moaner. His wife
raised her eyebrows.

'Personally I'll be happy with any of them. For heaven's
sake cheer up, darling. Times are changing. If you can pay
for them and have the leisure to go searching, you can get
things again. Winnie's back in Downing Street, there's a
young queen on the throne and things are looking up for
people like us.'

'About time too,' grumbled her husband.

'Cheer up,' repeated his wife. 'This will be a Christmas to remember - for us, and for Jeremy too. His first Christmas worthy of the name.' She turned to the boy who was just finishing his breakfast egg. 'Got to celebrate the birthday of Our Lord properly, haven't we?'

The boy nodded. He thought they meant Lord Cricklewood, the biggest local landowner. He was always a bit of a snob in later life.

It was quite true that things were beginning to come back into the shops, that ration books were shrinking in size, and 'cheese' no longer described exclusively dry mousetrap cheddar. For the first time in his five-year lifetime Jeremy's hunger for sweet things could very nearly be sated.

'You'll be happy to eat dinner in the servants' quarters, you and Gareth?' Veronica asked Susan, her maid, as she helped prepare her for bed.

'Of course Mrs Bing,' said Susan, a form of Veronica's name that they had compromised on for quickness's sake. 'We'd prefer it.'

'I'll make sure it's a good one,' drawled Veronica, spraying herself.

'No, *we'll* make sure it's a good one,' thought Susan, who had a cold and logical mind. 'We'll be doing the bloody cooking.'

The next day was the 23rd, and last minute shopping was the order of the day. Jeremy was normally a quiet, serious boy (slow, malicious neighbours said), but now he could scarcely contain his excitement- a quality remarked on many years later when a lady of Soho sold the story of their encounters to the newspaper popularly called The

News of the Screws, bringing to an end his short political career. The young Jeremy's excitement was fixed on knowing what presents he was getting for Christmas- one, he was sure, was a Dinky Toy, but which Dinky Toy?- and he tired himself out daily with anticipation. When he woke up that night at half past ten he took himself out to the lavatory, and saw from the landing his mother in a low-backed dress and high heels, and his father going through what looked like a pile of bright red blankets.

'They're terribly dusty,' he was saying.

'Well, there's no time to wash them now,' his mother said. 'Even if it were done tomorrow we couldn't hang them out - Jeremy would see them.'

'Not if we hung them in the kitchen garden.'

'At the moment he's so excited he goes everywhere. And we can't tie him to a table-leg.'

'Sounds like a brilliant idea to me,' said his father.

If Jeremy had only left his visit to the loo half an hour later, he might have seen his mother, standing under Dorleston Manor's mock-medieval wooden chandelier which hung from its roof down into the hall and was now decked with mistletoe, kissing a white-bearded gentleman dressed in white-edged red robes- kissing him gingerly, it must be said, so as not to raise clouds of dust that might ruin her make-up.

The morning of Christmas Eve was enlivened by the arrival of a crate of rather fine cognac, a present from Veronica's Uncle Ernest. 'Leaving present from Lloyd's, dear girl' he wrote, 'but forbidden on pain of death by my doctors, along with many other good things. Drink and enjoy!'

Henry examined the case and could find nothing to

grumble at. It was the sort of cognac he had drunk when he began drinking, before the war.

'Trying to make us feel guilty for not inviting him,' he said.

'Nonsense,'said Veronica. 'Uncle Ernest hates children. It's gratitude for our not inviting him.'

Christmas Day began with Jeremy's cries of delight (and the odd ominous silence of disappointment when the present did not live up to his expectations). The kitchen bore the brunt of his high spirits, because his parents stayed in bed late to prepare for the labours of the rest of the day.

Veronica had bought Henry a magnificent set of golf clubs, property of a nearby aficionado of the game, gone to the great links in the sky. Henry had bought Veronica art nouveau ear-rings and bracelet at an ill-attended Sotheby's auction. Old still meant better for the Threakleston-Bings.

Jeremy's presents, as he told Gareth and Susan over and over again (Susan hiding well the fact that she didn't care for children) were only half his store. Santa Claus would be bringing the rest of them personally during Christmas dinner. Major and Mrs Farnaby were the first of the guests to arrive. Derek Farnaby was an old army pal of Henry's who had bought and become headmaster of a prep school in nearby Peterborough. He knew nothing about boys, and ran the school like a training camp, fitting the boys ruthlessly to the regime and never varying the regime for an individual boy. The prominent lump in Hester Farnaby's stomach revealed that another victim of the Major's system could be on the way.

'And what did you get for Christmas, young man?' the major asked Jeremy.

'Sherry? Dry or medium?' interrupted Veronica. She didn't bother to offer gin and tonic. The Farnabys were mixing rather above their level, she thought, and were only invited because Henry insisted on it. It was a waste of an invitation. Jeremy certainly wouldn't be going to school there. Susan, taking time off from the parts of the dinner that Gareth was not responsible for, took them upstairs to show them the bedroom where coats and hats were to be left, as well as the guest bathroom. They were on the way down for their sherries when the doorbell went and the Cavendishes arrived.

The Cavendishes were much more to Veronica's taste. Cecily had been presented to King George and Queen Elizabeth at the first Queen Charlotte's Ball after the end of the war. She had married Gareth as soon as he completed his National Service, and his father had died on cue the day after they returned from their honeymoon. Accordingly they had taken over a fine Queen Anne house in Peterborough, and as things had livened up in the early 'fifties they and the Bings had enjoyed quite a lot of 'fun' events together. Veronica had detected that Gavin was beginning to lose interest in his wife, and this added to the couple's appeal. Veronica took them through to the estate office, where the drinks had been set out.

'Sherry?'she asked. 'Or gin and tonic? And just bear in mind that we've oceans of a rather fine cognac for later on.'

'And what did you get in your stocking, young feller-me-lad?' Gavin asked Jeremy when they all went into the sitting room.

Drinks took quite a while, because Gareth and Susan were snatching their Christmas dinner below stairs before serving the grander meal in the dining room. For fun Veronica put on the little maid's hat that Susan always wore when they had guests and went round with bottles. Jeremy had registered that no one was really interested in what he had got for Christmas, but his interest was maintained by the fact that more was to come: he had noticed small parcels being slipped into his father's hands by the arriving guests. He was a watchful, if not an intelligent, child.

Dinner, when finally it arrived, went swimmingly. The vegetable soup warmed all the adults up (Jeremy just said 'ugh'), and the various meats catered for all tastes and were well carved by Henry, who had plenty of his own preferred duck when he finally served himself. Gareth- he of the Welsh twinkling eyes- pressed steaming silver dishes of vegetables on everyone, and went around with a wine bottle in each hand, replenishing well before more was needed. Jeremy ate chicken and drank his favourite American Cream Soda. People sometimes threw questions at him, but mostly he just sat there watching, and sometimes commenting.

'She's got -' he began.

'Darling, not she,' said his mother. 'Mrs Cavendish.'

'Mrs Cavendish's got ear-rings like Christmas puddings.'

Everyone looked. They were circles of gold, flattened at the bottom.

'I suppose they are rather like plum puddings,' said Cecily Cavendish. 'How clever of you to spot it.'

'He's remarkable like that,'said Henry, who was proud of his son in public. 'He sees everything. You can rely on his observation.'

The same was said of the man who, thirty-five years later, in the dying days of the Thatcher government of which he was a minor member, said to his contact in the press: 'She's invincible' just at the time when the daggers were being thrust in. But of course they were metaphorical daggers, and it was only real, corporeal things that Jeremy observed so well.

When the pudding had been tasted Jeremy's father said he would have to fetch more wine. Jeremy pointed out there was some in one of the bottles, but Henry said 'That won't go far.' Five minutes later a figure entered the dining room, exuding bonhomie and dust. He didn't actually say 'Ho ho', but he rubbed his hands, felt into his sack, and said:

'There's'a young man here that I've got presents for!'

'Me!' shouted Jeremy.

Some of the presents were a disappointment, especially the My First Spelling Book from Major and Mrs Farnaby, which had all the hallmarks of a publisher's free sample. But Jeremy, under his mother's cold gaze, just said 'Thank you very much'and went on to the next package. And his presents didn't end the show. Santa dived into his sack again and drew out three identical packages. 'To make it a really happy Christmas,' Santa said, giving one to the Major, one to Gavin Cavendish and one to Veronica. 'Let's see who can drink theirs first!'

When the guest had disappeared to his waiting reindeer Henry returned to be told by Jeremy he had missed Santa. He just said he had seen him often enough in childhood. The packages were opened and the excellence of the brandy commented on by the visitors. They were less happy when it became clear that they were expected to

131

consume their own bottles for the rest of the day, but still it was a good brandy, and a generous gift. The Major inwardly vowed that his wife in her condition could drink none of it, that he would be abstemious, and that he would take most of it home for late night consolation against the trials of drilling thirty twelve-year-olds into a force fit to guard their Queen.

The party continued on its course. The new LP player was plugged in, and dance music furthered the process of softening up which the wine and brandy had begun. As Jeremy went out to kick around the new football from the Cavendishes (what finally put paid to his political career in 1991 was the revelation by a prostitute that he preferred to make love in Peterborough United's football colours- if it had been a smart London club he might have survived, but humble Peterborough had the nation chuckling), the three couples inside began dancing to Henry Hall and Glen Miller, first together, then after more drink with different partners, their cheeks getting redder, their eyes glazed, their innuendos more bed-orientated.

The Major and his wife dropped out. Their special reasons were acknowledged, and it left the more unbuttoned foursome more freedom.

First Veronica and Gavin went upstairs, and Veronica dropped her revealing dress to the floor outside the marital bedroom, as a sign that it was occupied. Soon Henry and Cecily followed, noted the dress, then made their way to the principal guest bedroom, where the bed had been made in anticipation of just such an eventuality.

Daylight faded. Jeremy came in from kicking the ball around and took to his room the clockwork car that sped round and round in dizzy circles. By now the bedrooms were quiet. The Major and his lady had been commenting on other people's conduct, manners and morals in the privacy of the estate office, and they now collected their bottle, still nearly full, and went down to the servants' quarters rather as the Major had been used to visit the Other Ranks' mess, and thanked Susan and Gareth for a wonderful meal. The pair were drinking a bottle of household brandy, superceded by the unlooked-for crate, which Henry had generously taken downstairs for their use. Gareth stood up for the Major but Susan forgot to, and they soon heard the Farnabys' Austin Seven chugging down the drive.

'Bloody Threakleston-Bings!' said Susan. 'I bet they're at it with each other's partners.'

'We could be -'began Gareth.

'Not yet!'said Susan, as she generally did. As she spoke Henry drifted blearily in, carrying his wife's dress, which he deposited in the laundry basket, and drifted out again.

As darkness fell Jeremy felt the need to go to the lavatory, and once again passed along the landing. Snores were coming from Mummy and Daddy's bedroom, but when he looked down he saw his father and mother in the mock-baronial Great Hall - his father having a white fuzz stuck on both cheeks below the ears, his mother in the low-backed dress she had worn at dinner. As Jeremy began back to his room he realized his father had pushed his mother back on to the table by the far wall of the Hall, under the hunting trophies of his great grandfather, and he heard the word, distinctly hissed, 'cow'. He had long since given up looking for a four-legged, contented-looking animal chewing grass when he heard that word, and he wasn't sure of the meaning of the other word he heard, so he went back into the nursery, wound up his lovely new car, and contentedly played with it until he heard a car draw up outside. He jumped on his bed to look out of the window above it, and thus was the first to witness the arrival of Inspector Pittock and Sergeant Fry.

****

It was Gareth who had called the Police, and Gareth who took the pair into the estate office after they had briefly viewed the body in the sitting room with the stab wounds to the heart. They called at once to Peterborough HQ for scientific backup.

'Where are the people of the house?' asked Pittock, looking around.

'You've just seen one of them.'

'Well, where's Mrs Threakleston-Bing? I presume she's been told.'

'No, she hasn't. So far as I know she's upstairs. It's awkward... a delicate matter.'

'Hmmm. There were two cars outside the front door.'

'That's right. There've been guests for Christmas dinner. Major and Mrs Farnaby have gone home. He's a headmaster. She's in the family way.'

'I know them. Fry - get on to the school. I want them back here ....What about the others?'

'Mr and Mrs Cavendish.'

'Mr Gavin. Cavendish?' When he nodded Pittock whistled. 'They have the reputation of fast livers.'

'You could say that.... I think that he and Mrs Threakleston-Bing ...'

'I see.' Pittock meditated slowly, distaste suffusing his

face. When Fry came back into the room with the news that the Major and Mrs Farnaby were on their way back to the Manor Pittock made up his mind. 'Go up to the bedrooms - which one? -'

'Second to the right at the top of the stairs,'said Gareth.

'- and catch them in flagrante. That will stop them trying any silly business and wasting our time. Tell them to stay where they are. If you can find Mrs Cavendish, tell her the same.'

As he stood there, pursing his lips. Inspector Pittock foresaw the results of this particular investigation: faithless wife, angry husband, and the husband it was who got it in the neck. Or in this case the heart. What a way to celebrate the Lord's birthday!

But two hours later he was not so sure. He talked to the Major and his wife first. Good, upstanding, truthful people in Pittock's view. He'd heard of the school, and knew the Major ran a tight ship, if that wasn't a mixed metaphor. When he heard about the bottles of brandy, the dancing, the disappearances to the bedrooms, the swapping of partners, Pittock was shocked to the core. Ten years later, in the swinging 'sixties, Pittock was frequently heard to say 'That's when I realized what was on the way. That's when I saw just how far standards were sliding. The descendents of Cephas Threakleston, swapping wives like bl- foreigners, like Frenchmen! I tell you, I was shocked to the core!'

It should be said that Pittock knew no more about the habits of Frenchmen and their wives than he knew about the habits of the Trobriand Islanders.

When he talked to the unfaithful widow she had obviously had time to get her story and Gavin Cavendish's to coincide. They had had too much to drink, they had gone off to bed together -'these things happen'she said airily to Pittock, to whom they did not happen - and they had been together the whole time. No, she had not slept, Gavin had not slept, (what, Pittock wondered, had they been discussing? The symbolism of the Wise Men's gifts?) and they neither of them had left the bedroom. Cecily Cavendish's plight was still deeper. She and Henry had - you know - and then he had dressed and gone off - gone downstairs, in fact, and then she had slept off the brandy - you know how it is - and remembered nothing until Sergeant Fry had knocked and come in - I mean the shock, hearing that someone you've just been ... you know.

After this testimony to the approach of a new Sodom and Gomorrah Pittock felt, as he said, the need for a bit of fresh air. He was, however, only speaking metaphorically, because when he left the estate office he prowled around the ground floor of Dorleston Manor, his piggy eyes going everywhere, noting the crate of brandy, the two half-drunk bottles, the hunting trophies of the ancestral Threakleston, with the empty slit where a hunting-knife had once been, the tidy dining-room table, with everything cleared away and a floral decoration in place in the centre. Then he saw in one corner of the room a Dinky Toy, a paper hooter, a spelling book and a knitted kangaroo.

'What's this?' he demanded of Sergeant Fry. 'Is there a child?'

'Jeremy,' came the answer from Gareth, lurking around the door. 'Just five. He'll be in his room.'

'Why wasn't I told there was a child?'Gareth didn't say 'You didn't ask', but wisely held his peace. 'And while he was in his nursery the parents were .... Oh, it makes my blood boil!'

'Shall I fetch him?'

'No. Show me to the nursery.'

The nursery announced itself by the noise of clockwork. When they opened the door a red car was spinning in circles of eight around the floor.

'I don't have to ask what you got for Christmas,' said Sergeant Fry.

'Everyone else did,' said Jeremy. Fry got down to the floor and wound up the car, sending it noisily on its way again.

'We're going to ask you some questions, Jeremy,' he said.

'Why?'

'Your Daddy has had a bit of an accident, and we want to know how it happened.'

'What sort of an accident?'

'Your Mummy will tell you later. When did you last see your Daddy?'

The boy thought.

'I went to have a wee-wee. I saw him and Mummy then.'

'When was this?'

'Oh, when I'd played with the car, and had a little sleep.'

'So you got up, and went out to the landing?'

'Yes. There was snoring coming from Mummy and Daddy's room.'

The two policemen looked significantly at each other. 'I thought they were asleep, but when I looked down they were in the hall. Sort of kissing.'

'Sort of kissing?'

'Their faces were close ....' The child seized on a new thought. 'I've discovered something about Daddy.'

The inspector and the sergeant both stiffened. 'Oh?'

'It was Daddy who was Santa Claus. I expect Santa couldn't come after all, so Daddy dressed up as him so I wouldn't be disappointed. He still had bits of white beard on his face.'

Again the policemen looked at each other.

'So they were kissing, or close to each other.'

'That's right. Mummy had her back to me, and it was dirty, and their faces were close. But when I came back from my wee-wee Daddy was bending her over the table in the hall, and saying words like 'cow' and that other word .... 'sluck' or something like that. It was one of their rows.'

'So what happened?'

'I don't know. I just came back here, and went on playing with my car.'

'Jeremy,' said Pittock. 'What do you mean by saying your mother's back was dirty?'

'It had a great big black spot on it. Like soot.'

Back downstairs in the Great Hall Pittock went over and inspected the table, then looked up to the landing to ascertain that the boy could have seen what he said he saw. Then he fingered the slit in the assemblage of hunting trophies and methods of slaughter that stood behind the table. The knife taken from the slit, judging by his expression, could indeed have inflicted the wound in Henry's chest. But he was not happy. There was dirty and difficult work to be done. Luckily it could be left to Sergeant Fry.

'You're going to have to inspect their backs. For a black mark.'

'Someone's got to do it,' Fry sighed. 'But she could have washed it off.'

'If she knew it was there. And if it wasn't a birthmark. Do all the ladies, and don't take any nonsense from them.'

'Starting with the wife?'

'I suppose so. But if it was a birthmark -'

They were interrupted by a scuffling sound from a door leading into the hall. Pittock, who had once been a nifty half-back for an amateur side, was through the door in a flash, through the hall, then down a long corridor, just in time to see a foot disappearing through a green baize door at the far end. Seconds later he and Fry were in the massive kitchen, and Fry had his hands on Gareth's collar and was forcing him down into a chair.

'So you were listening,' said Pittock.

'Don't get much excitement in this household,' said Gareth sullenly.

'I'd've thought you got all too much. But you're not just interested, you're involved, aren't you?' and to the man's vigorously shaking head he said: 'What do you know about a woman with a dirty back? Or a woman with a mark on her back? A birthmark?' Gareth shook his head again, but his heart wasn't in it.

'You the only servant here?' asked Fry, looking at the table where two desert plates with the remains of Christmas pudding were set. 'There's a lady's maid, isn't there?' Gareth nodded miserably. 'Tell us about the birthmark on her back.' There was a silence, then Gareth came clean.

'Susan. Susan Sullivan .... It's not as though I've seen it often. Snooty she is. It's very much a favour if she gives anything at all. Except to him. Of course.'

'Him?' asked Pittock. 'Mr Threakleston-Bing, I suppose?'

'She had her plans, had Susan. I've always thought that. She wasn't an ordinary servant - cut above us, and she knew it. So why was she here? Once she'd got him in her toils she was going to work the situation for all it was worth.'

'Blackmail,' said Pittock.

'That most likely. He had his eye on a political career. The descendent of Cephas Threakleston being member for the Peterborough constituency where his brick-factory had been. She'd like to have been mistress of this place, but failing that she was going to milk him. Nice little earner. Then she'd move on.'

'That is, failing divorce, then a remarriage to her?'

'That's what I thought.'

'You weren't in on the plan?'

'NO! .... Don't make me laugh. She was like a sphinx. I'd never have got anything out of her if I'd tried to discuss it.'

'When did you last see her?'

'Oh, over an hour ago.... Mrs Bing's car's gone from the garage.'

Pittock nearly swore (his bl's were always a sign that a case was getting beyond him), got the registration number, then sent Fry off to the phone again. Fuming, he turned back to Gareth.

'So let's make a guess. Susan dressed up in Mrs Bing's outfit. How did she get hold of it?'

'He came down and dropped it in the laundry basket. I expect she'd just taken it off somewhere. He was making a point.'

'Bl.... So she put it on, and went to find him to suggest that she made quite as good a Mrs Threakleston-Bing as the existing one.'

'Maybe.'

'And he, drunk, fed up with her, didn't react as hoped, called her a cow and a slut -'

'If you say so.'

'We have evidence. And she, in a fit of temper -'

'She had one. I told her it'd be her downfall.'

'- snatched at the hunting knife and plunged it into him.'

'And dragged him to the sitting room to delay his being found.'

'And then collected together whatever spoil she'd already got her hands on, got the key to Mrs Bing's car -'

'We often use it for shopping in Peterborough.'

'- and off she went. And all we have to do is pick up her and the car.'

But doing that proved more difficult than they expected. They first thought she would have gone to Peterborough, which even on Christmas Day had a first-rate train service. They thought she would choose London, or perhaps Cambridge, to disappear in. The newspapers carried descriptions only, there being no photograph available. They described her suitcase, and they described the strawberry-shaped birthmark just below her left shoulder-blade (they praised to the skies the observational powers of the dead man's little boy, though in fact the description owed more to Gareth).

On New Year's Eve the car was found abandoned in the Birmingham area.

The most reliable of various sightings had her on the boat from Fishguard to Dublin. It made sense to disappear in a crowd of Irish people returning home for the festive season, particularly as the Irish Republic had no extradition treaty with Britain.

****

Time passed. The grieving widow made a great show of
maternal interest in Jeremy, but soon cooled off. He went
through the usual cycle of parental neglect in the English
upper-classes: prep school, boarding at seven; public
school (i.e. private), at thirteen; then Oxford, the City, the
House of Commons. By then the case had long been forgotten. The police of course said they never closed the
files on a murder enquiry, but they buried in pretty deep in
their basement.

The next time the name of Threakleston-Bing got into
the papers there was no reason for the police to be
involved. The bizarre sexual habits of MPs were of no
concern to anyone but themselves. And the women who
serviced them. And the popular press. The woman who
serviced Jeremy, then junior minister at the Department of
Rural Affairs, was a lady from Tibilisi, an early refugee
from the Eastern bloc as the Cold War was ending, and
one with a concern for customer satisfaction unusual in
one nurtured by the Soviet system. No, the goings on in a
Soho brothel were of no interest to the nation's police
force.

However if they had got involved, someone with a long
memory might have noticed that the brothel employing
Varvara from Tibilisi was run by an older woman who
called herself Madame Susie. And if they had dug deeper
still they might have found that she had below her left
shoulder blade a black, strawberry-shaped birthmark. And

that this was a fact known to many people. Many men. Many, many men.

Forbidden Fruit
By Caroline Praed

Debbie searched through rack after rack before she found it. It was perfect! An extremely naughty silk and lace negligee - just £3.95 from the local charity shop. If Simon ever queried the credit card bill, she'd blame the Forbidden Fruit expense on that. She stroked the slick, heavy silk with trembling fingers. Debbie sighed. It seemed dishonest to be doing this at all, never mind having to think up lies to cover herself. Still, it would have seemed even more dishonest just to ignore things.

'Forbidden Fruit Detection Agency - how may we help you?'the voice had singsonged.

Debbie gulped. After getting the engaged tone so many times, she'd been shaken to be speaking to the Agency at last. 'Ah...um' she'd faltered.

The receptionist's voice had been warm and encouraging. 'Am I right in thinking you'd like to engage our services?' it had cooed.

'Er...yes,' Debbie had mumbled. 'It's about my husband.'

'Just a few details, then,'the voice had cajoled.

It was as easy as that. Debbie found she'd booked an appointment with a detective for Tuesday. She was to bring a recent photo of Simon. Oh, and her credit card.

So now Debbie sat edgily at home, very scantily clad, waiting for the call.

In many ways she was regretting going to the Agency. If she hadn't been so certain then she'd never have dreamt of paying all that money. Expensive, the Agency's services. But practically foolproof, she'd been assured.

Sighing, she started to walk towards the window hoping to see if - just this once - Simon had come straight home from work. But then, remembering her current deshabille, she retreated. Instead, pink-cheeked, she went into the kitchen, drew the curtains, and fiddled with the already-perfect place settings.

Everything was ready. More than ready. All she needed to know was whether to serve the chicken casserole on an elegant plate or over his lying, cheating, head.

If he passed the test, then she planned to serve herself up after the chicken. She'd had a long time to think about it, and to plan. In the large newsagents in a town 20 miles distant, and taking every precaution against being recognised by wearing sunglasses, a scarf, and her gardening clothes, she had made some 'top shelf magazine' purchases.

Actually the sunglasses had made it hard to see just what she was getting and the reality of what she had brought home shocked her ... then, though she could barely admit it even to herself, excited her.

Being rather wanton had seemed just the idea to perk up their marriage. She'd read the lot, cover to cover, finding herself almost unbearably turned on by some of the readers'stories. How shameless these women were. How casually they seduced these reluctant men.

She'd been so stimulated she'd almost been able to put

her own ideas into practice. Only a few weeks ago, lying there in bed as enticingly as she could, she had woken Simon earlier than usual.

'I'm feeling a little bit ... hot,' she'd breathed at him.

Sadly it had not gone to plan.

'So am I!' he'd replied, enthusiastically. Then spoilt everything by adding

'Perhaps you ought to turn down the central heating, darling, while I take a shower.' And he'd leapt from the bed and rushed for the bathroom.

Taking a long, honest, look in the mirror while he washed had persuaded Debbie that displaying herself naked had not been such a good idea. And she'd been looking for something a little 'different' in the way of nightwear ever since. Now she had found it. She was determined to bring spice back into their wedding bed.

And if that also meant 'learning to love your body' (something she had previously ignored when she'd seen articles in glossy women's magazines) then so be it. It might just be a question of practice...

A couple of weeks ago, still decidedly under-spiced, she'd watched from the bedroom as he bounded down the path for work, picking a rosebud as he went. The rosebud had decided her. She'd reached for the Yellow Pages.

Of course, there was nothing really concrete to prop up her instincts. The woman at the Agency had asked if he'd begun working late. 'Often the first sign,' she'd told Debbie.

Well he had been working later some nights, but it coincided with him getting a new, stricter, boss at work. And whenever Debbie had rung him late at work - to check on when he'd be back, or which pudding he'd prefer - he'd always picked the phone up after just one or two rings.

He'd never seemed flustered, or anything other than pleased to hear from her. Not unless the new boss was around; and Debbie always knew, because then he sounded colder and highly efficient - just as if he was talking to a customer rather than his wife.

And no, they hadn't had a spate of "Wrong Number" phone calls, nor lipstick on Simon's shirts. As for perfume, nothing could possibly compete with the aftershave Simon now favoured.

Still, and here the female detective had nodded forcefully in agreement, a woman sensed these things.

'Oh yes indeed, Debbie - may I call you Debbie? - a wife always knows.'

And so Debbie had parted with the holiday photo of Simon, and with her signature for a sizeable amount of money. It would be worth it to prove she was right, and the evidence would be admissible in a Divorce Court.

Why wouldn't that blessed phone ring? Still, she reassured herself, it probably meant all was going to plan. Nervously, she adjusted the straps on her negligee. Her breasts felt swollen. The décolletage was really rather frighteningly revealing. The lace had rubbed her nipples until they stood erect. The palms of her hands were slippery from nerves.

In the Saloon Bar, Simon was chatting to a young secretary. Attractive, with a fashionably short skirt and tightish top, and a little too much make-up, she and Simon were laughing about office politics.

Simon was listening to her views on life with an elaborate courtesy, although he suspected buying her the second gin and tonic had been a mistake. She was getting quite giggly.

When her hand trailed invitingly over his crisply-tailored knee, he consulted his watch, announced his wife would be expecting him, and retreated swiftly into the street. Young girls these days, he thought with dismay, were sometimes just asking for trouble.

'Hello, yes, this is Debbie.' It was the long-expected call. 'He didn't? He left? Are you sure? Well, I can hardly believe it!'

Debbie put the phone down and contemplated her brazen reflection in the hall mirror in disbelief. She rued the money wasted. She reproached herself for her lack of trust. She'd make it up to him, of course. It was the chance to make a fresh start in their marriage. Suddenly ashamed of the negligee - had she really thought that anything could improve their perfect marriage? - she ran upstairs to change into her usual clothes.

Still, she couldn't bring herself to discard the beautiful lacy silk entirely. Without knowing quite why, she didn't bundle it into the back of the wardrobe but draped and displayed it carefully on a padded hanger.

Simon was met with a warm hug from his wife and ushered into the dining room to a superb supper. He glowed with contentment. Everything in his life was working out perfectly. He had a good job, a wonderful wife and home, great prospects. Not many men could say the same.

True, when that young girl had practically thrown herself at him in the pub, he had been tempted. But only for a moment.

After all, when you had all your home comforts and a

terrifically exciting lover for a boss, you really didn't need anything else.

Memory
By Sara MacDonald

I watch the couple in the corner. They cannot take their eyes off one another. They could be in a box or a totally empty room, not a busy restaurant. Looking at them I think, a bomb could go off outside and these two would still be locked in cyc to eye contact.

Their food arrives and they remove their arms from the table, lean back still talking intimately as the waiter places dishes of food onto their table. Amazingly, they seem able to order and eat a whole meal without looking at anyone else. I have not seen them turn away from each other once, to view the room or the other diners. He is the most beautiful Indian boy I have ever laid eyes on. The girl is curvy with creamy skin, short hair and trendy clothes.

I am eating with a colleague, her back is to them and I have ample time to watch them as the conversation is desultory, needing no concentration; we are eating here from convenience not celebration and we are both tired after a long week.

I try to remember, as I sip my wine and eat my chicken, if I had ever, once upon a time, been so wrapped up in a man I was totally oblivious to my surroundings; everything narrowed to a pin-prick; every emotion, every sensation concentrated on a man you cannot bear to take your eyes off, a man you want so badly you can hardly breathe.

I can. But it seems a lifetime away; something that happened to the girl I no longer am. It was not with the man I eventually married and later divorced.

The boy in the corner reaches out for the girl's hand, turns it palm up and presses his mouth to the small hand, hard; closes his eyes to hide the strength of his feelings. It is a small act so nakedly raw and filled with intent that the girl swallows and her lips part in a small sensuous intake of breath. She turns her hand slightly so that her two fingers caress his cheek and she leaves them there in a touch as subtle as a brush from the wing of a moth. They stare at each other with open longing and slowly smile.

I have become a voyeur and long suddenly for my youth and a life that is gone, and my heart aches for their vulnerability in this uncertain world.

Under the table, below the crisp white tablecloth, their bare brown legs cross and touch. I can see silvery grains of sand adhering to their ankles as if they have just left the beach with no time to shower.

I visualise them in the long hot day that is gone, lying together on the hot white sand until the last moment when the sun slides into the sea and the sand loses its womblike warmth. I see them stretch, sit up startled to discover the beach is empty and they are hungry.

My colleague and I have finished eating; they have hardly begun, the food cools on their plates. We ask for our bill, halve it carefully. The boy leans towards the girl and says something and she throws back her head and laughs a long happy sound that seems to release the sexual tension in them both. She wrinkles her nose at him; he gazes at her in amusement, his head slightly on one side.

Suddenly, regardless of the crowded restaurant he leans forward over the table and reaches for her face. She leans towards him; they place their lips together, not a kiss, their mouths just touch in a blatant, overtly sexual exchange. Then, slowly she leans back and cups her thin brown arms around her stomach, offers herself to him and he closes his eyes, shivers.

I have watched them all through my meal and yet they are totally unaware of me. What would I have done if they had turned to catch me sitting here staring at them? I place a tip beside the silver wrapped mints and turn and make for the door. Outside I say goodnight to my colleague and walk slowly home round the harbour.

The black sea spins and sparks with the reflected lights of a small seaside town. Fishing boats bob and turn on their moorings. Seaweed and salt fill the night. I sit on the wall and get out my mobile phone and dial a familiar number. I know it will be turned off at this moment but I can leave a message.

'Darling,' I say, thickly. 'Ring me? I was wrong. I unreservedly withdraw my objection. You so obviously love him and life is a gamble; if you want to marry him…it's OK with me, really. Bring him home, it is the long summer break and I miss you.'

I see again my lovely daughter throw her head back and laugh for the sheer joy of being. See her cup her stomach as if to protect what lies there. I might never have known. I might have lost her for good. I could have forgotten for ever that time in your life when no one else exists. Just you and a man; lust and love in a bubble.

Single-minded passion cannot last but that is no reason to deny its existence. For my daughter it might be different. It might change to something long and lasting. And if it does not, she will one day be reminded, out of the blue, of moments, never regretted, when a touch of a hand scorches the skin; when sex will never be so searing or so erotic again.

Even after nineteen years she will find that the memory is still alive and lies painfully and shockingly visceral. She will double up in the dark at the sudden clear vision of that beloved and forbidden face.

After all, that moment is the reason my daughter exists and my greatest, lasting happiness.

The Edward Lewis Gambit

By Sophie Weston

'And that tee shirt won't do,' said Lucy with intensity. 'Oh you make me so mad sometimes, Alice.'

I was hurt. She had said dress down. This evening was supposed to be just the three of us going on the town for her mother's birthday. Think student style, she said.

So I'd unearthed a pair of jeans (last worn a year ago, thank God they still fit) and, rummaging, found my only tee shirt. At nearly thirty-seven I didn't have a lot of student gear. Okay it had the company logo on it, DFTC, but it was thin and much washed and I thought it looked scruffy enough.

Only I was wrong. Lucy didn't want scruffy. She wanted, as she explained patiently to Rachel and me, young, hip and up for it.

We glugged a bit. But when she sent us off to the Ladies with a couple of shiny carrier bags, we went.

They turned out to contain cropped tops. Mine had sequins round the neck. Very cropped. Lots of sequins. Rachel's was so pink it hurt the eyes.

'You need to look okay to get into the club,' Lucy told us, reasonably satisfied. 'And, of course, I know the bouncer.'

I should have realised she was up to something then. Her tone was just on the windy side of martyred. But I didn't. Not an inkling.

Not until – many, many drinks later - she yelled, 'You've written yourself off as a human being, Alice. These days you're just a brain attached to an airline ticket. Why can't you *see* it?'

Lucy, I should explain, is my Jiminy Cricket. She was born when her mother and I were both eighteen and sharing a flat on the central mouse motorway in Southampton. Rachel limped through her degree while the rest of us in the house took turns minding the baby.

Lucy has been a sort of shared talisman ever since. I don't babysit her any more. But I talked – well listened - through her first adolescent crush. I walked her through banks and stockbrokers when she thought she might like to be a financier. And I sent her the ticket to get home when she was dumped in New York by a man old enough to be her father and Rachel thought she was partying with the girls in Ibiza. Lucy and I know stuff about each other.

So when she said, 'You've written yourself off as a human being,' I listened. Not enthusiastically. But I did listen.

I'd been clubbing before, of course, but never quite as we did that night. The average age must have been about nineteen. The noise was indescribable. On the heaving dance floor, I was drilled into some rudimentary salsa moves by a sweat-slithery young god with a safety pin in his navel. Actually, I was just starting to enjoy myself when Lucy swooped again.

This time she shot us off to a late night showing of "Pretty Woman" on the South Bank. Well, at least we got our breath back. We had popcorn and sang along to the soundtrack. Then all blew our noses, hard, when Vivian said she wanted the fairytale.

And we came out into the crisp January night – early morning by that time – with a big fat smile on our faces.

'Oh isn't it perfect?'said Rachel, putting one arm round Lucy's waist and one round mine.

We swung along the Embankment. The wind was icy. But the lights reflected in the Thames were magical. There were great swags of them, like necklaces, along the water's edge. Behind them theatrical spotlights hit towers and palaces which were probably accountants' offices if only we knew. The new Hungerford footbridge glittered like a path of moonlight. And all of it gleamed and shifted like fairy gold reflected in the dark, dark water beneath.

All this sumptuousness went to our heads. In the sleety early morning we danced like Hades' handmaidens until we were out of breath all over again.

And that was when Lucy started in on me. Alcohol and long disapproval made her wise.

'The trouble is, Alice, is not the girl,' she pronounced, slurring only a little.

'*What*?' Rachel missed a step.

Lucy and I held her up.

Lucy can be a bit abrasive when she is in one of her truth telling moods and she had shipped enough rum cocktails to get her there. Rachel, on the other hand, has a heart of warm butter, even when awash with alco pops.

'Think about it, Ma. You and I think we're Vivian.' Lucy knows the script of *Pretty Woman* off by heart. It was her first grown up movie. 'But Alice doesn't. Alice is Edward Lewis.'

'Alice has never looked at another woman,' said Rachel foggily. She weaved a bit. Lucy steadied her. 'I mean *a* woman. I mean – '

'We know what you mean, Rache,' I soothed. 'Lucy isn't calling me a closet dyke. She's saying I blow into town for two weeks; then zip around in a limo doing deals. Then head back to London.'

Lucy nodded. 'You even,' she was warming to this, 'have an ex spouse and an ex dog.'

'Not together,'I said, revolted.

My dog Elephant is a poodle - one of the original normal size ones that can give a Shetland pony a run for its money. He had moved in with Lucy and Rachel about a year ago when I started going to Almaty every two weeks. My ex husband was in Corfu with a succession of leggy blondes, as he had been for ten years and more. (I'm short and freckled with hedgehog brown hair I never get round to doing anything about.) Elephant and ex never even met.

'Don't be silly, Lucy.' Rachel sounded almost angry. She looked at me worriedly. Did I say she was all heart?

'It's not silly. Alice's life is nothing but business. True or not?'

'We-ell,' said Rachel reluctantly.

I was more robust. 'Yup. All business it is. That's how I like it.'

Lucy clicked her tongue. 'You can do more than one thing, you know. Women are multi-taskers.'

I stopped dead. The wind off the river lifted my hair like icy fingers. Suddenly I was sober. This was something on which I felt strongly.

'Look,' I said. 'Some time in the sixties, some damn

silly woman wrote a book saying women could have it all. Love. Family. High powered career. Great sex. And her own choice of hair colour thrown in. Women have been breaking their backs to do it ever since. And I'm here to tell you, it can't be done.'

Lucy looked mutinous. 'You've got the high powered career.'

'Sure. And I enjoy it. But – and this is important Lucy. Are you listening? - that's because it's what I *chose*.'

'You're saying if you want a decent job, you have to give up all the other stuff?' She sounded scornful.

'The gods say take what you want – but pay for it.'

'Like you do, you mean? Borrowing other people's children?'

At that Rachel went stone cold sober too. 'Lucy!'

Oh, she's good my Lucy. Stiletto in under the third rib when the opponent least expects it! And all for my own good, too. We ignored Rachel, eying each other like duellists.

'There are women down at the gym three times a week at six o clock in the morning, trying to have it all,' I said. 'They live on the edge of panic. And their husbands leave them anyway.'

Beside me, Rachel gave a sharp intake of breath.

'Get real Lucy. Life is about choices. I made mine.'

She was a bit taken aback, I could tell. But she doesn't give up easily. 'Don't you ever regret it?'

Rachel moved in closer. I could feel her at my shoulder, just as we had sat all those years ago in the draughty Southampton flat, while the baby cried and cried and none of the books told you what to do about it. That was three in the morning too, now I come to think about it.

'Oh sure,' I said steadily. 'You regret the path not taken. You wouldn't be human if you didn't. My point is, you take one path. And do it properly.'

'No fun? Ever?'

I sighed. She didn't understand. But then very few people did, no matter how many times I said it.

'For me business *is* fun. I love it. I don't need anything else.'

Lucy dismissed that with a wave of a hand. I saw that she wasn't wearing gloves. She was crazy. Sharp little splinters of January sleet sliced down onto any bit of exposed skin.

'I'm going to bring you back some fur mittens from Khazakhstan,' I said, momentarily distracted. 'Your hands must be freezing.'

She gave a little crow of triumph. 'You see. You *don't* think about business all the time. You *are* still a human being underneath.'

Rachel put an arm round my waist. 'She's got a point there.'

I didn't deny it.

'What you need,' said Lucy thoughtfully, ' is to try the Edward Lewis gambit.'

Her mother and I exchanged confused glances. 'Sorry?'

She was impatient. 'Edward Lewis. Out of *Pretty Woman*. Find yourself a bit of rough and give yourself a week of adventure. Well, a night, anyway.'

'*Lucy!*' Rachel looked agonised.

But I was intrigued. One thing Lucy has learned from me is how to plan. For all the winsome partying, I began to suspect a quite careful strategic design to this evening.

'Practical problem,' I said casually, cunningly. 'It's not

that easy to bump into a bit of rough.' And I watched her.

She is promising; but still too inexperienced to hide it when a ploy begins to work. She grinned.

'No, it isn't. You can find it anywhere. There was Ben at the club tonight.'

I feigned puzzlement. 'Ben?'

'He was teaching you the merengue.'

Rachel moaned.

I didn't. I was starting to enjoy this. I'm a negotiator, after all.

'Lucy,' I said softly, 'I am not going to bed with a man with a safety pin through his stomach. It might catch on something.'

That brought her up short. For a moment she just glared. Then she broke into the frustration hop. I first saw her do her little dance on the spot when I picked her up from pre-school. It was enchanting – and very funny.

Rachel and I collapsed.

In the end, Lucy stopped dancing; even smiled reluctantly; and I called my chauffeur on the mobile to pick us up on Westminster Bridge.

He took them home first. Rachel lived out in the suburbs and I didn't rely on either of them to give him decent directions.

'Oh you,' Lucy said, hugging me, as she scrambled out at Rachel's cosy garden gate. 'I suppose you'll go on your own way, as you always do.'

'I suppose I will.' I hugged her back.

But as the car slid through the silent streets back to my riverside penthouse, I did think about what she had said. Of course I did.

Though I would have died rather than admit it to Lucy,

she was right. Horribly right. Even more right than she knew. Because the business, though I loved it to bits, was coming slowly to a natural end.

Actually, I was really lucky that it had ever started at all. I mean, I'm not what you'd call natural millionaire material. I'm not brilliant and I don't have Contacts. I do now. I didn't twelve years ago. That's when it all began to happen.

There were three of us. First of all Haroun who is a computer geek. Well, he is probably a genius but he can't talk to people. I think he keeps expecting them to have binary brains. The first sign of illogicality in someone and he starts throwing up his hands and saying he can't cope. Haroun's software was the reason there was a company at all.

Then there is Will. He could sell you a dead rat if he put his mind to it.

And me.

So what do I do? Good question. They made me Chief Executive Officer. Basically because I'm a planner and I did the bits they didn't like. And I'm good.

For instance, I'm responsible for the DFTC on the tee shirt. My first bit of company policy. In a lively six weeks Wil had dated and discarded our lush Australian temp and the despatcher had started writing sonnets to Haroun. The cramped office was a hotbed of hormones and hysterical weeping. Everything was getting done wrong and the clients were yelling.

'Right,' I said in the end. 'Enough already. From now on, an interoffice affair gets the sack, instantly.'

I had company tee shirts printed: a lozenge with DFTC round it. It stood for Don't Fuck the Company. Haroun used to spend his coffee breaks making up dog Latin tags that would fit too. He even offered a prize for the best at the Christmas party, as we grew and were big enough to have a Christmas party.

But everyone knew what it meant. And it worked. Like I said, I'm good.

We started in the heady days of glasnost. If you were doing business in the Wild East then, you know that the most critical thing was that nobody knew who to trust, on either side. Well, they trusted me. I told the truth, in spite of Haroun yelling that it was suicidal to be straight with a bunch of Mafiosi who were in the KGB last week. Also I didn't let us take bribes or give them, although Wil said that was hopelessly naive. But I said we had to start as we meant to go on. And we did.

So, while other IT consultancies grew and grew until they blew up, we went steadily on at 15% growth a year until we made some serious money. Money enough to buy me a penthouse overlooking Chelsea Bridge and keep a chauffeur driven Jaguar on call, anyway.

Not money enough to give Elephant a decent quality of life or keep a relationship going.

So yes, I earned my salary. And no, it wasn't going to last. We all knew that, though the other two had been carefully skirting round the subject since Christmas. The truth was, you see, that they didn't know what to do about me.

We had a buyer for the company, which would be good for everyone. Our employees would get more money and a whole lot more opportunities. The shareholders (including us) would all get very rich. And the other two both had jobs to go to.

Haroun, being a genius, could do anything, of course – stay on as Head of Research with the new owners, teach, invent, write books. And Wil, I knew, was being wooed by a multi national.

Which just left me surplus to requirements. Everyone knew it. No one actually talked about it. They were all waiting for me to call Time!. And soon – *soon* – I was going to have to do it.

So after I got out of the Jaguar and said goodnight to Gordon the chauffeur, I didn't go to bed, that cold January dawn. I went out on my penthouse terrace and watched the ghostly greyness brighten along the dark snake of river. A few birds started a brave dawn chorus across the way in Battersea Park.

Dawn is not a good time to think. Especially not when it's really, really cold. Especially not on top of too many rum cocktails with an empty flat behind you.

I liked my life. I didn't want it to change.

I could see all too clearly what would happen if the company was sold. Oh, I'd get another job. But it wouldn't be the same. It wouldn't be with friends I'd worked through the night with, who'd seen me through the divorce.

Face it, Alice – *they are your family*.

Without them, I knew all too well what I would turn into - a hanger on with a job anyone could do. Plenty of money , sure. Nothing meaningful to do with it. Lucy was right, damn her. I'd turn into a highjacker of other people's children

That was when I thought *the Edward Lewis Gambit? Well, why not?*

At once, I caught myself. It was too crazy. I'd given up

sex pretty much when marriage gave up on me. Apart from the odd wistful moment looking at honeymooners on my plane sometimes, I'd never really missed it that much. As I said to Lucy, you take what you want; and you pay for it.

So I put the nasties out of my mind and went back to work, blessed work. And forgot the Edward Lewis Gambit. Or at least, I thought I did.

But the next morning, I pulled myself together and did the decent thing. Everyone in the company heaved a sigh of relief. It took some intense negotiating to get a fair deal for everyone. I enjoyed that.

But then the deal went through and Haroun and I went on whistle stop tour of the clients with the incoming CEO.

The last place was Almaty. It felt appropriate somehow, the meeting point of the mighty Tien Shan Mountains and thousands of miles of frozen prairie. Believe me, Khazakhstan in January is bleak. And wind blown.

The wind reminded me. 'I must buy Lucy some of those fur mittens,' I said to Haroun. 'This will be my last chance. I doubt if I'll ever come back.'

He knows Lucy. Rachel has invited him over for family meals a couple of times, in spite of his hopelessness with people. Or maybe because of it. He does a very good lost little boy genius when the mood takes him. And he has eyelashes to die for. They help.

He said, 'I'll come with you.'

But thinking of the mittens and Lucy must have made the Edward Lewis Gambit bubble up out of the hot geyser of the subconscious. And suddenly I thought – *this is my last chance for that too.*

So I got vague and said I didn't know when I would go,

I would just squeeze it in during the day.

Maybe he was a bit hurt. I was never sure with Haroun. But I didn't have time to think about it. I had to concentrate during the day's meetings. And all the time, the little pendulum was clicking away in my head.

Last! Chance! Last! Chance!

Go on Alice! Are you a woman or a mouse?

So I said to the interpreter – 'Where would you go if you wanted to – well – meet people?'

The trouble was the interpreter already knew me. He would never have imagined that I was on the hunt for a bit of rough. Never in month of Sundays. He told me kindly to go to the open air skating rink, up the mountain.

I sighed. I'd been before. It was terrific. On a Sunday afternoon, half the families of the city seem to get out there. The ice turns to slush round the edges and kids fall over and lovers show off to each other. They play a lot of ABBA and it is all incredibly wholesome and friendly. Not what I was looking for at all.

So I tried the concierge, the maid, the student moonlighting as barman at the lobby bar, a couple of waiters. They suggested everything from a primary school (cultural exchange) to the space museum (historical interest). Nobody came up with anything remotely useable. It was profoundly depressing.

And then there was a knock on the door of my room. I opened it.

'I hear you want to do the town,' said Haroun without expression. 'Get your coat.'

I flushed. I mean, an adventure on my own, in decent privacy was one thing. Having my friends along to do the driving was something completely different. Besides –

Haroun!

Perhaps this is where I should explain about Haroun. Yes, he's a geek. Yes, he's blank about people. He's also *beautiful*. Quite apart from the eyelashes, he is tall and walks with that liquid rhythm that makes you think that's how angels must move in Heaven. He has that far away poetic look – usually because he's not paying attention but I've always understood why the smitten dispatcher went for literary tributes – and a mouth that makes even quite sensible people like Rachel think hot and lustful thoughts.

In the matter of girl friends, he has even more blondes than my ex husband. They don't last. But, to a woman, they are stunning.

And this was the man intending to accompany me on my last chance adventure. I went pink to my freckled ears. I mumbled something about not wanting to interfere with his plans. Even to me it didn't sound convincing.

Haroun didn't even pretend to believe me.

'You want to go clubbing? Fine. Let's go.'

It wasn't exactly an alluring invitation. He sounded grim. I said so. I got quite indignant about it.

'Aren't I allowed to enjoy myself? Is that just for the chaps?'

'You've never wanted to before.'

I sniffed. 'How do you know?'

'DFTC,' he said wryly.

'Oh that's just nonsense. Just because I didn't date the payroll . . .'

'Or anyone else,' said Haroun between his teeth.

'You don't know that,' I said, glaring.

'Yes I do.'

'You don't know everything about me.'

His teeth flashed in a really nasty smile then. 'Want a bet?'

Oh God, I thought suddenly. It's happening already. This man was my friend, my family. And next week he'll be across town in a building I don't even know and we won't speak every day any more. And already he's behaving like a stranger.

It was like divorce all over again. Worse.

I said abruptly, 'I've changed my mind. I don't want to go out after all. I'll just stay here and wind up my valedictory report.'

'Oh no you won't,' said Haroun. 'You're coming with me.' And he put his shoulder against the doorjamb so I couldn't close it.

He's like that. He doesn't argue. He focuses. And waits.

So I went. Mutinous and muttering. But I went. It was easier. When Haroun makes his mind up about something, it usually is.

The club wasn't at all like Lucy's heaving strobe-stroked cellar. For one thing it was cavernous. For another the music was live. But the dervish dancing was the same. And so were the sweating stripped-to-the-bone bodies.

Haroun left me the moment we walked in. An exuberant group of girls waved him in and absorbed him. Pretty soon he was dancing with the whole damn bunch of them.

Khazakhstan isn't just a meeting point for geographical features. There was every shape and race in that room. Square faced, muscular Chinese; small mountain men with eyes as far away as Haroun's; slight, graceful Pakistanis; ginger haired Ukrainians; ice blond Estonians;

men with triangular faces and the half closed, slanted eyes of the cruel Mongol invaders.

Actually it was a Genghis Khan look alike who bought me a vodka and came closest to fulfilling the evening's objective. He was an economist called Ivan and he told me in his fluent moviegoer's English that he thought English women were hot. He had a nice body, no safety pins and he kissed nicely. Only – I'd lost the urge somehow.

Across the room, Haroun and his netball team of admirers were punching the air to the music. He had his back to me.

I said to Ivan, 'Look, I'm sorry. I've just thought of something I ought to put in my report. I really ought to go back and finish it.'

He was amazingly nice about it. Nicer than I deserved in the circumstances. Economists, he said largely, understood the importance of reports. He called me a taxi, took me out to it and then stood there in the snow, the sweat evaporating off him in cloud of steam, waving me off. Much, much nicer than I deserved.

I sat in my luxury suite and looked out over the ice landscape. Well, I'd blown my last chance at adventure. Obviously I was just the wrong type. Too hidebound. Too critical. Too *old*. Not too old because of the thirty seventh birthday on the horizon. Too old because of the person I was. And probably always had been.

I barely noticed the scratch on the door. When I did, I ignored it. It was two o'clock in the morning, for Christ's sake. It occurred to me that the student barman would just have come off duty and might have decided to check whether I still needed company. I knew I wasn't up to any further failed adventures. So I went on ignoring it.

And then a small piece of paper shot under the door. I got up wearily and read it.

Open up it said in Haroun's unmistakable black slashing letters.

I was astonished. Surely Haroun would still be dancing with his chorus of houris?

But the gentle scratching came again. There was something about the way he did it that told me he wasn't going to go away. Par for the course, that.

So I squared my shoulders and opened the door. 'Back already? I thought you could party for Britain – '

And suddenly there I was, with Haroun's arms crushing me, not able to speak, not able to *breathe* any more.

It was really very odd. I mean, I've known him forever. We've kissed lots of times. Hello … goodbye … celebrating success … hanging on after failure …

But not like this. Never like this.

I suppose it could have been the full body contact. Or the dark. Or the unpeopled hotel, with all its electric and water systems purring and gurgling like a sleeping mastodon. Or the fuzzy moon outside my balcony and the silent night snowscape below. Or - or –

Or shock, actually.

Full body contact with Haroun wasn't what I was expecting. I mean – you get used to people being that critical nine inches away. I'd concentrated on the eyelashes and the intellect and I'd put him in the No Sex With Me Box. Even before the instigation of the DFTC policy.

But when you're too close to see the eyelashes and the intellect isn't in evidence, you start to take in other things. Like his smell – sort of toffee with a hint of oregano. And his hair – kind of crackly under my fingers. And his hands – frankly, everywhere.

'Good God.' I said, when I could breathe. It came from the heart.

'About time,' said Haroun, taking my clothes off.

He was surprisingly good at it. Well, maybe not surprisingly, now I come to think about it. Only *my* clothes hadn't been taken off by anyone else for a long time and it felt a bit embarrassing to be honest.

Except Haroun doesn't do embarrassment. He does, with total concentration, the thing he happens to be engaged with at the time. That night it was me.

He's a geek, I kept reminding myself, as clothes flew and pillows thumped. Okay a geek with eyelashes. But still a geek.

I found my hips still had full backward rotation. Just as well in the circumstances.

And it wasn't just the chandelier-swinging potential that was a revelation either. Because suddenly Haroun was transformed. He was murmuring things like, 'rarer than rubies' and 'a pearl beyond price'. And he was kissing me. And I mean kissing. All over. Like I'd never been kissed before. Like I'd never imagined being kissed. As if it was scheduled to take a hundred and one nights and he wasn't about to hurry it.

I made some interesting discoveries. Geeks are thorough. And original. And they don't care how long it takes.

Oh boy, they don't care how long it takes.

We did fall asleep in the end. Well – fall. In my case crash would be a better word. I was shaken to the core. One or two muscles were in deep shock, too. But the real hit was – the feelings. Laughter, lots of it. Passion of an eye-watering intensity. But there turned out to be kindness too; and an odd rueful fellow feeling. It was as if Haroun and I were a pair and I had only just realised it.

When I woke up, my first thought was Wow.

My second was, I don't believe it.

My third – how the hell am I going to make Haroun see that we belong together?

The last was so depressing that I could have screamed. I mean Haroun has many qualities, and I admire nearly all of them, but he doesn't listen to anyone else. He works stuff out for himself or it stays unworked out.

Listen to me? Fat chance.

But my body hadn't grasped that. My body was all soft and purring and ignored my brain when it screamed, 'Get up and *do* something.'

My body was still snuggled up to Haroun when, eventually he stretched and yawned and woke up.

'Morning,' he said not opening his eyes.

I wondered bitterly if he knew which member of the netball team was beside him.

I swallowed. 'Good morning,' I said politely.

His eyes flew open at that. At three inches distance, the eyelashes were *amazing*.

'Now what's wrong?' he said patiently.

I suppose I could have said, I've just realised that I'm in love with you and it's absolutely no use because you don't think of me like that and my body thinks you do and this is going to be worse than divorce and the sale of the company and no Father Christmas all rolled into one . . .

And he said – he said –

'Your place or mine?'

'*What?*'

He shifted himself onto one elbow so he could look down at me. We'd made love in the moonlight last night, so I hadn't really taken in the beauty of his colour scheme: dark toffee eyes, golden fudge skin, liquorice eyelashes. Scrummy.

He said patiently, 'Where are we going to live? Your place or mine?'

I gagged. I mean, how many breakthroughs is a girl suppose to make in a day? Only yesterday he was the genius I worked with who I was never going to see again after this trip.

'L-l-live together?'

'For a start. What did you think last night was about?'

'Sex,' I said, shaken into honesty.

The dark toffee eyes went wicked. 'Ah, we're talking about the Edward Lewis gambit are we?'

Oh Lucy, you traitress!

I went scarlet from toenails to hairline. I would have pulled the covers over my head and gladly died. Only he wouldn't let me.

'You had your chance at a one night stand last night. You could have had Ivan or one of his mates,' said Haroun, like a judge summing up. 'You blew it.' He started to do seriously disturbing things without taking his eyes from mine. 'I claim my prize.'

A long, long *long* time later, I said dreamily, 'Of course you can't really have it all. Not for long. But just sometimes you get a perfect moment. . .'

'And this is your perfect moment?'

I could hear the smile in his voice. I had my head on his chest by this time and I could hear it, all echoey, as if the smile was going round and round inside his body. It set up a nice little reverberation in mine too.

I sighed blissfully. 'Nothing left to wish for.'

I thought he'd say likewise or something similar. But he didn't. He lay under me. I could almost *hear* him smiling. But he didn't say it was perfect.

'You?' I prompted, piqued.

He stretched. 'I've got one thing left to wish for.'

Aha, I thought suddenly, here it comes, the proposal of marriage. How glamorous! How romantic!

'Yes?' I said starry eyed.

But Haroun was on another tack altogether. Like I said, a geek at heart.

'DFTC,' he snorted. 'When we get home I'm burning those bloody tee shirts.'

Christmas Wish
by Tina Brown

'Oh shoot,' Caroline cursed and ducked around the back to the store room.

'What's the matter?' Lia asked, moving away from the counter where she had just laid down a plate of chocolate covered rum balls. They were in the lingerie department, but with Christmas not far away, each section of the store had their own little treats to give away to customers.

'It's the Jamison brothers doing their Christmas inspection round,' Caroline hissed from behind the curtain. 'If they ask where I am, just tell them I've ducked out okay. I've had enough of Mark's so called observing comments this morning.'

'But ...' Lia didn't get a chance to question her supervisor's actions since she was promptly pushed towards the counter and told to stay there and make herself look busy. Lia knew that Caroline had already been given a rap over the knuckles from Mark this morning.

There were four Jamison brothers, all tall and handsome with dark burnished hair. They were drop dead gorgeous to a man and they all knew it, this apparently bringing them to the conclusion that they were God's gift to women, except for maybe Jerome.

Each of them ran their own chain of Jamison's Department Stores. Mark, the oldest, had control of this, the original store in Sydney. Terence ran the store out at Penrith, Sam had opened a Jamison's in Melbourne last year and the youngest, Jerome, had recently opened a store on the fashionable Gold Coast in Queensland.

'Good morning, Lia,'Mark said as they came closer. He glanced around the ladies' lingerie department and then asked casually, 'Caroline around?', before picking up a chocolate covered rum ball and popping it into his mouth. Lia wondered if her boss had a romantic interest in Caroline. He came to this department an awful lot lately.

'No, sir.' Lia flashed each one of them a quick look, catching Jerome's eye last and longest. He was the most handsome of the four brothers, no doubt about it. They all had their attention focused on her as if she was going to say something else. Suddenly feeling very self-conscious she continued, 'She ... um, has just ducked out.'

'That's a shame,' Mark said with a raised eyebrow as if he didn't believe her excuse. He reached for another rum ball.

'She mentioned something about an errand.' Which wasn't exactly a lie she consoled herself.

'We're doing our Christmas wish round. You did get your ribbon?'Jerome asked as he helped himself to one of the coconut covered treats. Lia couldn't help but be mesmerized as she watched him lick the last bit of chocolate from his lips. She swallowed the dryness in her throat and ignored the funny tingling sensation running down her back.

'Yes, thank you.' Lia felt a blush spread across her cheeks. She had been working here now for five years and each Christmas the Jamison's gave their staff a ribbon with their name on it and the opportunity to pick something out of the store that they would like to have for Christmas. The longer you had worked for them, the more expensive the gift you could choose. It was upgraded every five years, so this year she was allowed to step up a level. On Christmas Eve they draw a raffle and one name from each store would be chosen as the winner.

'Have you made your choice yet, Lia?' Jerome asked.

'No, sir. Not yet.' There was something about the look he was giving her. She wondered what she had done for his attention to be so focused on her. She had always had this strange sensation when she looked at Jerome right from the time she had been interviewed by the brothers. 'I'm still considering.' She almost stammered under his intense gaze.

'We'll come back later,' Mark said as he started to walk away. The others followed, apart from Jerome.

'Everything alright?' he asked and Lia swallowed trying to wet her dry throat.

'Fine thank you, sir.'

'I told you to drop the "sir" when there's only you and me around.'

'Sorry.' She couldn't bring herself to say his name without giving herself away.

'I was sorry to hear about your grandmother.' He stepped closer.

She flashed startled eyes up at him. He had been in Queensland when her grandmother had passed away. 'How did you ...?' His crooked smile brought her words to a stop.

'I keep track of the people that interest me.'

'Oh,' was all Lia could think to say. She didn't know quite how to take that comment so she changed the subject. 'How is the new store going?'

'Very well. Actually, the position for lingerie manager has just become available. Are you interested?' He shot the question out at her so quickly Lia gasped and stepped back. His eyes were watching her carefully.

'I ... I haven't seen it on the notice board.'

'It's not on there. Because I want you.' The way he said those words made her swallow hard.

'Oh.'

'I've been impressed with you from the very first day Lia. I wanted to take you to the Gold Coast from the beginning, but Emily Bradshaw showed her interest and since she had been with us for a long time I could hardly refuse her. She's now decided to retire so the job's yours if you want it.'

'Oh, but Caroline was here before me ...'

'I doubt my brother would allow me to steal Caroline from him.' His smile and his eyes twinkled with a secret, which only confirmed what Lia had thought for some time.

'Do you think you can work with me? And I shall need a hostess on some occasions, as well as a dinner partner.'

'Did Mrs B do that for you?' Lia's eyes nearly popped out of her head.

Jerome laughed. 'No, but it's a condition of *your* employment.'

Lia's mouth opened but nothing came out. Jerome was watching the movement of her lips. Without thinking, her tongue came out and licked the dryness away. She saw and heard him inhale sharply.

There was a noise from the storeroom and Lia held her breath. She knew a look of guilt was covering her face as she had never been good at hiding her emotions.

'You'd better go and see if Caroline's alright,' Jerome said with an amused tilt to his lips, but before Lia could do anything further Caroline came out with a sheepish grin on her face.

'Hiding from my brother again Caroline?' He raised one dark quizzical eyebrow.

'I knew I should have taken today off sick. Why didn't you warn me you were making your Christmas wish rounds today?' Caroline grumbled.

'And miss out on all the fun?'

'Some friend you are,' Caroline muttered, but in a cheerier note asked, 'So what's your Christmas wish stuck on this year Jerome?'

'Nothing at the moment.' He gave Lia a quick look. She was about to turn away when Jerome said, 'Before you go, I've got something I have to do.' He reached out and grabbed her hand.

'Yes?' She turned back to him and waited, the heat of his fingers sending shards of pleasure up her arm.

Slowly he pulled his other hand out of his pocket. 'I'm making you my Christmas wish.' Before she could react, his hand went under the collar of her shirt, his knuckles grazed the top of her breast as he pinned on his wish ribbon. Then he tilted his head and kissed her.

Lia felt as though her bones had turned into melted chocolate. Shocked at the stirrings of delight he sent through her body with just one kiss, she stepped back when he finally lifted his head away from her.

'You can't!' Lia was stupefied. She tried to step back more, but Caroline was there pushing her towards Jerome so her toes wouldn't get squashed.

'Why not?' Jerome grinned.

'Of course he can,'said Caroline. 'He's the boss, he can do anything he likes and if you're going to Queensland ...'

'But I'm not ... I haven't said ...' Lia had trouble finding the right words. Yes or no was all she had to say really. She knew what she wanted to say, but would it be the right word, would it be the right choice?

'Let's talk about it at dinner tonight,'Jerome suggested.

Lia couldn't believe this. For five years now she'd had a secret crush on Jerome Jamison and now he was asking her out on a date. Not only that, but had made her his Christmas wish and wanted her as manager in his new store.

'On second thoughts, forget about dinner. I've waited long enough. Caroline, if my brothers ask, tell them I'm stealing Lia away for lunch ... we might be some time ... if we come back at all.' He grabbed Lia's hand and started for the front door.

She let him lead her out under the curious eyes of the other staff members and his brothers, but when they reached the sidewalk in front of the shop she stopped abruptly and tugged at his hand.

'Now hold on just a minute,' she began, giving him a serious look, and Jerome's eyebrows rose up in surprise. 'What makes you think you can just waltz in there and drag me out without even asking? Don't I have a say in these matters? I may be just an employee, but I'm a person too.'

Jerome blinked. 'But, ... of course you do. It was just that ... I got the impression you felt the same.'

He looked sheepish now and was staring at her with confusion clearly written all over his face. Lia repressed the urge to laugh. She pulled her own ribbon out of her pocket and stepped up to him.

'Well, as it happens, you were right, but from now on we make decisions together, okay?' She tagged him with her wish ribbon and stood on tip toe to kiss him. She felt his arm snake around her waist as the kiss deepened and their Christmas wishes were sealed with the lingering taste of chocolate covered rum balls.

Mixed Messages

By Bernardine Kennedy

Simon instinctively knew his wife was up to something. He didn't actually have any proof but then he didn't need any, not really, his finely honed adultery antennae could swiftly pick up on and recognise even the slightest of unconscious signals.

After all, he'd been there before, he'd lived with affairs for as long as he could remember and experience had taught him to interpret the tiniest of signposts so well that he didn't have to wait for all the boring, well-documented signs.

The Talking Heads of Psychology always cited the hoary old chestnuts of the guilty party buying new clothes, embarking on a new diet or a changed appetite in the bedroom as signposts, but Simon thought that was a load of old codswallop.

The best way, he had discovered, was to observe constantly and watch out for the slight quickening of body movements, the involuntary blink of eyes or the nervous fidgeting of fingers.

He almost prided himself on his expertise as he silently watched and listened, just as he had been doing for the last two months.

Ever since he had first picked up on Emily's luminous pink cheeks when she had nonchalantly pulled her ringing mobile out of her handbag and clicked the answer button.

'Sorry, you've got the wrong number', she had muttered sharply, holding the phone close to her mouth and then blinking rapidly as she instantly deleted all the information of the call.

'I get a lot of those as well', Simon commented to make sure that Emily knew he had heard. 'I just wish these morons would take care when they're dialling, it's so irritating to keep getting unwanted calls at inconvenient moments'.

Simon had leaned back in his chair and smiled quizzically as he waited for the verbal flow about the ins and outs of wrong numbers.

Too much information on the minutiae of daily life was another signpost.

He didn't know who it was she was seeing but he didn't really want to know because he was determined that the affair wouldn't be a threat to them as a couple. He hoped that if he ignored it then it would run its natural course and he could pretend it had never happened.

It was just an affair, he told himself. A fling. Just the same as every other affair that hadn't wrecked their marriage and had eventually fizzled out, because deep down he and Emily were meant to be together and hopefully they would stay that way forever because they truly loved each other.

He guessed that, for Emily, it was simply the thrill of the chase, the excitement of the secrecy and of course the irresistible pull of illicit sex. It certainly wouldn't interfere with their relationship, he wouldn't let it.

Simon had been reading the paper and munching happily on a slice of buttered toast when Emily cleared her throat.

He carried on reading but his antennae twitched an alert signal. A little nervous cough before speaking usually intimated an oncoming lie.

'Bill's working away for a couple of days so I'm going out for a drink with Sophie tonight, is that okay with you?' Simon noted that Emily's voice was slightly higher than usual as the nerves in her throat constricted.

'Mmmm, no problem. It will do you good to get out', Simon had murmured, 'I've had so much on at work lately I was thinking of having an early night anyway. Will it be a late one do you think?'

'Probably, so don't wait up for me', Emily studied her cereal as if it was a riveting page of an encyclopaedia, 'Sophie's been having a few husband problems with Bill, she thinks he's playing away and she needs a shoulder to cry on. You know what she's like......'

Simon had stood up and walked around the table.

'That's what I love about you', he whispered as he affectionately kissed the top of her head, 'you're so kind and caring. Sophie's very lucky to have you as a friend. I hope she appreciates you giving up your time for her'.

He watched through his eyelashes as the vivid red hue of guilty embarrassment crept slowly from his wife's chest all the way up to her hairline.

Just as he had intended.

Simon knew the power of guilt and he knew that Emily wouldn't be able to deal with it for very long and then they would be able to get back to normal.

That night, true to his word, Simon was in bed nice and

early and it was barely nine o'clock when the phone on the bedside table jumped to life.

Just as he had expected.

Although he had been wide-awake and anticipating the call he let it ring a few times before answering and feigning drowsiness.

'Hello...'he yawned down the line, 'who is it?'

'Hi Simon, it's me'. Emily's voice crept quietly down the line and Simon guessed someone else was nearby. 'Sophie isn't feeling too well, she's really down and has had too much to drink, I think I'd better stay overnight just in case, do you mind? I'll go straight on to work in the morning......'

'No problem, you do whatever you have to do to make her feel better, I hope she's going to be okay! I'll see you tomorrow....... Be good!'

Same old line about a friend in need, Simon thought wryly, surprised in a way that an intelligent woman like Emily couldn't come up with something a little more original.

Replacing the phone he stretched and flexed his arms over his head before rolling his naked body over and reaching an arm out across the bed towards the woman smiling beside him.

'Well, well, well, Sophie my darling, looks like you're going to have to stay the night, apparently you're drunk and incapable and need looking after!'

The pair of them giggled hysterically at the irony of the situation.

'Emily has really dug herself into a hole with this one', Sophie laughed, 'and you tell me she's intelligent?'

They laughed again, in fact they laughed so loudly

under the covers they didn't hear the door open and they certainly didn't see Emily and Bill standing there with their arms around each other grinning victoriously.

Just Like Old Times
By Pam Weaver

'I never realised what a restriction the kids were!' Freya sank back onto the pillows with a warm glow.

'Umm, you sexy thing...' Tom murmured contentedly.

This was the first time in ages that they'd been on their own. Jason had moved out to live with his long-term girl-friend, Suzy was abroad backpacking somewhere in New Zealand and Tonia was spending a few days on a house-boat with some college friends. That left Freya and Tom with an empty house, all to themselves...

'I'd forgotten how vocal you can be,' said Tom. 'You moaned like a good 'un.'

Freya feigned indignation. 'And you encouraged me every step of the way!'

After twenty-four years of marriage, he could still excite her and their newfound freedom had certainly perked up their love life.

'It felt like the first time we did it without having to worry about your mother bursting in on us,' grinned Tom.

'Back then we were pretty clever at finding places to be alone, weren't we?'

'Do you remember that night in the woods?'

How could she forget it? Laying on a blanket under the starry sky... probably the moment when Jason was con-ceived. She liked to think so anyway.

'I bet it's a housing estate now.'

Freya suddenly propped herself up on one elbow. 'Let's see if we can find it again.'

They set off the next night, a bottle of wine and a blanket in the boot of the car. Freya felt eighteen all over again.

Surprisingly, the place was still there, although there was a housing estate and a motorway slip road nearby.

The ground was soggy, but eventually, Tom found a dry patch under the trees where the motorway lights didn't penetrate. In the distance, a dog was barking.

'Where's the blanket?'

'I thought you had it. Shall I go back?'

'No, ' he said. 'I'll put my coat down for you.'

Freya sighed. So gallant... so Colin Frith... so Mr Darcy...

They settled back on the coat and Tom took his trousers off.

'The ground's cold.'

'I'll soon warm you up.'

'Ouch!' Freya whispered urgently. 'Something stung my shoulder!'

It was difficult to see in the gloom, but Tom leaned over her to feel the ground. 'Ah! We're lying on a bed of nettles.'

There was a sudden rustling sound and a dog burst through the undergrowth.

'What the...' Tom leapt forward as the dog's cold nose touched his bare buttock. He fell with a loud curse into the middle of the nettle patch. Freya scrambled nervously to her feet. The dog thought it was a great game and barked excitedly.

'Haven't you kids got a home to go to?' A man's angry voice boomed out from somewhere near the edge of the woods. 'Get out of here before I call the police.'

Back in the safety of the car, parked in a secluded lay-by, they took stock of the situation. Freya had some stings on her shoulder, but not as many as Tom. His face was a mass of red weals, his trousers were covered in muddy paw prints and they'd left the wine behind.

Tom sighed. 'Let's go back home.'

'This car is bigger than your old Ford Anglia,' Freya smiled remembering another time, another place. She raised one eyebrow.

Tom shook his head. 'You wanton hussy.'

'Wanton..? Ooh, yes please.'

They climbed into the back seat and were enjoying a cold handed fondle when the car was flooded with light. A Police car was turning in the lay-by.

Tom leapt up like a scolded cat. 'Aggh! My leg!'

The policeman tapped on the glass. 'Good evening, madam... sir.'

'Hello,' said Freya sweetly.

'Ouch,' moaned Tom.

'Are you all right, sir?'Freya couldn't help noticing the policeman had a silly smirk on his face.

'My husband has cramp,' she said quickly. 'I was just... er... giving him a massage.'

'I see,' said the policeman, staring at Tom's bare buttock.

Oh, lord, thought Freya. Please don't arrest us. What'll we tell the kids?

'Is there...' Freya was conscious that her voice sounded high pitched and strangled. She cleared her throat. 'Is there something wrong?'

'I wonder,' said the policeman holding something up, 'could this be your jacket, sir?'

It was, but it was another twenty minutes before he was fully satisfied that the man in the family photograph he'd found in the wallet, and Tom were one and the same person.

Freya and Tom drove home in silent embarrassment. Back in the kitchen they began to see the funny side.

'My calf muscle's still a bit niggly.' Tom stretched.

'Why don't you have a bath and relax,' Freya suggested.

'I will... if...' Tom gave her a wicked grin, 'you promise not to go off the boil.'

'Ooooh, Tom,' Freya said, lowering her eyes and looking at him through her lashes. 'What do you mean?'

Tom hobbled upstairs. 'We can still make it special,'his parting words as the bathroom door closed.

Make it special...

When she heard him coming back down, Freya was ready for him. She'd showered in the downstairs shower, she smelled of the expensive perfume he'd given her for her birthday and the sitting room was ablaze with candles. She slipped out of her dressing gown and waited behind the door.

The door opened slowly and Tom hopped inside. 'Oh no...'

As she closed the door, she saw him for the first time. He was wearing the Roger Rabbit outfit he'd bought for the kid's party about ten years before. She stared in disbelief.

'Sorry...' he said, beginning to take the head off. 'I was

just mucking about. Have I spoiled it?'

Freya laughed out loud. 'No, don't take it off!'

'But you've made this room look fantastic...'

Freya pulled him closer and giggled. 'I've never made love to a rabbit before.'

He kissed her naked shoulder. The whiskers tickled her breast deliciously.

'Think of me as an early Easter present,' he murmured.

The Roger Rabbit head was soon discarded as they made love on the floor. It was wonderful, sensual and Freya murmured, 'well worth waiting for...'

The gravel crunched outside.

Tom stared at her wide-eyed. 'Who the devil's that?'

Freya was already on her feet. 'How the hell should I know?'

A car door slammed and a voice called, 'Do you want me to help you with those suitcases?'

'Your parents!'cried Tom

'My parents!' cried Freya.

The next few seconds were frantic. Candles out and cushions up. The TV News went on and Freya fumbled for her dressing gown. Tom stuffed the bunny costume behind the sofa and switched on the lights.

The door bell rang.

Freya patted her hair tidy while Tom, still naked, flew up the stairs two at a time.

'I'm not so sure this was a good idea.' Freya could hear her father's voice on the other side of the door.

'Nonsense,' snapped her mother. 'Dropping in like this will be just like old times.'

Ten
By Hazel Cushion

The bath is getting cold, the edge rimmed with soap and leg hair. We'd joked once, Stella and me, about how you could always tell if I really fancied someone because I'd even shave the backs of my legs. Would tonight be the night for a perfect ten? Surely it was time my luck changed. There'd been nine - nine fabulous fucks in my life, except they hadn't been. In fact, the first had been so appallingly dismal that I'd pretended to be a virgin for the next three. I'd certainly wished it was true, and anyway, they'd believed me. Men were so bloody gullible when it came to sex.

Stepping from the bath I wrap myself in a large, soft towel. Surely this time I'm due some glorious passion but perhaps it's all just a con, a myth created by magazine editors so they can fill their column inches. Hah! Column inches, I smirk lewdly at myself in the steamed up mirror. Perhaps the world is full of people thinking everyone else is having great sex, except them. God, I hope not – I'm still too young to give up on my dreams.

What shall I wear? I've been planning different outfits all day. There's the black but it's a bit tight for dancing. Would we dance? I'm not sure. Or the boot leg trousers and that new top. But is it too low, too tarty? Drying myself I head for the underwear drawer. Not the usual grey, saggy comfy ones tonight – sex and comfort aren't easy bedfellows. Instead I reach to the back of the drawer and hesitate, virgin white or seductive black? Stupid question really. I laugh and grab the black.

Number seven hadn't been so bad. In fact, the way the skin near his eyes had crinkled when he laughed had been lovely. He'd been better in the sack too. Slightly more advanced than 'the quick tune in on the nipples and in like Flynn brigade'. Still a bastard though. He really should have mentioned his wife before he shouted out her name as he shot his load. Nothing can make your insides curl quicker than that.

God, I'd better hurry, – we're meeting outside the Town Hall at eight. Umm, number eight, I remember, had been quite different – the deeply committed, spiritual type. Sex for him was a tantric union that required enormous preparation beforehand. I'd liked the idea of a cleansing candlelit bath together until, to clear his chankras, he blown out his nasal passages underwater. The thought of those grey submarines of snot lurking in the depths had definitely spoiled the moment. I should have called a halt then. If only I'd realised that his 'cleanliness is next to a fantastic fuck' routine didn't extend to his bed sheets. They definitely hadn't seen the steely drum of a washing machine for many a month.

Oh Christ! What am I going to wear? Why am I so nervous? God knows, we've known each long enough, since that shy first year at Blackwater Comprehensive in fact. Funny how they'd never really thought of each other 'like that' until now.

We were laughing over number nine when it had happened. I'd just been describing how he'd come faster than Concorde when suddenly, our eyes had met and held. Who had looked away first? I can't remember. But I know now there's no looking back. How was it you could be friends with someone for so long without really noticing them?

Okay, decision time - trousers or the black dress? All right, the dress and then I can wear stockings – tart that I am. But I like stockings, I like the way they pull at my thighs, how you can't forget them so they make you feel like you've got a naughty little secret all evening. Make-up, not too heavy, just some grey around the lids to give that heavy, sleepy look and some lippy. Fluff up the hair, spritz on some perfume. Final check in the mirror, quick twirl – go for it girl!

I'm going to be late. Oh Christ I hate being late. Calm down, you're fine – look there's a parking space and it's only two minutes walk. My suspenders pull slightly as I step from the car. I smooth my dress down in nervous anticipation. It's one of those wonderful, mellow summer evenings – a lifestyle ad sort of evening that shows soft focus friends beside a river sipping white wine. It's an evening heavy with potential and promise. A rich golden gleam is reflected by the Town Hall windows and so, just for a moment, I'm blinded, dazzled in the honeyed light before I see the familiar figure standing there, smiling.

'Hello Stella' I say, 'Where shall we go?'

Nibbling At Nachos
by Bill Harris

I am invisible. Brian can't see me hiding with my pizza behind the potted palm. I watch him lean across and brush his lips against her neck. She touches his cheek and carries on chatting to the woman seated opposite. All four of them sip their wine, eat and chat. She's nothing like he described her. Not fat, not loud, not common. She delicately nibbles a nacho and smiles as the woman opposite says something.

'I'm there for the kids, just for the kids,' Brian said in my bed this afternoon. 'They're all that's keeping us together.' And he touched my belly and his hand slid tenderly down. I felt his desire. And he ignited mine.

'Really?'I whispered, scraping my nail across his chest.

'Course it is.'

Deep inside I was trembling, so wanting to believe. And for those few minutes I did believe. When he was inside me, I believed completely. Until we erupted.

He held me while our breathing returned, while our heat cooled, then looked at his watch.

'Jesus, is that the time?'

I looked into his eyes.

'What's the matter?'

I didn't reply.

'Look I haven't got time to sod about. What's the

matter?'

'You have to go.' I said.

'I told you I've got the kids concert, remember?'

'Oh yes,' I said brightly, 'so you have. So that's all right.'

He swung his legs over the edge of the bed and stood before me. 'Well don't make me feel guilty then.'

'You look ridiculous just in your socks.'

He glanced down and frowned. 'Thank you,' he said, 'for making me feel stupid.'

'Thanks isn't necessary, you manage quite nicely.'

And he was gone, a draught of anger and stripy socks followed by a slamming door.

Maybe that's why he's all over her now. Maybe that's why she's suddenly this sexy woman he wants to touch. I'd certainly like to have her bra size. The palm fronds wave as I poke them with my nose. They rustle. Loudly. I sink back into my seat and pretend to hack away at the pizza.

When I raise my eyes, he's at the bar glaring at me. He glances at his table then mouths, 'What are you doing here?'

I put on my sunny expression and mouth back, 'Why shouldn't I be?'

He frowns. 'Eh?'

I mouth, 'Colly iddy do dah icky poo.' And I raise my eyebrows.

'Eh? What?'

Her voice carries across the restaurant, 'Where are our drinks darling?'

'Well? Answer me,' I mouth.

He lets out a piercing giggle. 'Won't be long sweetie,'

he calls, and glares in my direction.

The bartender wears a bemused look. Especially when I put on my best sexy pout and stroke my left breast, some-what lewdly. In fact the bartender is quite tasty in a Brad Pitt sort of way. I throw him a wink that zooms across Brian and has the desired effect.

Turning, he growls his order across the bar. Now I'm no longer invisible, I saunter slowly over and stand next to him.

'What are you up to?' he mutters from the side of mouth, then grins across at his table. I notice a slight dampness on his upper lip. Tiny drops of sweat are form-ing nicely and his hand has adopted a shake.

I perch on a high stool and allow my thighs to cross extravagantly.

'Don't look over there,' he hisses. 'Please.'

'Your wife doesn't look fat to me, Brian.'

'Ssshhhh.'

'And I'm sure she isn't a gravestone in bed.'

The sweat on his lip has travelled over his nose and now smothers his cheeks and forehead.

'Okay, what do you want?' He manages to say these words while glancing airily at his wife. But a tic has started in his right eye.

'Nothing. Just letting you know I'm really a bunny boil-er. Me and Glenn Close are like sisters.'

Brian just groans. But cleverly he smiles at the same time and carries the tray of drinks back to their table. The smile now resembles rigor mortis.

I order a drink from Brad Pitt and sit while Brian squirms. I hadn't realised just how talented at squirming he is. I do know how talented a liar he is. But his charming wife is looking at me curiously and I know it's over. I'll have to find another job of course. And another man. A real man, one who exists. I turn to Brad Pitt.

'Do you exist?'

He watches me carefully, is there a little fear in his eyes? 'Wot?'

I shake my head then swig my wine, stand up and smooth my skirt over my hips. Brian twitches. The twitch turns into vibration as I head toward them, my gaze fixed on him. As I draw closer I can see his mind working. What's she doing? What's she going to say? What the hell can I say. Help!

As I reach them he stands up, abruptly. 'Hi Babs, what are you doing here?' His voice cracks slightly. He looks like a little boy in need of the toilet.

I nod faintly as I pass. I hear a quiet sigh and his wife saying, 'Are you all right darling? You look like you've seen a ghost. Do you know that woman?'

I open the door and sweet night air brushes my face. The street is empty but for the car waiting by the kerb.

'You're late,' he says grumpily, when I get in.

'These work things go on sometimes,' I tell him. 'Have you eaten?'

'Had chips and a pint earlier. Let's go home.'

As my husband starts the car, a woman appears and walks straight across the road toward us. He stiffens, jerks the car into gear, and we howl off up the road. In the mirror, she turns and follows us with her gaze. And I smile. And wonder. Did he wear stripy socks this afternoon?

Stormy Weather
By Sue Dukes

Huddled against the cold, Jane drove slowly and confidently through the first smattering of white flakes. So much for it being too cold to snow, she thought. Still, a little adverse weather was all right as long as you took the right precautions. Like the full tool kit, the torch, the change of clothes which always lived in the boot, and to which she had recently added the down-filled sleeping bag. Her friends laughed, but she just smiled, shrugged, and went her own way happily. One day she would be vindicated by the attention to detail which her friends called paranoia.

It wasn't that she was afraid of life. Quite the contrary. Life was there to be lived, to the full. She had tried parachuting, diving, skiing, rock climbing, and just about every water sport going. Wasn't it dangerous? she had been asked on many an occasion. Of course it was dangerous, she thought, that was part of the attraction, but she would just quote her philosophy with a bland smile: 'It's only dangerous if you get it wrong'.

So when the steady chug of the engine first missed a beat, then faltered and died altogether, she wasn't totally disconcerted. At best she could fix it, at worst she could climb in the down sleeping bag and stay warm till morning.

She climbed out of the car, and the freezing wind bit instantly through her clothes. Not dressed for this, she thought, looking down at her silk trousers and silly shoes. Opening the back of the car she rooted around and hoisted out a green boiler suit and climbed quickly into it. It might protect her evening clothes, but did little to buffer her against the bitter cold.

She popped the catch on the bonnet, shone the torch in and ran through the possibilities with calculated calm. Though she knew she could not stay out in the chill for long, she had to be systematic, or she might as well not bother to look.

Engrossed in the logics of the internal combustion engine and all its satellite parts, she didn't hear the other car drive up until it pulled in carefully before her, and the door slammed. She glanced up. A tall man in a dark coat had eased his long legs from the confines of a small car, and was walking up to her.

'Need any help?' he yelled as he got closer.

'Not unless you've got a set of internally heated underwear handy,' she replied.

A white smile flashed across dark features, and she noticed the way tiny flakes of white snow adhered to his abnormally long eyelashes. He flapped arms around his torso. 'Jesus it's cold.'

'You'd be best getting on home, then.'

'I can't just drive on and leave you here, miles from anywhere. Do you want me to look?'

She lifted up grey eyes, amused. She hadn't missed the slight hesitancy in the noble offer. 'Would you know what you were looking for?'

'Not really, but I'll give it a shot,' he said honestly.

God, he was sexy. She turned away quickly, disguising the flash of interest which must surely have sprung from her eyes. 'Trust me, this won't take long. You don't have to wait.'

She hoped it wouldn't take long, for the weatherman was perhaps, for once, right. The snow suddenly changed to freezing sleet, and the shoulders of her boiler suit were soon running with water. She shivered dramatically, knowing if she stopped she would turn instantly into an ice sculpture. This was not good.

The stranger leaned over and peered in at the incomprehensible intricacies of the engine, and in the harsh light of the torch his features took on a sinister appearance, all angles and shadows. 'Are you sure you know what you're doing?'

'I'm fine,' she said. In spite of her outward calm, he worried her slightly.

'Do you think you ought to leave the car here, and I'll take you somewhere?' he said, worrying her further. Just where did he have in mind?

Out of the car, on her own, on the middle of a moor, she was vulnerable, and knew it. Not, she thought, that anyone with any sense would try a rape in this weather, it would probably freeze solid and fall off. The thought made her smile slightly.

The stranger thought she was smiling at him, and responded.

God, he had a nice smile.

She bit her lip, and stood up. 'I'll give it a try, now,' she said.

He stood back while she passed, stuffed his hands deep

in his overcoat pockets, and stamped his feet. The car turned over once or twice and roared into life.

She grinned with vindication, climbed out and shut the bonnet.

'I'm impressed,' he said through chattering teeth.

'Well perhaps you should be impressed somewhere a bit warmer,' she suggested, wiping the water droplets from the rats-tails of her hair. 'And thanks for stopping, I appreciate your concern, really.'

'No bother. Where are you going? Shall I stick with you for a bit, just in case?'

'In case of what?' she said quickly. 'The Hall is only three miles or so from here. Even if I get stuck I can walk.'

'The Hall?' he said quickly.

'Bridington Hall. Why do you know it?'

He gave a rueful smile. 'You're going to think this is the most corny line ever, but that's where I'm going, too. I suppose you are coming to the Art History Group Funding Dinner?'

Her brows raised with amusement, and her fear fled. 'So it would seem. I don't suppose you know how to get there?'

'I should, I live there.'

'Oh. In that case, I will follow you after all.'

'You're very independent, aren't you?'

She flashed him a smile. 'If you mean I like to make my own decisions, then yes.' She climbed in the car, and slammed the door, and she could still see him shaking his head as he walked to his own vehicle. Whether with laughter or confusion, she wasn't sure.

Once again the weather changed, though. As she drove

along, following the taillights of the stranger at a (hope-fully) safe distance, the sleet thickened, blurred, and turned into a real snowstorm.

She parked alongside the other car and climbed out gin-gerly; the concrete drive was extremely slippery. 'I'm beginning to wonder whether I've made a bit of a mis-take,' she said over the top of the car.

The stranger flashed a smile. 'What an admission from such an independent lady. But don't worry, there are plen-ty of beds here. You don't have to worry about driving back if it doesn't ease off.' He lugged a small wooden box from the back seat, and closed the door with a practised swing of his hip.

They hastened through a large, oak front door, and into a flag-stoned corridor. The silence as the door slammed was extreme. The stranger balanced the box on one hip, and held out his hand. 'Mark Waterhouse.'

Her brows rose. 'Good Lord, you're the Professor? I'd expected a much older man.'

'Sorry.'

She took his hand, and grinned, unabashed. 'Jane Macklin. From the library service. It was just the list of titles that misled me, you see. Professor of both Ancient Art and Archaeology, you know.' She glanced around at the low ceilings, the ornate wooden scroll at the bottom of the stairs, and the uneven walls. 'Very nice,' she said approvingly, extracting her hand from his very strong grip.

'Parts of the building actually date from mediaeval times,' he explained, dumping a large crate on the floor, and removing his coat. 'The original building was once a monastery, and the Hall was built on top of partial ruins. They incorporated a lot of the old stone into the walls, too.'

'The odd gargoyle or two, eh?'

'And the odd bit of carved graffiti, believe it or not. May I take your coat?'

She shed the coat almost reluctantly. 'I think I'm wet right through,' she said ruefully.

'No problem. Follow me. Just let me get shot of the strawberries.' He collected his crate and pushed through a far door into a large and welcoming kitchen draped with stainless steel utensils, brass ornamental pots, and plaited strands of onion and garlic.

'Strawberries?'

He smiled at her surprise. 'Bribes. Strawberries and champagne in February. The wonders of the twentieth century. All mod cons. Except that we couldn't do much about the weather. The worst winter for fifteen years, and I have to choose it for my presentation.'

'I have serious doubts as to whether many people will turn up on a night like this,' she offered candidly. 'I only came early because I was on my way home from a lecture. If I'd gone home first, I probably would have phoned in with my apologies.'

'I'm glad you didn't.' His warm gaze incorporated her boiler suit, darkened from the sleet. 'Follow me.'

He went up another set of back stairs, and led her to a bedroom complete with four-poster bed. 'I'm not suggesting getting warm in there,' he assured her, casting a speculative glance to the contrary, 'though the thought is not unattractive. It's just that this room has a heater and an en-suite shower. 'Come and find me downstairs when you're dry and warm.'

Almost self-consciously she locked the door behind

him, and stripped. The common sense behind his sugges-
tion was undeniable, but somehow being naked and alone
in the house with this man turned her thoughts very much
towards carnal pleasures. He had an extremely sexy smile,
and a nice body. The thought, as he had said, was not
entirely unattractive. She turned the heater up full, and
left her clothes steaming before it, and wallowed beneath
the hot shower until her shivers ceased.

Half an hour later the only thing not dry was her shoes,
and she wandered in stockinged feet down the wooden
staircase in search of her host. He must have heard it
creak, for a door opened, outlining him in the flickering
light of a real fire. His eyes lit appreciatively at the finely draped silk. 'I'd expected something a bit more - ah -
butch,' he commented.

'I can be a woman and still understand engines,' she
said, slightly sharply.

He held his hands up in mock supplication. 'Sorry. It's
my two thousand year-old gender stereotyping. And that
from a man who doesn't know a petrol pump from a water
hose.'

'It's OK. I shouldn't get so defensive. Sorry.'

'Come on in.' He stood back, and she passed him. The
living room was long and low, probably spanning the
width of the house. It had been furnished with large
pieces of oak furniture from different eras, and dotted with
a variety of collapsing old stuffed chairs each loose-cov-
ered in a different fabric, each piece obviously chosen
with a loving care which had nothing to do with colour co-
ordination. But it was the fireplace which dominated the
room. It was a vast affair, in which the logs were piled to
one side, and the fire-basket stood on two dog-faced triv-

ets. And above it a tall mirror reigned, heavily decorated with gold-painted plasterwork cherubs. 'This is cosy,'she said appreciatively.

'I've had the heating on all day,' he explained, closing the door behind her. 'And the fireplace has got a damper just inside the chimney. When I first moved in I could have heated the upper stratosphere before the fire touched the living room. I like old houses, but I have to say I like my comfort, too. Now do you want the bad news or the good news?'

'Bad,'she said with resignation.

'Sixteen people have sent their apologies, and the storm is turning into a blizzard. The road down to the Hall is already impassable. We're marooned.'

'Ah. And the good?'

'You and I have ten pounds of strawberries and eight bottles of champagne to help us through our exile.'

She chuckled. 'One could almost wonder whether this wasn't a part of some dastardly grand plan.'

'If I had seen you before I might very well have organised it that way. That outfit, silk trousers with the ankle cuffs, has very much the overtones of Arabian Nights.'

'I bought it because it was comfortable. Had I met you first, I would have worn something a bit more - butch.'

'I'm glad you didn't.'

His voice was low, and internal fires coiled and writhed behind the reflection of the amber flames. She looked around and stared, mesmerised. 'Is that a compliment, or another bit of gender stuff?'

'Oh, gender stuff, without a doubt,' he said cheerfully. 'I have never felt the least inclination to make love to another man.'

'Oh.' She was taken aback. 'You are very forthright, aren't you?'

'Not always,' he admitted. 'But the moment I saw you standing there out in the freezing cold, something moved inside me. I don't think I've ever met a woman who has made me so thoroughly interested quite so instantly.'

'Oh.' She gingerly sat on the edge of a small chair by the fire. She had never before met a man who was quite so forward quite so quickly. 'Do you say that to all your women?'

'All?'

'Arabian Nights,' she reminded him.

'Just because I dream doesn't mean I am entirely without morals,' he said. There was an explosion and she jumped, looking round as the cork came out of the champagne. He gave a child-like grin, tipped the overflowing bubbles into two waiting glasses, and handed one to her. She sipped it and stared at him over the rim. 'Is this the softening procedure before the seduction scene?'

'Yes. But of course, you can press the stop button at any time.'

She giggled, wondering which button he meant, but said nothing. He came and sat on the floor beside her, and for a moment there was silence, broken only by the hiss and crackle of the log fire. She stared surreptitiously at him. Why was he so sexy, so desirable? He was older than her by several years, and yet there was something impish and innocent in his open desires; he was hiding nothing, just taking advantage of a situation which had just happened. He glanced up, met her gaze, and once again, the strong lines of his face suddenly seemed devilish and slightly evil.

She shivered, and gave an internal laugh at the fantasy, but her heart leapt in another gear. She recognised it instantly. It was the same feeling she had when about to ascend a difficult rock-face, or the leap of adrenaline which preceded the moment she leapt out of an aeroplane.

It was the excitement of fear.

He saw something flit across her face, and knelt up. He pushed her silk-clad knees apart and leaned forward to kiss her fully on the lips. There was no hesitation, no doubt. Just the fullness of his kiss, the long, slow enjoyment of his tongue tracing the line of her teeth.

She shuddered with expectation.

Her hands reached around strong shoulders, pulled him strongly towards her body, and as her inner thighs touched, she burned with a different kind of fire. Now it was not just him kissing her. Through the heady taste of champagne she knew that she wanted to make love with devastating desperation. What was he doing to her? She had never felt like this before.

Now his hands were sliding with jerky movements against her silk clothes, and her own hands were tracing the hard muscles of his tense shoulders, and their bodies were weaving together in the age-long tune of desire.

Eyes wide, each saw the reflection of passion in the other, and sensed a foreknowledge of the inevitable. In that instant they knew that they were going to lie naked, entwined in each others arms before a roaring fire, come what may tomorrow.

There was a thundering sound on the front door.

'Shit,' said the professor.

He waited a moment, but the knocking came again, more urgent. He sighed and stood up.

A moment later a large, red-faced man in a flat cap entered, slapping gloved hands together. 'Aye, 'tis warm enough in here,' he said in jovial tones. 'I was just telling young Mark here that I came over in the Land Rover just to see if anyone was stranded and needed rescuing. I only just got through, myself, and given another hour, I doubt I'd have even attempted it.' He glanced at her. 'If you want to get out before Friday, you'd best come along with me, my dear. Shame about the party.'

'A great shame,' Mark said, a rueful light in his eyes, and she knew what he meant; that it was a great shame that the Land Rover had made it here at all. She felt like the proverbial victim suddenly released from the hypnotic effect of a snake's eyes. Good God! She had been about to have sex with a complete stranger. She moved with sudden haste.

Doubt filled her mind, she stilled her urge to run.

So why did she suddenly feel saddened by the loss of that experience?

It was like going up in the plane and chickening out, not having the courage to jump. Damn it, that wasn't her style. 'I don't need rescuing,' she said slowly.

Realisation dawned in the farmer's eyes. 'Oh, sorry, my dear,'he said in confusion, 'I just thought you were one of the guests, stuck in the snow, like. And seeing as how the lines are down, you couldn't even phone out.'

She smiled, and saw it echoed in the soft curve of Mark's lips, in the dark and sultry promise in his eyes. 'No, I think I am slightly more than just a guest,'she said. 'More like a sort of dream incarnate.'

The farmer looked confused as the professor ushered him back out into the cold. A flurry of snow entered as he thrust the door closed against the elements. She heard the Land Rover pull away.

Mark came back into the room, his dark eyes pools of lust, his smile one of sardonic amusement. 'So, embodiment of my dreams, fulfil me.'

His voice was so low she only just made out the words, but the stance of his whole body was that of burning need, and with echoing needs and just the faintest stirring of fear, she walked decisively into his embrace.

Crumbs of Affection

By Biddy Nelson

'Cicely St-John-Smith,' she said, waving her glass and spraying me with asparagus roll.

'Gosh, what a mouthful,' I said ambiguously.

'I believe you know Johnny?'

I did. Very well. I kept looking for him but he hadn't arrived at the party yet. He was late, but being a hospital doctor he kept funny hours.

'I can see you're his type. You must get asked out a lot,' she said, smiling gamely, 'lucky old you.' She blushed and laughed rather loudly.

I wasn't sure what to say to her, but then I looked across the room and saw Johnny. He's tall and thin, dark and quite irresistible. I crossed the room to him and knew from the way he looked at me that we wouldn't be staying.

We didn't. We raced back to his flat and threw everything off the bed. My zip was easy, but I remember buttons from his shirt flying in all directions. Afterwards we sat up and he ate bread and marmalade. Johnny was always hungry, but making love made him ravenous. I licked a bit of marmalade off him and thought how brilliant life was. Then, as we wondered whether to go back to the party, Cicely came into my mind. Life wasn't so great for her.

'Johnny, why are some girls simply not attractive?'

'Oh you're not that bad, sweetie,' he said with his mouth full.

I stopped licking and bit him instead.

'Serves you right,' I said when he yelped. 'But seriously, there was this girl tonight...' and I told him about Cicely.

'The latest medical research indicates,' Johnny said, doing his doctor bit - then pouncing, 'that if you think you turn a girl on then it's whoopee - viagra all round.'

Marmalade became mutual.

I forgot that conversation until I saw Cicely wandering through Harvey Nicks a few weeks later.

'Time for a cuppa?' she asked. I couldn't think of an excuse fast enough, so we drifted upstairs.

'Sorry I moaned at you the other night,' she said, after we'd settled at our table.

'Did you moan?'

'You know, about not being asked out much - you'd think I'd be used to it by now. Sad old me, just not sexy.' She laughed and shrugged at the same time, then poured out. How do you respond to that? I had to say something, because she obviously minded, so I decided to tell her what Johnny had said.

'A chap told me,' I said, ' that to be sexy you've got to feel turned on and show it, of course that's if you really like the guy. So who'd you want to go to bed with? Decide, then... try it out,' I added.

Just after that Johnny disappeared from my life, no visits, no phone calls. I kept going over the last time we'd been together. We'd made love, then I said it - the no-no word. Didn't mean to, it just popped out.

'Johnny, do you love me?'

'Course,' he said.

'Say it.'

'You know I do.'

'Well say it then.'

'Sweetie, I'm a do-man, not a say-man.'

Why couldn't I have left it there? But I didn't. I had this great need to hear him say the words.

'Johnny, the Victorians may not've done as much in bed, but at least they could talk about love.'

'Yeah - while they made it in the dark so they didn't see each other. Where's the honesty in that?'

'But they weren't frightened of the emotion.'

'Busy, busy,'he said, climbing out of bed. 'Must get on, save a few lives.'

He left.

I stuck it out for a bit then caved in and phoned.

'Shall we meet?'

'Sorry, concentrating. Membership exam next week, and I'm job-hunting too. See you sometime.'

Brush off words. Don't plead, I instructed myself, just move on. I was still young, it was still party-time, wasn't it? Uneasily I realised I'd done that bit. My job was a nothing-job, there to support my nightlife. I was filling in time until... silly old fashioned me. But maybe my parents were right?

'Get a husband. Didn't that school teach you anything, Emma?' my father had grumbled. 'Cost enough.'

'Em, darling, it's great fun being married. I mean, just look at Daddy and me - well anyhow, I'm sure *you*'d be good at it.'

Oh Johnny. Can't think straight when you're there.

Can't think straight when you're not.

I nearly didn't go to Cicely's party. I'd just arrived when Johnny pounced.

'Where've you been?' I said, going for cool.

'Told you. Membership exam. Done it. Passed.'

'Congratulations,'I said, aiming at the stand-offish side of enthusiastic. But Johnny had enough enthusiasm for two and refused to notice.

'Em-my-gem,' he powered on, 'has it occurred to you that there are too many people around here? We must talk - amongst other things.'

I let him cave man me out of the party and back to his place. Later he sat up in bed and ate pate from a tin.

'I think it's possible,'he said, 'we ought to get married.'

Warm, happy relief of the long-term variety spread through me, but as token resistance - who was being Victorian now? - I said, 'What would someone like me do getting married?'

'Breed,' he said. 'You're going to want to breed.'

'Am I?' I asked, realising that was true.

'I've been offered a partnership in Hereford.'

'Good for breeding?'I asked, 'For me as well as cows?'

'Excellent.'

'Johnny? Why me?'

'Because you're a miracle in bed and...' suddenly he looked shy, 'you're kind,'he mumbled.

'Kind? What makes you think that?'

He was embarrassed. Amazing. People like him can talk bodies until the cows come home - cows had obviously become an obsession in my life - but when it comes to feelings...

'Cicely,' he said, 'she's a cousin of mine actually. She

said you bothered with her, made all the difference.'

'How?'

'You told her to think about who she wanted to go to bed with and she realised it was Maggie Palmer. They're the happiest couple in town, except us. She even looks different, goes to my Father's tailor, looks very spruce.'

Good for Cicely.

'Could you manage to say how you feel about me?' I asked.

'You know.'

'Do you love me?' I persisted.

'Yeah,' he said. 'Look, I'm on call, must go.'

I knew then that for the rest of my life I'd have to settle for actions and do without the words.

'Am I engaged?' I called after him.

He stopped, turned, and said, 'You are engaged, booked, occupied territory, situation filled - it's a full time job.'

And so it's turned out to be. There's Johnny to look after, and the babies, and always, always crumbs to brush out of our bed.

Something in the Water

By Sarah Salway

Jane sat on the edge of the swimming pool, dipping one toe into the water to test the temperature.

She told her husband that she liked to come at this time of the evening because there were always so few people. It wasn't a complete lie; more of a half-truth. Fewer people meant she had more space for the one she had come to see. She spotted Patrick immediately over at the far side, but didn't acknowledge him straight away. They had so little time together that ignoring him had become a precious luxury.

A bored father was standing in the shallow end watching a group of children bob up and down on brightly coloured fish-shaped floats. Two pairs of women were chatting together as they swam lengths in unison. The middle of the pool was given over to the serious swimmers. A man was ploughing up and down the fast lane, putting his face up too often to gasp for breath, churning the water with his arms. Jane watched the other swimmers smile tensely at each other to acknowledge the inconvenience. When he was safely out of the way, she slipped into the water.

She realised she'd been dreading this moment. It was

like a sacrifice. The fear was out of all proportion to the action, as if a transformation would have to be effected by the time she got out of the pool. She would give something up through her immersion.

Now she hung on to the metal bar at the end to get her breath back before starting to swim. She took her time, concentrating on building up the structure of the stroke. It was the first chance she'd had all day to stretch her body. She reached the other end and floated on her back, her arms bent behind her grasping the bar, her legs scissoring slowly through the water. When Patrick came up, she made her face blank. 'Is everything alright?'he asked and she nodded, focusing on how his legs had joined hers moving in distorted shapes under the ripples. 'Why won't you look at me?'

She turned her face round, opening her eyes comically wide to stare at him. His blond hair was plastered to his scalp, showing ridges left by his fingers where he'd scraped it off his face. It accentuated his broad nose and fleshy cheekbones.

She knew his face so well. There were times when she would be talking to her husband or helping the boys do their homework and she'd have to catch her breath. An image of Patrick would hit her so hard it was as if he were there in the room with her. When she closed her eyes every night, it was Patrick's face she saw next to hers on the pillow. She had imagined every inch so vividly, it was almost disappointing to see him in the flesh.

She shut her eyes briefly now but it was Harry, her eldest son, who floated before her, his dark hair tousled over Thomas the Tank Engine pyjamas, his cheeks red and round with laughter. When she opened her eyes again, it was to find Patrick had put his face close up to hers, almost touching. She hissed at him and he laughed, throwing his head back as if he was putting the line of his neck on display.

The violence of her feelings towards Patrick shocked her. When she thought about her husband it was always with respect, a little distance, but Patrick broke down all her defences. Crossed all her boundaries. She imagined slitting his neck then, a clean cut across the Adam's apple, using the same precision as when she was carving the Sunday roast. The blood would stream out across the surface of the water, rippling over to where the children were playing, interrupting the women gossiping. Most of all it would curl round and round her, trussing her up with strings she couldn't escape from.

'We have to be kind to each other,'she said, more fiercely than she meant to. 'Otherwise there is no point.'

She moved to swim off but he lunged down and grabbed hold of her ankle, tightening his grip so she had to hold on to the side or sink down, unable to kick. He inched his fingers round, moving them individually. It was the same hand action she used with the children. Incy wincy spider. But then Patrick clenched his fist, digging harder and harder into her flesh to push beneath her anklebone and the rest of her foot. The pain was so unexpected it made her gasp.

'Did you hear about the girl who wakes up one morning and decides she's a masochist?' he asked.

Jane shook her head. She had let go of the side by this time and was trying to look as if she was floating on her back. As if no one was holding onto her ankle. As if nothing was happening.

'She meets a sadist and everything's fine until he finds a way to really hurt her. Each time she begs for pain, he's nicer and nicer to her, brings her flowers, chocolates, everything. And do you know the thing that really pisses her off? She can't complain to anyone, because they're all so fucking jealous of the way she's met the perfect man.'

Patrick pushed Jane off then and she trod water for a few minutes, listening to him laugh. 'I love that story,'he said. 'Causing pain through kindness, and everyone thinking you're some kind of saint.'

Jane turned her back on him, and told herself that if she managed to swim to the other end without making one splash, without causing one ripple in the water, then everything would be alright. She didn't even come up for air until she'd reached the halfway mark, and then she took care to emerge very gently.

She swam a few more lengths on her own, trying to fill her mind with thoughts of home. She pictured her children sitting round the kitchen table, Tim reading them stories. It soothed her until she believed she could forget Patrick. By her eighth length, she'd entered the dream zone. She was dimly aware of the other swimmers but it was her body, her place in the water, she was focusing on. All she had to do was to get to the white tiled end, cling on to the silver rail, turn herself round and aim for the other side. The smoochy, late-night music had been turned on now, the over-bright striplights switched off so the building was lit up by spotlights from below the water. Everyone had the same dazed expression. This was the twilight hour and none of them were rushing home.

It was at this hour she'd first met Patrick. She'd swum herself into a trance so when he'd come up beside her, it had been a surprise to look around and see they were alone in the pool. Even the lifeguard had his back to them as he spoke on the poolside telephone. It had seemed natural then to swim side by side. They'd nodded to each other a few times before that, exchanging the sort of half smiles you do with someone who shares the same hobby as you do. But that evening had changed everything. It was the water that had done it. It had suspended reality, encouraging them to talk not about the actualities of their lives but about their dreams.

Later that night, sitting in front of the television beside her husband, she started to shake with the enormity of her betrayal.

'What's wrong?' Tim asked.

What could she say? She had often wondered what would have happened if she confessed how a stranger knew that every morning she sat down to breakfast hoping this was going to be the day she would have the courage to run away and leave them all, Tim and the children.

Tim would never have believed her. She was a good mother, a good woman. She wasn't the type to run away. It was Patrick who had seen through her straight away because he had the same unrealistic fantasies. Only his were that he would one day settle down.

'We are so completely opposite,' he'd laughed that first time, after they had swum a length in silence taking this in.

'We'd pass each other by in the street without even noticing,' Jane had agreed. 'You are the type of person I would never, ever want to meet.' She looked across at him as they swam. 'Normally,' she added.

But the next Thursday, Jane stood outside the Leisure

Centre and paused a second in front of the revolving doors. 'If I can get to the other side without having to touch them again, Patrick's going to be inside,' she told herself, giving the doors one big push. She'd managed, of course, but then she'd known she would. Jane wasn't the type to play a game of chance unless the odds were heavily stacked in her favour.

Neither Patrick nor Jane had missed a Thursday since.

It hadn't taken them long to find a rhythm to their swimming. They would swim individually at first and then drift together. After a while, they stopped talking and just rested, letting their hands trail out with the water's flow towards the other's body before pulling them back. Just in time.

They used never to touch. It had been one of their rules. Jane told herself that it was so she could go home with a clean conscience. A clean mind in a clean body. The water washing everything away. All their dirty secrets carried off by the waves.

Two women in their fifties came up in the medium lane, skirting round Jane. She nodded them on to show she wasn't moving anywhere and they smiled. 'Give me some inspiration,' Jane overheard one woman say. 'What are you feeding him for tea tonight?' She thought of the lasagne she'd got simmering in the oven for Tim and her to share later, but then Patrick kicked his foot out at her calf.

'I'd like to eat off your body,' he said. 'I'd start at the top. Put canapés over your face. Olives, salami, salty cheeses. I'd have to bite at them, nibble very gently, peck with my lips, and then I'd lick the juices off.'

Jane swam off, picking up speed, kicking at the water

with her legs. She wondered if she'd put enough tomato sauce in the lasagne, covered it with enough cheese. It would spoil if it dried out. Patrick caught up with her.

'You'd have to lie absolutely still because you'd be the table. Your neck would be covered in the thinnest slices of smoked salmon so I'd need to bend right over you to get hold of one of the ends. I'd have to use my teeth to pull it off, layer by layer. I'd pause a bit then. It would be important to be able to take my time.'

'That's hackneyed, trite,' Jane said. 'A schoolboy's fantasy.' She didn't say what she really felt. That it was the strange innocence of their meetings she had liked. It had been this feeling of talking to a best friend, a mirror image, that had kept her coming back to the pool week after week. Now, she just felt let down by the one-sidedness of the conversation. Patrick had changed their relationship from the shock of shared intimacies to a sordid predictability.

He fell behind her then, tapping the soles of her feet as she swam. She kicked out, splashing wildly until he came back beside her. 'There lies the crux,' he said. 'If you're turned on, there's no point to the game. You mustn't move a muscle otherwise you'll spoil my pleasure.'

'And the main course?' she asked. 'I suppose you'll put slabs of beef on my breasts and fill my navel with gravy.'

They were silent as they turned around for another length, weaving through the other swimmers who were congregating in the shallows. They had found a rhythm now, were matching each other stroke for stroke. Apart from the background music, the pool was unnaturally quiet so Patrick started to whisper.

'I'd turn you round then and eat from your back,' he

said. 'A Chinese banquet, so I could dip in and out as I choose. Fill the hollows made by your shoulder blades, the valleys beside your spine, the dimples just above your buttocks. Nothing too much of anything but just enough to whet my appetite.'

She tried hard to feel some frisson of arousal but as she thought about lying there with Patrick bent over her, she started to shudder. In the pictures she was creating in her mind, her hair had turned to seaweed and her legs fell to each side uselessly. If he were to turn her over, her eyes would be gaping holes, her flesh would fall off with each bite. She tried to dismiss the images but a final picture of Patrick licking his lips above her wasted body lingered on.

'Time to go,' she said. 'I've been in too long.'

He nodded and still swimming in unison, they made their way to the metal steps. He moved round to encircle her with his arms as she climbed out in front of him.

No Running. No Jumping. No Shouting. No Petting.

In front of the notice, a bored lifeguard sat, looking through Jane as if she didn't exist so she shook her wet hair as if by accident and watched the drops of water land on his bare sunbed-tanned thighs. He brushed them off still without reacting, semi-focusing on a spot in the distance.

'Pudding from your legs.' Patrick was whispering behind Jane as they walked towards the Jacuzzi. 'Custard to suck from between your toes, jelly up and down your legs and ...'

She turned round and put her hand over his mouth as the two women from the pool shuffled round the Jacuzzi bench to make room for them. Jane and Patrick sat there in silence, legs and hands entwined under the cover of the bubbles, heads resting back on the ledge.

After a while, the women resumed their conversation. 'No, swimming's the thing,' one said. She was wearing a pink and orange flowered swimming hat which clashed with the red flush on her neck and cheeks. Jane closed her eyes. 'I've tried all sorts of exercise but when you get older, you've got to be careful, haven't you?'

'I tried jogging once,' volunteered the other woman. Patrick made running movements with his fingers along the inside of Jane's thigh. She squeezed her legs together to catch his hand, knowing he wouldn't try to free himself.

'Never again,' said the woman. 'I couldn't walk properly for days. It turned my legs to jelly. Jelly and custard they were.'

Jane gasped, and when she turned to look at Patrick, he'd ducked his head under the water. Jane passed her hand several times over where he'd been as if she was showing off a magician's trick. The Disappearing Man. When he surfaced, she pushed him gently down again, holding her palm flat on top of his hair.

Later, Jane lay in bed with her legs drawn up to her stomach, her back to Tim. He tapped her on the shoulder but she shrugged him off, pretending to be half-asleep. She could feel him kiss her back gently, his tongue grazing her skin, but then he stopped, rolling away to the other side of the bed.

'You taste different,' he said. 'What is it?'

She lay there, not breathing, holding her arm up in front of her to see if her hand was shaking. Slowly, she moved it to her lips and licked it tentatively. Then she laughed.

'It's just the chlorine,' she said. 'I didn't have time for a shower.'

'I like it.' He shifted onto his side so the bed creaked. 'It reminds me of those American swimmers, all shoulders and smiles.'

She turned to face him and took his face in between her palms, studying it hard. 'You,' she said seriously, 'are my anchor in life. You tie me down. Without you, I'd float away.' Then she gave him her version of a wide American smile.

'You're always happy these days,' he said, as if he was accusing her of something.

She was happy. The thought surprised her. She pushed both - the thought and her surprise at it - to the back of her mind to consider later.

'I'll have to come swimming with you.' His fingers were playing with the hair that curled at the back of her neck. He was always touching her, playing with her. 'If it's so much fun,' he added.

She flopped down on her back and sighed. 'I'm not going again,' she said. 'It doesn't do me any good. I think it must be all the chemicals they put in the water,'

'But...'

She interrupted him then, reaching out to stop him saying anything else. But as they moved back across the bed towards each other, she tried not to notice how clumsy their movements were, swimming on land.

Comfort and Joy

By Christina Jones

The bus crawled along the dark, damp High Street. Multicoloured lights, reflected in the puddles like fallen rainbows, made a sad attempt to brighten up the grey shops. Carrie, on her way home from work, stared at the trashy brash windows with their tinsel and baubles and garish gaudiness.

Christmas. Again. She hated it.

As the bus rocked to a halt and the woman next to her gathered a mass of carrier bags together, Carrie shrank back in her seat to avoid being smacked round the head by a gameboy.

'Sorry,'the woman laughed, dragging her parcels over Carrie's feet. 'You go mad at this time of year, don't you? Still, it's all for the kids, isn't it? Spoil 'em rotten, don't you?'

Carrie shrugged. 'Not me. I haven't got children.'

'Ah...' the woman looked a bit askance. 'Right. Sorry...'

'Nothing to be sorry about.' Carrie was used to it. People looked at her, guessed her age, looked at the wedding ring, and simply couldn't understand. 'I manage to enjoy Christmas - even without children.'

It wasn't true of course, but the woman looked less

embarrassed as she hauled her shopping off the bus. Carrie had said it so many times to so many people that she'd even managed to convince herself that the Christmases she and Frank shared were bearable rather than bleak and miserable. Just the two of them, with very little in common these days: ten years married and light-years apart. Mind you, this Christmas might be different - and next year certainly would be...

The bus stopped on the edge of the housing estate and Carrie stepped off into the blustery darkness. Christmas trees twinkled in every window and a fair few Santas leered in neon splendour from chimney pots. There was no-one around. It could be the middle of the night, she thought, snuggling deeper into her coat. Frank would already be home, it being Friday, but he wouldn't have started the dinner. He thought that was woman's work.

Pausing at the end of the road, Carrie glanced at her watch in the smoky glow of a street lamp. Why not? What difference would another half an hour or so make? Frank would probably be snoring in front of the telly anyway... She tucked her wind-blown hair behind her frozen ears and hurried back in the direction of the town.

Ten minutes later, Nick opened the door of his flat. 'Carrie!' He pulled her into his arms. 'Oh, wow - I didn't expect to see you tonight. I thought Friday was Frank's early finish day?'

'It is,' Carrie grinned, relaxing her icy body against him. 'I just wanted to see you.'

Nick kissed her tenderly. With love. Her eyes, cheeks, lips. Slowly. He pulled a face. 'Angel - you're freezing. Come on in and get warm. Have you got time for a drink?'

'Tea would be lovely. I'd better not have alcohol - and

anyway, Frank would smell it from a million paces. And I am supposed to have come home straight from work...'

Nick unbuttoned her coat, unravelled her scarf and pulled off her gloves, kissing her all the time. Carrie felt her body melt with lust and longing. No-one but Nick could do this to her...

She took his face in her hands and kissed him back. 'I love you. I can't keep away. You're even harder to give up than cigarettes.'

'I hope you're not thinking of kicking the habit?'Nick whispered, his tongue circling hotly on the frozen skin of her neck.

'Not a chance,' Carrie sighed. 'I'm hooked. But we can't... Not now... I've got to go home...'

'Sod it,' Nick said good-naturedly. 'Just a cup of tea, then? Boring old bag...'

Carrie punched him cheerfully then kissed away the punch.

He made tea while she leaned against the kitchen table, all the time fighting the urge to grab him and rip his clothes off and drag him on to the kitchen floor. He was beautiful, fifteen years younger than she was - and looked it. She loved his young lean body, his face, his silky hair, his joy of life - but most of all she loved his love for her.

He handed her the mug of tea, stroking her fingers. 'How are you feeling?'

'Fine,' Carrie sipped the tea. 'Positively blooming.'

'You look it. It suits you. Makes you even more gorgeous - if that was possible.' Nick took her free hand and led her into the tiny living room where a fire flickered cosily in the hearth, holly and ivy tumbled from vases, and gold and silver streamers sparkled across the ceiling.

'Have you told him yet?'

Carrie sank down on to the sofa and stretched her toes towards the gas logs. 'No. It's going to be my Christmas Day surprise. A sort of extra special present.'

'Yeah, right!' Nick laughed. 'Some present! But - are you sure - ?'

'Absolutely,' she sipped her tea, then placed the mug on the floor. Nick sprawled beside her, unable to keep away from her for long. She snuggled against him. 'Nick, darling, I love you very much. But you're twenty one. The last thing you want is to get saddled with an old bag like me -'

'But I love you,' he interrupted. 'I'll always love you. You know that.'

'I hope so...' Carrie kissed him again. 'And I hope you'll always be around for me, but Frank's my husband and however bad our marriage is, it's still a marriage. And this -'she stroked her stomach, 'could make all the difference.'

Nick lifted her sweater and unbuttoned her skirt. He ran his fingers slowly, tantalisingly, across the swell of her belly. Then he lowered his head and kissed her pale, translucent, slightly stretched skin. 'Incredible... totally incredible...'

She wriggled down beside him, unable as always to resist him, and shuddered with exquisite pleasure as he undressed her, expertly, erotically slowly...

Afterwards, totally satiated, curled together naked in front of the fire, Carrie lazily stroked Nick's hair from his eyes. She adored him. She adored the sex. she adored being wanted. She always would - but this wouldn't last. He'd changed her life, but it couldn't last. Not now.

Her inability to have a baby had caused endless rows with Frank. They'd had all the tests. There was nothing wrong. It simply hadn't happened... and now.... She looked at Nick - and now it had. She'd tell Frank on Christmas morning. It would be the making of their marriage and would make it the best Christmas ever.

'I wish you'd leave him,' Nick whispered against her hair. 'You could move in with me and -'

'Spoil everything,' Carrie interrupted. 'Nick, darling, we've been over this hundreds of times. You'll meet someone of your own age one day and then I'll be ancient history - but I hope you'll always remember your fling with the boring old bag with love...'

She was giggling as he pulled her against him again.

Christmas Day. Lunch time. Carrie had been cooking all morning while Frank and his equally po-faced parents sat in front of the television looking about as happy as patients in a dentist's waiting room. Not that it mattered. She'd soon cheer them all up.

'Come and get it!' she sang out happily, carrying the first of the dishes through to the table. 'Don't let it get cold!'

She'd tried really hard to add a bit of festive sparkle. The Christmas tree was baubled to the hilt, and she'd criss-crossed crackers on the red tablecloth. Frank had grumbled about the expense but she'd told him it was to make an effort for his parents and he'd shut up. Eventually.

They'd already opened their presents. She'd brought Frank a shirt. He'd given her a CD she'd already got. His parents had given them a pot plant. Nick's present, a crystal heart on a slender gold chain, was tucked away in her knicker drawer.

'More sprouts?' Carrie pushed the vegetable dish towards Frank's mother.

There was a grunt of acceptance. Frank's parents, who had never liked her, had been very disappointed that their only son's wife hadn't managed to make them grandparents. And said so. Many times.

Waiting until all the plates were filled, Carrie leaned across the table. 'I've got another present for you all... well, a bit of news, actually.'

'Really?' Frank looked surprised, a roast potato suspended on the fork prongs halfway between plate and mouth. 'So have I.'

His parents perked up, looking from one to the other in anticipation.

Frank put down his fork. 'I should have said something sooner - but I thought I'd save it for today. Make it special.'

'Me too.'

Frank looked at his parents, then at Carrie. 'I know how bad it's been for us all these years, with you not being able to have a baby...'

'Ah, yes, but -'

'So,' Frank beamed, 'I thought I ought to do something about it. Put an end to all the disappointment. Every month. All the tears...'

'So have I.' Carrie grinned. 'And so -'

'So,' Frank interrupted again, 'I thought, well, we've been on our own for ten years now and it's been okay, so I thought I ought to take the bull by the horns and -'

'Me too,' Carrie wanted to laugh out loud. They were on the same wavelength for once. Anyway, she wasn't that interested in Frank's Christmas surprise. She had a pretty major one of her own of only he'd shut up. 'Which is why I wanted to tell you today that -'

Frank's parents were practically on the edge of their seats. It was probably the most excitement they'd ever had at Christmas.

'I know you'll see the sense in it,' Frank almost smiled. 'It's all for the best -'

'I expect it is,' Carrie said indulgently. 'But let me have my say first -'

'I hope you won't be angry but -'

Carrie couldn't wait any longer. They spoke at the same time.

'Happy Christmas Frank! I'm three months pregnant!'
'... so I had a vasectomy six months ago...'

Are Diamonds Forever?
By Sue Moorcroft

If ever I'm glad to reach home, it's today.

For a week I've been staying with my cousin, Carly, in her modern, soulless city-centre flat, and the visit wasn't a great success. Maybe I just don't 'get' cities, maybe I just get on Carly's nerves. Probably I shouldn't have aired my opinions of her boyfriend – but Luke's such a weasel.

So, definitely, it's a relief to regain my own home-sweet-home. I shove in a week's worth of undies and tee-shirts to whizz round in the washing machine and lug my bags upstairs, just pleased to be back among my own things in my own little cottage down leafy Ladies' Lane with ...

'A new neighbour?' I halt at the little landing window to peer through the old, streaky glass at the neighbouring garden, a portion of which has apparently turned into a builder's yard in my absence. 'Looks like they intend to get busy.'

The next cottage has been for sale forever. It's also been a neglected mess, but now, even through the dusk, I can see someone's been getting a move on. The grass and the shrubs crowding the path have had a thorough haircut, more in keeping with my own patch of trim lawn, pink foxgloves and twilight blue delphiniums.

'Well, good for whoever,' I mutter, yawning as I move on up the stairs. 'It's about time number 2 stopped bringing down the price of property in Potato Row.' Potato Row stands alone down Ladies' Lane on the very edge of town, and it'll be reassuring to have another neighbour.

For now all I want in the world is a whisky and a hot soapy bath, both deep. Introductions can wait until tomorrow.

'Fancy meeting you here!'

'Chris*sake*.' I nearly shed my skin in fright when I round the corner of the house next door and find myself looking up at dark hair falling into darker, laughing eyes, and a square chin.

'*Richie!*' I do an inelegant buck backwards on the path between the house and the shorn shrubs, eyes swivelling in horror. 'What are *you* doing here?' Then a little dart of panic. 'You're not my new neighbour, are you?'

Richie taps his sandpaper on the window frame and slouches against the wall in a patch of sunlight on the dusky old bricks, looking thoughtful. 'That depends on where you live.'

I hardly dare say it. 'Next door – 1 Potato Row.'

His eyes gleam. 'And I live here – 2 Potato Row! What a coincidence.'

'Unbelievable!' I glare, trying to ignore an alarming thumping in my chest.

Richie's eyes are still alight, being serious doesn't come easily to him.

But this is a grave matter. As far as I'm concerned, ex-fiancés are better at a distance. A big distance. The other side of town. Or in another county. A different galaxy …

He returns to rubbing down the window frame. A nearby door's already prepared and primed and another window replaced. Evidently, a lot has happened while I've been visiting Carly. I watch his sure movements, rub-rub-rub, rub-rub.

He's not a decorator, but Richie seems to be able to do anything he sets his mind to. And he's good with his hands.

I remember … whoops, don't even go there. Don't think about how it used to be with Richie, all those delicious, libidinous nights … 'Still working at the vet's?' I ask, hastily.

He nods. Rub-rub. 'Still there – still bringing my work home.' He indicates a fat, black, three-legged cat who's just limped up to be fussed.

I drag my attention from those hands. 'What happened to him?' I stroke the sleekness of the cat's black back.

Richie shakes his head. 'Don't know, we never traced an owner.' He tickles the cat briefly beneath its chin. 'You should wear something to show you belong with someone, shouldn't you, Cat?'

His words jar an uncomfortable thought to the front of my mind, and my heart executes a quick loop-the-loop as I realise what an ideal time this is to sort out a bit of unfinished business. 'Back in a minute.' I leave Richie to his repairs while I race back to number 1.

By the time I get back he's stroking off-white primer onto the window frame with a narrow brush. His tee-shirt rides up as he reaches higher, and I hold my breath, waiting to see, edging above the waistband of his jeans, the familiar tattoo of tiger's eyes. Remembering how we chose it together … But he alters his position and his tee-shirt shifts again. He glances up calmly. 'Fancy seeing you again so soon.'

I hold out my hand. 'I've come to return this.'

He stops, brush poised. Regards the little square box resting on my unsteady palm, dark red plush with a golden clasp.

'I want you to keep it.'He dips his paintbrush, and turns back to his work.

'But I want you to take it back.'

Richie shakes his head, head bent over his painting. 'As it was "all my fault" and I "threw your love back in your face" with my "disloyal antics", I think I forfeit my claim. In fact – I don't want to ever see it again. Who said diamonds are forever, eh?' His voice is hard and uncompromising.

'Well, *tough*. You've got it.' I slap the little box on an unpainted bit of the windowsill, spin on my heel and march off.

'It's her red hair, Cat, she can't help it,' I hear him explain as I leave.

At the corner of the house I pause. Look back.

He's gazing at the box. Now he's wiping his hands, picking it up gently, opening it to study the contents. He's tipping the box to read the inscription inside the gold band that supports the diamond cluster. *Richie loves Beth*, it'll say.

Carefully he shuts the box again and drops it in his pocket.

Eyes stinging, I walk home.

It's a mistake to look back.

After a few weeks I stop fretting.

Why should I be ruffled because Richie's my new

neighbour? We were over ages ago. There are worse people to live next door to, and Richie's putting endless hours into transforming 2 Potato Row from eyesore to show house.

Which is exactly what I want, bearing in mind boring realities like property prices, so I haven't really got anything to complain about, have I? I'm even getting used to him being there, chatting over the fence, helping with heavy jobs. He seems perfectly content to be friends. We often pause in working in our respective gardens for a companionable cup of coffee among the bright flowers, the buzzing bees and the singing birds – it's all very sociable, we're becoming really neighbourly.

The engagement ring came straight back to me, of course. I wasn't even surprised. He had it delivered by courier. Neither of us wants to be the ring-keeper now, and palming it off onto the other person has actually become a game.

I drop it through his letterbox; he slides it through my open window. I leave it stealthily in his kitchen when I've been round for a cuppa; he hides it in the bag of rosy apples from his tree that he passes over the fence. Back-and-forth it goes in its little plush box. I'm not even exasperated any more. It's all part of the Richie sense of fun.

Early one bright morning an urgent rapping at the front door brings me haring downstairs. Almost before I get the door open, Richie bursts in, hurrying me before him. 'Upstairs, quick!'

Hustled unceremoniously into my bedroom, I tighten the belt of my green satin dressing gown suspiciously. 'What's going on? Why are you peeping through the curtains?'

He reaches out a long arm and pulls me hard against his side. He pulls the golden brocade curtains open a crack and peers into the early morning light. 'Look! Isn't she marvellous?'

I lean my head against his chest to see through the break in the fabric. And draw in my breath, forgetting any irritation. 'Oh, wow, what a beauty.'

On the flat roof of the outhouse, curled round like a doughnut, basks the biggest fox you ever saw, fur blazing amber in the sunshine.

Richie laughs softly. 'What a stop-out, Mrs. Vixen should be home in her lair with the family by now, instead of being out on the tiles.' As if on cue the fox stirs, slinks easily to her feet, slithers over the edge of the roof and steals along the fence before jumping down between Richie's shrubs.

I sigh in disappointment as she disappears. 'She's beautiful.'

'You make a good pair.'

I look up in surprise.

Richie puts up a hand to touch my hair. 'A pair of foxy ladies.'

I try to laugh, but it snags in my throat. I'm suddenly aware – acutely aware – of only the thinnest of fabrics between me and the heat of Richie's hand on my hip, the firm length of his body pressed against mine pretty much from chest to toes. I swallow.

The hand moves slightly, reflexively. I shiver as goosebumps sweep up my back.

Then he steps back, smiling crookedly. 'Got to get to work.' And he's gone, jogging down the twisting stairs and clattering through the front door.

The moment stays with me all day – the morning sun burnishing the fox's coat to absolute beauty, Richie rushing to share the privilege of the sighting. We're evidently great friends now. I mean, if he can stand to feel my scantily-dressed body against his, so warm, the bed so temptingly nearby ... There can't be any desire left, can there?

At least not on his side, if that moment of proximity, of opportunity, passed him by without reawakening the lust we used to share, if his hand didn't automatically glide into the folds of my robe as they once would've done, knowing all the right places ...

Well, surely that's a good thing?

And so what if he used the opportunity to tuck the wretched engagement ring behind the curtain? I'll bribe the paper boy to take it back tomorrow.

'Coffee.'

Richie clears a space for me on his bench. 'I thought you were never bringing it, I fetched the biccies ages ago.'

'I've been on the phone to my cousin Carly for the last hour, on-and-on about her problems.' I set down the chunky green mugs with the funny handles and accept a choccie biccie, settling down on the worn bench. 'Of course, nothing she told me came as a surprise.' I do a big theatrical sigh as I pick up my mug and messily dunk my biscuit. I love the way the dark chocolate melts and slithers off the biscuit and into the coffee, and I don't have to worry about good manners or anything when I'm with Richie.

Richie raises his eyebrows, scoffing his own over-dunked biscuit quickly before the wet bit falls on the grass and managing, through his steaming, soggy mouthful, 'Wha' not a su'prise?'

I sigh. 'Carly's boyfriend, Luke – he's been two-timing her. I suspected, but she wouldn't believe a word when I tried to warn her. *He's only flirting*, she insisted, *we under-stand each_other*. Only now, it seems, he *wasn't* only flirting, and *I* understood him better than her, because she's caught him with a girl from his office wearing nothing but a condom and a horrified expression.'

Richie plonks down his coffee on the bench beside him. 'And doesn't that just suit *you*?'

'Suit me?' I'm stunned by the edge to his voice. 'What do you mean? I didn't want Carly to get hurt.'

Richie glares, eyes blazing, reminding me that he's not always all laughing fun. 'I mean that you assumed the worst, as usual, and you're absolutely delighted that this time, it's true.' His voice becomes louder. 'Long before Luke toppled off his pedestal you were predicting disaster – have you ever heard of the benefit of the doubt? Or *trust*?'

We finish our snack in near-silence. As soon as I can, I abandon him to his mood and scamper back to the sanctuary of my own place.

Fumbling through the door I wonder what on earth I did to bring all that on my head. He's so angry. And it's so not Richie – except …

Except the odd occasion. Like at that party, last summer. Not one of my finer moments.

Late and tired after some crisis at work, threading my way through a smoky room and an annoyingly drunk and raucous crowd, I had a job finding Richie.

And when I did, it was to discover Annabella, blonde and beautiful, in his arms.

Oh my, I made a good, old-fashioned scene, right there

in front of Richie's friends. God, I still cringe at the memory.

Because then I found out that Annabella and Richie's mate Ian had just that second announced their engagement. 'Or perhaps you expect me to kiss Ian, instead?' demanded Richie, dangerously.

It became only one of a long line of similar misunderstandings.

Like when the opportunity came up to go climbing for the weekend, Richie saw no reason to decline just because I didn't fancy it.

'We're not connected at the hip,' he declared, 'we're independent people. It's mainly an outing for the lads, anyway.' But then girls joined the climbing expeditions and I didn't handle that very well. Or very politely.

Eventually came the row to end all rows. One of the girls showed a particular interest in Richie, and I wouldn't accept that the attraction was all one-way.

I exploded. And Richie just walked away ...

The door knocker clatters, making me jump back into the present.

Lemon-faced, Richie stalks in. 'Let's talk.' Without asking, he makes fresh coffee, slapping the mugs down opposite one another on the kitchen table.

I take a seat, feeling as though this is an interview with my old headmaster. 'I don't know why you're getting so steamed up,' I begin in an effort to placate.

'No, unfortunately, you probably don't.' Richie takes a hasty gulp of coffee. 'But let's put that to one side for a minute, and just get a couple of things out in the open.'

He thinks for a moment before speaking. 'Now I've made progress with my house I have to decide whether to sell and bank the profit.'

'Sell?' I blink. I didn't realise selling was a prospect.

'Or whether to live here, whether I *can* live so close to you.' He rubs his fingers over his eyes. Silence. Then he sighs. 'Look, Beth, perhaps I shouldn't have blown up. We've got along okay until now, haven't we?'

I nod.

'I like living in Potato Row. But if we're going to get along, you must spare me your *just as_you always sus-pected* and *knew it all along*. It's always going to be a sore point between us.'

He's gone. My face is red.

As red as the little plush box he's managed to deposit behind his empty mug on the table. I glare at it. Then laugh. Tricky bastard.

The lane is very beautiful this afternoon, the hedgerow starred with perfect spider-webs, the nettles pearled with little creamy flowers under each rosette of leaves. I set off to walk down the lane to Castle Lake, about a mile away, and enjoy the birdsong and the blue sky.

Passing Richie's house, the noise of the drill through the half-open door indicates that he's engaged in his usual quest to renovate his home. He's put the little table that usually stands in his hall on his front lawn with a rug and a lampshade, I suppose he doesn't want them covered in dust.

I grin, and, one eye on the doorway, creep across the lawn. Then I tuck the ring box in the shallow drawer of the table. When Richie retrieves his furniture he'll automatically take possession of the ring.

I poke my head around the front door and into the cool hall. 'Don't you ever stop? Fancy a walk?'

He lays down his drill and lifts up the hem of his tee-shirt, a black one today, to wipe the sweat from his forehead, giving me sight of his flat stomach with it's fine coating of soft hairs. 'Too much to do.' He sighs.

Aw, poor Richie, I don't suppose it's much fun, working every weekend on the cottage. I step inside. 'How about some help?' I flex my muscles, like Popeye, posturing to make him laugh. 'Tempted?'

After a moment he turns back to the radiator he's fixing to the wall, vertically to fit the only piece of available space in the little hall. 'It would be nice if you wanted to hang around and chat. Makes the time go more quickly.'

So, abandoning my walk, I make myself comfy, back against the doorjamb, and ask him about his job and his family, and complain a bit about mine. He pushes his face against the wall to peer down the back of the radiator, his back to me, his shirt riding up.

'So Mum and Dad are supporting my little sister, Yvette, while she bums about, *thinking* about going to uni …'

His tattoo of the tiger eyes stares at me from the gap which has appeared between shirt and his jeans. A shiver, a memory, flits through me. That tattoo always turned me on.

'And Yvette doesn't even get a temporary job, she just flops about all day …'

All around the eyes the skin is very smooth and brown. 'I don't know where she got the idea …'

I tail off. My mind seems to have emptied itself. Gently, I reach forward and touch the eyes with my fingertips.

Richie jumps as if my fingers were wasps.

Then he turns slowly so that he's close, very close, and I have to look up to meet his eyes. I can smell the plaster dust on him, overlaying his shampoo. 'Sorry,' I say, vaguely. 'I forget what ...'

His gaze drops to my mouth, and then flicks back to my eyes. His fingers catch hold of mine. Slowly he lifts my hand and slides it around his waist to place it on the tattoo, at the top of his left buttock. The flesh is warm. My hand seems to have a will of its own as it touches, strokes.

Now there's no sign of laughter in Richie's eyes, as he holds my stare with his. Then his hungry mouth drops down to mine.

At the first hot touch of his tongue-tip between my lips I jump, a shiver sizzling down my spine. Then I sag, eye's closing. God, Richie always made me feel like this, that melting, burning, fizzing feeling. Made me want him with such a fierce desire that everything else ceased to matter.

He presses against me. I'm wearing a new halter-top which ties, and his fingers pick impatiently at the knot, sweeping my hair aside. Then it's free. The fabric slides slowly, slinking over my skin as he pushes it down, slithering across my breasts, my belly ...

'I want you.' His voice is hoarse.

I nod, too many times, too fervently, to be cool. But the only cool thing about us at the moment is the wall at my back as he finds the fastening of my bra, between my breasts.

He groans. Then he glances back at the still half-open front door. 'Upstairs. I don't want ... Not the floor ...'

We mount the stairs, slowly, kissing, sliding along the wall so as not to fall, taking two attempts to find the way into his bedroom. 'Beth ...' His hands are gentle as he removes the rest of my clothes, hot when they touch me. But not as hot as his mouth fastening on my breasts. I gasp, squirm. Push him away. Pull him back.

He laughs. Breaks away to pull off his own clothes, then yanks me back against him, his back is strong and smooth under my hands, his chest hard against mine. I draw in my breath as his fingers walk across my belly, down, down ... to probe, to explore. I can't think past the most delicious and well-remembered feelings ... that *rhythm*, slow, languorous, deep ... mmm ... deeper ...

Oh ... I ... have ... missed ... this ...

'I never stopped.' His voice is husky in my ear.

I press against his hand, concentrating, building the urgency.

Understanding, he slides himself between my legs, rising above me. And I think, *y-e-ssss!* But then he pauses, just there, not quite inside. Holding back, teasing ...

I open my eyes. His eyes are smiling, waiting.

I gasp, 'I never stopped wanting you, either!'

And then he's inside me, and the world is exploding with pleasure.

It's a long time before we're in the hall again, stepping over his discarded drill to reach the kitchen, driven by hunger, an insatiable desire for replacement energy in the form of chocolate biscuits. I open the tin. 'What happened to that little table? Aren't you keeping it in the hall?'

He opens the fridge. 'There isn't enough space. The van should've picked it up by now.'

I sit down suddenly on a cold wooden stool.

I have to swallow before words will come out. 'Picked it up?'

He pours tall glasses of mineral water and pineapple. 'This charity scheme.' He shows me a leaflet. 'They pick up unwanted furniture and pass it on to someone in need.

As I couldn't use it I thought … What's the matter?'

Richie drives, every movement betraying his irritation. 'The things you'll do to throw that bloody ring back in my face!'

Miserably, I huddle in the passenger seat. He's being very unfair about this. 'How was I supposed to know the furniture was awaiting collection?'

But I feel empty with guilt, nevertheless. One of us ought to have kept the ring instead of playing silly games with it. It once cost Richie a lot of money – more than I thought he ought to have spent.

I remember how he laughed at my protests. 'But that's how much I love you.'

Once it was a symbol of our love. Forever. Tears fill my eyes.

The depot's crowded with household goods. Acres of old furniture, a clearing house for leftovers and discards. I wait, dismayed, while Richie consults a man with a clipboard.

'Smaller pieces are sent straight to a warehouse,' he reports briefly, entrusting me with the directions, and we drive onwards through the heat and fumes of noisy and frustrating rush hour.

The warehouse is already locked when we arrive. 'Fuck's sake,' he hisses loudly. But he manages to intercept a man leaving for home, and after another head-scratching conversation comes away with a different set of scribbled directions.

'Sorry,' I offer quietly, as Richie flops back into the car, every movement a weary protest.

'It's not really your fault.' His anger's evaporated, he just sounds endlessly sad. 'We have to find a Mrs. Lyons.'

He passes over the address. 'She takes home any items of value found in cupboards and drawers.'

Mrs. Lyons, round, grey-haired and cheerful, invites us into a back room stacked with paperwork and dusty boxes.

' 'Scuse my mess,'she says, not seeming too worried by it. 'Now.' She swings round suddenly, beaming. 'Are you who I hope you are? I've been praying you'd turn up, ever since we found it. Tell me you're Richie and Beth?'

Through a giddy rush of relief I hear Richie's voice as if from another room as he agrees that we are, thanking Mrs. Lyons when she produces the little red box, shaking her hand and leaving a grateful donation for the charity.

'And you know how to avoid losing it again, don't you, sweetheart?' Mrs. Lyons' shiny face is one big smile. 'Keep it where it's safe.'And she takes the diamond cluster from the box and shoves it unceremoniously onto my finger. 'Oh, bless her, look at her tears. I'm so glad for you both.' Then she admonishes Richie, 'Now, you see she keeps that ring on her finger.'

Outside again, into the car. Once Mrs. Lyons' door has closed I gaze down at the ring, sparkling on my finger as if glad to see the light again.

Heavily, I make to remove it.

His hand closes over mine. I look up into his eyes. They're laughing. 'Fuck's sake,' he murmurs. 'Can't you leave it on? At least we'll both know where it is.'

Wanting, Wanted, Wanton

By Linda Mitchelmore

'We shouldn't have done that,'Kate said.

'Because?' Tom propped himself up on one elbow and looked at her, still with his bedroom eyes which was no surprise to Kate because that was exactly where they were. Room 23. The Redcliffe Hotel. 'One good reason...'

Because of a lot of things. Because Kate didn't know what sort of wanton madness had made her buy new underwear only to rip off the price tags and the washing instructions with indecent haste, slip it on over specially waxed and expensively creamed skin and then take it off again. And all within minutes of buying it. Because Kate's less than perfect body was lying next to Tom's younger, leaner one and even with her eyes closed she could tell the difference. And because she feared it would probably all end in tears. Hers.

'Didn't you want to?' Tom asked.

Oh yes, Kate had wanted to. Had wanted to very much. 'Yes, but...'

'You're thinking about Jason? Right?'

'Hmmm,' Kate said.

'That's a 'yes'?' Tom said, trailing a lazy finger along

Kate's collarbone.

'I suppose.'

'That's okay,' Tom said. He moved his head closer to Kate's. He replaced the finger on her collarbone with his tongue, making tiny licks that sent jelly-shivers through Kate's body. 'I was thinking about Natalie just now as well.'

'You mean just *now*? The just now when we were making love?'

'We still are making love,' Tom said, turning his licks into the soft pressure of a kiss.

Yes, Kate thought, we are. And isn't it all a bit of a cliché? The hotel – the curtains drawn to shut out the afternoon sun; the DO NOT DISTURB notice hanging from the door handle outside; the bottle of champagne – empty – on the bedside table.

And Kate with Jason in the equation, and Tom with Natalie.

'It all happened a bit fast, didn't it?'

'What?' Tom said, 'The sex?' He looked at Kate in mock-horror because hadn't they both known the sex had been delicious and satisfying? And slow. Just as Kate liked it and had almost forgotten about. She'd thought she might just evaporate from the tenderness Tom had shown her; his courtesy in making sure she was pleasured before himself.

'No, silly. Us getting together.'

Which it had been. Just three weeks from the day Kate had had her accident with her bike on the corner of Hyde Road.

'Well, if you must ride a bike in a long skirt, what can you expect?' Tom had said, not unkindly - the way Jason would have done, making her out to be some sort of lesser form of life - but with infuriating male logic while extricating her skirt from the chain, as Kate propped herself up on his bent back. 'Shorts would be more practical. Or jeans.'

He'd appeared seemingly from nowhere just as Kate's front wheel had hit the kerb and her skirt got caught and she wobbled, sure she was about to hit the pavement in an undignified heap. Instead strong hands had grasped her, steadied her.

'I'm not a jeans person,' Kate had said, her voice still shaky from the shock of the near accident. 'Or shorts.'

A skirt could hide a lot of wobbly sins, couldn't it? And besides, Kate liked the feel of a skirt whirling around her thighs, swishing as she walked, sending cooling draughts of air up as far as her bottom.

Tom, his Sir Galahad gesture over, straightened and looked at Kate. Smiled. Goodness but he was handsome. Dark, almost Latin looks with eyes like those chocolates – Minstrels – that Kate loved so much. Hence the need for long skirts to disguise fleshy thighs.

'I'm too much of a gentleman to comment,' Tom had said. The right-hand corner of his mouth twitched up a little as he said it, and Kate blushed imagining Tom doing all sorts of un-gentlemanly things to her. And when their eyes met, Kate knew he was thinking along roughly the same lines.

Wheeling Kate's now buckled bike with one hand and cupping the other under Kate's elbow he steered both towards The Backstage Bistro.

They sat outside at a metal table which had once been painted white but which now had a verdigris finish from long days in the sun and the rain.　Tom erected the umbrella with a flourish, gave it a twirl, sending trapped fallen cherry blossom to scatter like confetti on the tiled terrace.　And Kate had been charmed.

'Your skirt's done for, I'm afraid,' Tom said.　He bent down and lifted the hem just a little and examined the rip and the oil.

'I can get another,' Kate said.　She wondered why she felt disappointed when Tom let go of the hem, severing their physical connection.　'It was cheap anyway.　From the market on the ring road.'

Kate had fallen in love with the colour – swirls of different shades of turquoise all shot through with a shimmer of silver.

'I could come with you,' Tom said.　'There might be some cheap CDs.　Bob Marley.　Don't you just love Bob Marley?'

'Well, yes..'　Yes.　As it happened Kate did love Bob Marley.

So they went to the market in Tom's battered VW Golf.

And Kate bought another skirt exactly the same as the one she'd worn at that fateful encounter, as all worthwhile encounters are fateful.　And she also bought a cheesecloth cotton top with intricate embroidery, the fabric so fine that when she tried it on in a corner of the field which acted as a car-park as Tom turned his back to preserve her modesty, Kate's breasts were only just decently veiled in all their voluptuousness.

Turning round to Tom she had seen his Adam's apple gulping up and down but no words escaped his lips.　Only his eyes told Kate he liked what he saw.　Very much liked what he saw.　And when Tom took Kate's hand to walk back to the stalls she let him, feeling sixteen again with all the attendant rush of nerves and indecision, recklessness.

It had been a wrench to give Tom back his hand so he could drive back into town. Kate had folded her hands one on top of the other in her lap and felt bereft.

'I have something I need to tell you sooner rather than later,' Tom said as the car rattled down over Tarraway Hill. His voice (had it been fabric it would have been amber velvet) held that inevitability that he and Kate would have more than just the two brief encounters they had had to date. 'I have a daughter. She's three. I love her very much.'

'Tell me about her.' And Tom did tell Kate about his daughter, Kate shutting from her mind the fact that the child must have a mother somewhere.

'I come with baggage as well,' Kate said. 'Sixteen stones of strop called Jason. The term 'angry young man' was coined for him.'

'He doesn't hit you, does he?' Tom said, taking his eyes from the road to look at Kate. The way he said it told Kate that Tom would pulverise Jason if he'd been hitting her.

'Hey! Watch out! That car's stopping in front. No.'

No, Jason didn't hit her. Lots of shouting, lots of angry words. Silences frosty enough to keep a branch of Iceland going for a week at least. But no violence. She wouldn't stand for that.

And here they were, her and Tom, lying replete on a king-size bed in The Redcliffe Hotel.

'Films and books get it all wrong,' Kate said.

'Eh?'

'You know. The tangled, rumpled sheets. When were you in a hotel with sheets on the bed?'

'I don't make a habit of this,' Tom smiled.

'No? Kate reached out a hand for the twelve-pack of condoms, picked it up, waggled it in Tom's direction. She wondered if either of them would have the stamina to get through the entire packet.

'I also have a 32 pack of paracetamol and a box of 25 mixed plasters in my rucksack. I don't suppose I shall need all of those either.'

A wave of slight disappointment rippled through Kate. 'Perhaps just half the packet?'

'My mother warned me about older women.'

And Kate tried to laugh but much as a sneeze can threaten but doesn't bring relief, it wouldn't come. She took her hands from where they'd been behind Tom's neck caressing it and covered her breasts. She would have liked to have grasped the duvet to pull it up over her thighs, but films and books got that wrong too – lovemaking couples didn't perform some sort of bed ballet under its soft, moundy mass because in reality a duvet simply slid silently to the floor with the first pulsating moves of orgasm.

'Kate,' Tom said, 'Don't cover up. You're lovely.'

'I'm feeling a bit exposed,' Kate, who couldn't remember the last time she had been called lovely, said. She moved to make one arm cover both breasts, ran her free hand over a dimpled thigh as though by some divine intervention it would become sleek and silky again as it had been when she was the age Tom was now.

'I'm a breast and thigh man,' Tom said. 'The plumper the better.' He prised Kate's hand from her thigh, kissed the palm, as Kate wondered just how many women had been delighted by Tom's lovemaking as she had just been.

'Breast and thigh man?   Then shall I ring down for a

chicken?' Kate quipped.   She had read somewhere that
men appreciated humour in a woman. She liked Tom
appreciating her but the words 'chicken' and 'spring' and
'no' formed in all the wrong sequence in Kate's mind.

Tom's face creased into a smile but he didn't laugh.
And Kate could count on the fingers of one hand the
paucity of age-related laughter lines that crinkled at the
corners of his eyes.

'No phone calls,' Tom said. 'That was the rule, wasn't
it?'

'Hmmm,' Kate said.

'Ready for another round?' Tom licked Kate's palm,
making a firm point with the tip of his tongue.

As if of its own volition Kate's arm uncovered her
breasts and she offered them to him. A gift. Oh yes, oh
yes, oh yes.

She almost passed out with pleasure when her hands
found Tom's bottom which was so high and so taut she
could have used it for a shelf for the champagne glass if
only they'd had some champagne left.

And then it hit her.   It didn't really matter if this thing
with Tom was forever. Or not. It was for now. And now
was all any of us have really, isn't it? She moaned with
real pleasure as she gave body and mind up to this new
experience.

'I'm going to break our self-imposed rule,' Kate said.
She reached for the phone, knocked it from its rest.

'Hey!' Tom said, 'This is not exactly a compliment.'
But he said it with humour in his deep, velvety voice and
not in anger as Jason would have done.

Kate pressed 3.   And when reception answered she
requested a bottle of chilled champagne to be left outside

room 23. She slithered from the bed, went to the door and pressed her ear to the wood until she heard someone place the champagne on the floor outside; heard the bottle clink against the metal bucket, and the chink of ice; heard the gentle tap on the door to let her know the champagne had arrived.

Later, much later, as the first fingers of dawn spread across the sky, Kate knew she'd been right to spend this time with Tom. Tom was sleeping deeply beside her, his chest barely rising and falling with his measured breaths. How quickly she was becoming used to the timbre of his breathing, his unique body scents, the feel of his skin on hers. How very quickly she had fallen, if not in love, then in lust with Tom.

And how right she had been to leave her relationship with Jason to which she had given everything but received not a lot in exchange.

Should she ring now to tell Jason she definitely wouldn't be coming back? That she wasn't at her mother's as she'd said she would be? Tom had no one to leave because he'd been the one to be dumped.

A day and a night of glorious loving wasn't exactly a lifetime's commitment, was it? They were both playing cautious, weren't they? Making their first intimate time together on neutral ground. They could both just pack their respective bags in a short while and leave, couldn't they? Or not. Kate pondered all these things and reached for the phone, raised it ever-oh-ever-so-slowly from its cradle.

'Beat you to it,' Tom said. 'Natalie's been making gingerbread men with Mum.'

'Aah,' Kate said, wondering if she would ever meet

Natalie and make gingerbread men with her. She had a feeling she would but it really wouldn't matter if she didn't.

'Go on,' Tom said. 'Your turn. Phone.'

But Kate put the phone back on its rest. It was amazing how sexy sleeping naked with the right man made her feel. How wanted, how wanting. And how very wanton. And there was still half a packet of condoms left, wasn't there?

First in, last out
by David Wass

'In - out - in - out…' Sharon urged him on breathlessly, her heels pounding the floor faster and faster with each stroke. 'Out - in - out - in…'

She had no idea who the broad-shouldered guy with the shock of black hair was, but it didn't matter. All she knew was that she was with him all the way - the panting, the sweat dripping from his brow, each long thrust…

'Pssst!'

The sharp hiss to her left made her jump. She jerked her head round. Beneath her feet, the moving belt slowed from a frantic gallop to a stroll.

'What?' Sharon gasped at her friend Zoe next to her.

'Carry on like that and you could do yourself an injury,' said Zoe, without breaking her stride. 'I've been trying to tell you for ages that you win on the treadmill.'

'Good,' Sharon puffed. 'What's the score now, then?'

'Three-three, but that's not the point. You were miles away. Where were you?'

'Not that far.' Sharon nodded towards the other side of the aisle that separated the treadmills from the rowing machines. 'Third from the left. How about that for an adorable hunk of manhood?'

Zoe glanced over. 'Yeah, not bad.'

'What d'you mean, not bad? Look at those shoulders, biceps, thighs, the way he's pumping that machine. I mean if I could get him...'

'Yes thank you, Sharon. I've got your drift.'

Sharon smiled. She wasn't really surprised that Zoe wasn't too impressed. Even at school they'd had different tastes in the opposite sex. It didn't stop them discussing the talent, though. Like it didn't stop them competing against each other whenever they spent a couple of hours in the gym.

'What I meant,' Zoe continued, 'was that I can better it. Look.' She pointed a discreet finger to where a figure on a bike at the far side of the gym was pedalling like fury and getting nowhere fast.

Sharon studied him. He was tall and slim, and looked as if he might be a long distance runner. As did Zoe. Neither were anything like her, short and stocky with enough curves to slow down Jensen Button.

'Yup, he's right up your street,' Sharon agreed, switching off the machine and stepping down.

Zoe jumped to the floor and smoothed her shorts. 'Where next?' she asked, glancing towards the bikes.

Sharon grinned. 'Somewhere I can win again. I don't want to buy the dinner twice in a row.' She looked over to where the rower was still pumping hard. 'To be honest I've had enough of this routine stuff. What about you?'

'Whatever takes your fancy. As long as you promise me you won't be a bad loser.'

'Now there's a promise I don't need to make. See you in the changing room.'

Laughing, the two friends headed off in different directions. Sharon strolled across the aisle.

As usual on a Tuesday afternoon the gym was almost deserted, so the rowing machine next to the Steve Redgrave wannabe was vacant.

Having folded herself into it, Sharon grabbed the oars and pulled. Soon she, too, had settled into a rhythm, going at precisely half the pace of the powerful guy next to her.

She closed her eyes, allowing her imagination free rein, picturing them together on a king-size waterbed, a field of yellow corn, a tiny, beeswax-scented broom cupboard, a hot, sweaty changing room…

'Oh, no!' Sharon cried out, letting go of the oars with a clatter and curling up into a ball.

'Hey, are you OK?'

He looked even better close up, with his blue, take-me-now eyes, and bulging muscles

'It's…like…cramp in my back,' she wailed, grimacing with pain. 'Happens sometimes. It's just a pity my friend's not here, she knows exactly where to massage it for me.'

'Maybe I can help,' he said, bending over her. 'Tell me when I hit the right spot.'

'Yes, thanks. Up a bit…Down a bit…There.' Sharon squeezed her eyes shut, almost purring as his hand drew warm circles through her T-shirt.

'Any better?' he asked at last.

'A little. If you could just help me up. This way's best.'

Following her instructions, he faced her, put his forearms under her armpits and lifted. She leaned close, scuffing her chest against his damp singlet, smelling the salt from his perspiration. Slowly, they rose erect.

Wincing as though still in pain, she looked up into his eyes. 'I don't suppose you'd mind helping me to the changing room?'

'Of course not.' His arm encircled her waist. 'Here, put your arm round my neck.'

A shiver ran through her. There was that lustful huskiness in his voice that no man could conceal.

They reached the changing room. He shoved open the door with his spare hand.

Still hanging on to him, Sharon limped in. She threw a glance along the twenty or so cubicles. Only one had its curtain drawn.

Suddenly she was better. She dropped her arm and grabbed his hand. 'Come on,' she whispered, tugging him towards a cubicle at the opposite end.

She drew the curtain. His kiss took her breath away. Frantically, she tugged down his tracksuit bottoms. He yanked off her shorts and hoisted her into the air.

They made love, hurriedly, with sharp, shuddering passion, until Sharon collapsed in a heap in the corner of the cubicle.

She checked her watch. The rower must have noticed.

'You're right. I'd better get out of here,' he said, tucking in his singlet and leaning forwards to give her a long, lingering kiss. 'See you around.'

Sharon heard the changing room door slam. Seconds later, it banged shut again. She pulled herself together and swished back the curtain.

Zoe was at the far end adjusting her bra.

'Seventeen minutes from first contact,' said Sharon. 'You?'

'Nineteen,' Zoe tutted. 'So I've got to buy dinner. And to think I was here first.'

'Well you know what they say,' laughed Sharon. 'First in, last out.'

Liberation

By Sophie Weston

Being a good girl is hell.

My exclusive boarding school said, 'Be a comfort to your father, Melissa.' As if a world-class shark with scores to settle needs *comfort*. When Donny ran out of enemies he bought a boat. And started winning races ruthlessly.

Me he turned me into something between Shirley Temple and Miss Moneypenny. Well, I was an only child so I got his full attention. And Donny never did anything by halves. I had a strong bump of intuition, which he said was essential in sailing and business.

I didn't like the sea but by ten I was reading balance sheets. At college I had frizzy brown hair and was Treasurer of everything. I went home one weekend a month. And never dated the Wrong Sort.

My career, of course, was already decided. I enjoyed it but Donny swamped me. And men either wanted to date Donny's millions, or recoiled from him. Neither sort noticed *me*. I was just the female shaped thing in the middle with the key to the executive washroom as a sort of extra limb. Not very female shaped, actually.

Donny fought it when I decided to move out of our Wimbledon home. Then I moved into this luxury

Kensington block and he met my next door neighbour. The Duchess.

She was vile to him in a terribly clipped voice. That impressed Donny.

I thought she was like an elderly Pekinese that had been cooped up too long – desperate to bite something just to prove she still could. She was conducting a poison pen war with the Naval Commander who lived in the flat below hers and she terrified the porters. Donny said she had class.

She liked me! Well, I never played loud music. (The Commander was a Stones fan.) She gave me a thin smile when we met and sometimes asked me in for eye-watering dry martinis. Usually when she was mounting a campaign against someone and wanted My Father's Advice.

Donny said she was an interesting person and got her free legal advice when she demanded it. Well, it wasn't free. He paid. I had the feeling that men had paid for a lot of the Duchess'fights over the years. But when I said so, Donny told me that it wasn't like me and I was usually more sympathetic than that. And gave me two tickets to take her to a revival of "Salad Days".

She sang along with the performers. Even amidst a lot of strangers there wasn't one who was brave enough to tell her to shut up. In the interval she shot into the bar like a Pekinese off the lead for the first time in twenty years. All around us heavily coiffed ladies in elastic stockings called pitifully for tea, while the Duchess instructed the barman loudly in martini making. And I murmured apologies.

See what I mean? Good girl equals hell.

But it stayed at martinis and malice until one bright spring morning she bumped into The Hooligan. She told me all about it when I trailed in from work around ten o'clock.

She was in the deeply carpeted entrance lobby. I suspect she had been lying in wait for me. She was quivering like a Pekinese sighting a burglar.

'The hair! The dirty old clothes! I think he's squatting in the boiler room,' she said intensely. 'The porters are in on it. We should sue.'

It was not a good day for me. My latest date had proved to be just another guy who wanted to be Donny's son-in-law and I got rid of him at lunchtime. Then that night I'd stayed at my Docklands desk until California signed off. All I wanted to do now was have a drink and forget.

So I pushed back my now fashionably cropped hair and said wearily, 'Sue for what?'

'He lowers the tone.'

'Don't think that's actionable. Sorry.'

I escaped.

But the next morning when I left at seven she was sitting in the sumptuous lobby again. This time she was in a floaty Marlene Dietrich number, looking like a hanging judge.

'You'll see,' she said grimly.

And he came in.

He must have been out on a run. My eyes zipped out on stalks and returned to the launch pad severely shaken. I sat down rather suddenly.

He was *gorgeous*. All right, there was a lot of hair – quite a bit of it on his chest. And his clothes were rudimentary. His denim shorts looked as if they were about to disintegrate.

But he did not lower anybody's tone. Raised the blood

pressure, yes. Lowered the tone, no. He was big and brown and totally at ease.

He had wonderful blue eyes that creased knowingly when he saw us.

'Good morning.'

'Grr,' said the Duchess.

'Hello,'I said faintly. Which was quite a triumph, given how dry my mouth had gone. He nodded pleasantly and disappeared into the porter's flat.

'See?' hissed the Duchess. 'I bet the porter's letting him sleep on the floor somewhere. It's disgraceful.'

I thought about those hazardous shorts and said from the heart, 'It is indeed.'

I went to work in a dream and went three stops past my station. Jesus, I thought. This is what comes of a lifetime of being a good girl. Absolutely no sense of proportion.

I was struggling hard to be sensible – good girls are *always* sensible – when there was a knock on my door that night. The Duchess, I thought. I put my head down like a bull charging and flung the door open, ready to tell her that there was no way I was going to war with a half naked man whether he lived behind the bike shed or not and -

'Hi,' said the Hooligan.

'Glug,' I said, falling back.

He took it as an invitation. He came in, hand out. 'Jack Dangerfield.'

I shook his hand in a dream. Again.

He was wearing jeans and a navy sweater this evening. Shame, I thought.

He seemed faintly uncomfortable. 'The porters suggested we talk. You're the only one who gets through to the Chorus Girl.'

'Chorus Girl?'

Jack grinned. 'In the lobby with you this morning. Pissed off party in full slap and negligee. Hates me.'

Negligee? This morning? The Duchess? My father's favourite aristocrat? *A chorus girl?*

It was irresistible. 'You'd better tell me everything.'

We ended up sitting side by side in front of the fire with a bottle of rioja, exchanging life events. He clearly wasn't a boiler room squatter. Carefully, I came round to my father.

'Donny Tate?' Jack trawled his memory, polite but not very interested. 'Sails? That was a nice race he had in Australia.'

I drew a long breath of pure happiness.

'Was it?'

He can't not have known about my father's millions. Donny even called his bloody boat Million Dollar Mouse. If he knew about the race, Jack had to know about the man's millions! He just didn't care!

It might be that his only use for me was to neutralise the Duchess. But he definitely didn't see me as the key to the executive washroom.

Now if *he* asked me out . . .

'What do you mean, calling the Duch- –er – my neighbour a chorus girl?'

'Grandfather recognised her. Came clean after the third brandy one night. My guess is he dated her when he got shore leave.'

'But – a chorus girl? She's always given me to understand that she is frightfully upper class.'

He laughed heartily.

I had a flash of that intuition my father is so proud of.

The Navy runs in families, right?

I said slowly, 'Can you be the Commander?'

Jack pulled a face. 'I see you know all about it.'

Unlike the Duchess. She had no idea about his grand-father – or that her Hooligan was the neighbour she had reported for noise pollution.

He stretched. Even wearing clothes it was pretty spec-tacular. I felt a slight thrumming in my ears.

He didn't notice, thank God. He said, 'I saw the poor guy from the council today. Chap who's supposed to measure the noise levels. He agreed –she's nuts. But what can I do?'

He leaned back against the leg of the armchair and his eyes crinkled up wickedly. He had the sort of eyes that made you want to be wicked too. Well, me anyway. It was a new feeling.

I mean when all the other girls at school were laying traps for the gardener's boy, I was sitting in my study working on economic graphs. I'd moved from theory to practice since then, of course. But not really in the matter of gardener's boys. These days the graphs showed real international sales but in lots of way I'd stayed sort of stuck. Being wicked was something that braver and pret-tier women did in the shrubbery while I worked away con-scientiously at my desk.

Not that I was a virgin. I was a good girl, not a freak. But the few men I'd known carnally had all been terribly careful of me, if you know what I mean. I suppose it was that extra limb. They didn't want to do anything too frisky in case the key to the executive washroom fell off. What's more, if they were careful of me, I responded in kind. It's quite difficult to fling your inhibitions to the four winds when the flingee, as it were, is constantly looking beyond your shoulder at the reproving shade of his prospective father in law.

Not that my father would have cared. But they thought he would. It was another variant on those three-in-a-relationship things. Kept my sex life a bit - well - muted So it was a surprise to find myself sitting on the carpet now thinking about being wicked and wondering how you went about it. Quite suddenly, I regretted, burningly, the evenings with the gardener's boy that I'd passed up all those years ago. It was tough having to work out seduction from first principles at my age.

And then I found that he was looking fixedly at my mouth. And I thought: *maybe it won't be so tough, after all.*

'Half my kingdom if you get the old bat off my back,' he murmured.

I swallowed hard and said brightly, 'Make it dinner, and you've got a deal.'

His eyes got all heavy lidded. 'Done.'

So I went to see her. Asked – terribly casually – when she left the theatre and what it was like in those days.

I don't know what she was more scared of – people finding out that she'd high kicked her way to marriage with the Right Sort, or people actually doing the sums and realising how old she was. Either way, she had a secret to keep – and we had a price.

She paid up.

So, I'm glad to say, did Jack.

He took me to an Italian restaurant down a sinister alleyway somewhere off Trafalgar Square. It was so small we had to sit knee to knee. We ate artichokes. I was so flustered that I managed to drip the dressing down my front. He ran his finger round the fortunately low neckline; and then offered it to me to lick off the olive oil. Then he taught me to eat pasta one handed, so he could hold the other one. I stopped being flustered. I mean, after that, you know where you're going, right?

And I was right. It wasn't tough at all. Not even when we got back to the apartment building and got so carried away that we managed to jam the lift and had to be let out by the porter. A small audience had gathered and normally I would have been deeply embarrassed. But I just floated out, smiling at all of them, even the Duchess.

Mind you, I'd got my skirt straight and he had my underwear in his pocket by the time the doors actually opened. They think on their feet, in the Navy.

I fully expected her to be on the doorstep the next day, complaining. But she wasn't. As Jack says, she's a realist. And we have a bargain that suits everyone.

Everyone still thinks she's a Duchess.

Jack plays his music. It doesn't raise a peep out of her.

And I have learned to do some truly astonishing things to *Jumpin' Jack Flash*.

Being a bad girl is *wicked*.

Carla's Gift

by Jane Wenham-Jones

What do you say to a woman who has just had her first orgasm on the top of the multi-storey in a Ford Fiesta?

Congratulations was the word that sprang to mind but the others were strangely silent.

'Good for you,' I muttered to a cold shower of black looks.

I have always liked Carla. I liked her when she was married to Stuart and so I like her still. Round here, however, things are not so simple. I had witnessed a definite ripple of unease running around the circle of women I call my friends ever since Stuart walked out of 25 Arnold Drive and Carla - dry-eyed - walked out into the world and started to enjoy herself.

It was as if they feared that having gasped her way to ecstasy with her garage mechanic today, the next logical step would be tempting away their husbands. Frankly she was welcome to mine. If she could stir Norman into producing the merest erect nipple, I'd cheerfully buy her gins all night. And quite honestly, by the look of the other lot's assorted and spreading spouses I thought they should be jolly grateful for any spark of enthusiasm injected into their drooping genitals too.

Muriel, after a lot of sniffing, eventually said that Carla

should be careful not to catch anything. Sylvia swallowed and did a lot of what I think the novels call, 'dabbing one's eyes'with a pink tissue, before twittering on about the terrible ordeal that Carla had been through and how we were all so sorry and how she couldn't imagine how she would cope if Roger left her because he was such a *comfort*.

And I was just reflecting on the way we all just sat there, simpering, even though we knew that Roger had systematically got his podgy white leg over every barmaid the squash club had ever had, and that Carla had got totally slaughtered on champagne when Stuart had finally stopped just screwing them and had the wit to imagine he was in love and piss off, when I caught Carla's eye and she gave me the most enormous wink.

It was then that I decided to discover her secret. For actually I had never had an orgasm either.

It sounds ridiculous I know. Especially to a generation who have been encouraged by Cosmopolitan to have them every lunch hour. *Be responsible for your own!* the front covers exhort.

I would have been glad to, if only I'd known where to start.

Carla, with all the zealous conviction of the newly-converted, was full of enthusiasm for my plight. Before I knew where I was, she had me firmly by the arm and I was gazing at a mind-boggling array of battery-operated rubber and plastic in various eye-watering shapes.

'My God, what do you do with that?' I hissed, intermittently taking surreptitious looks at the other customers. I could not believe the neat navy blue suits and court shoes to be found in a sex shop.

'What did you expect?' asked Carla smugly, as she

expertly jiggled one of the more painful-looking contraptions.

'I don't know,' I muttered, hastily averting my eyes from the front cover of a particularly disgusting-looking magazine.

'But I don't think this is really me, Carla, not me at all,' I added nervously as she began to propel me towards the counter.

'She'd like one of these,' said Carla unperturbed, pushing a long cardboard box into the hands of the multi-pierced shop assistant.

'I'm not sure really,' I squeaked, my eyes riveted by the woman's naval.

'And batteries?' she asked Carla, totally ignoring me.

'Heavy-duty,' replied Carla firmly while I tried to bury my scarlet face in the rubber corsets.

On the way home, Carla screeched to a halt outside the bookshop and leapt out.

'Stay there!' she called, leaving me on a double yellow line peering nervously up the road for traffic wardens while I clutched my guilty package in hot hands.

'Here,' she thrust a paper bag at me seconds later. 'Never mind the stuff about self-esteem and letting go of guilt. Go straight to chapter seven and switch on! You don't know what you're missing.'

Four days later, after my deep warm bath, massage oil gleaming on my limbs, trying not to feel ridiculous for wearing a satin nightie at three o'clock in the afternoon, I lay back on the bed and tried my first session of what the book called 'pleasuring' myself. It wasn't easy.

I listened to the soft music, I ran a hand up and down an oily leg, I tried to keep my mind firmly fixed on what I'd seen Mickey Rourke do to Kim Bassinger on last night's video and I kept buzzing away.

But try as I might, my mind would keep wandering to the brussel sprouts waiting downstairs and how I was going to fit in getting Norman's brown suit from the cleaners. The vibrator gave me a pleasant tingling feeling, but frankly I was no nearer to experiencing *it.*

Carla was reassuring.

'Early days,' she said cheerfully. 'When I think how many years it took to get my first one out, but, now, well I can hardly stop.'

And she rang off quickly to attend to something that was evidently more pressing than talking to me.

I was not convinced. But the next evening, with the ironing complete in a pleasingly folded pile and the shepherd's pie already reclining in the oven, I found there was still forty-five minutes before Norman was likely to appear and since I had to admit I'd been feeling oddly unsettled all afternoon and Mickey Rourke had broken into my potato-mashing reveries more than once, I thought I'd have just one more tiny little go.

I didn't go through the focus-on-your-body-and-seduce-yourself-you-are-beautiful routine this time. I simply pulled off a few clothes and lay there thinking how times had changed.

The first time Carla had given me advice it was on a drop scone recipe. Now here she was casually adopting the role of sex therapist and here I was, lying around with a funny-shaped bit of white plastic pressed against me, waiting for heaven.

And then as I lay there further, idly wondering how Kim Bassinger's bottom got to look so muscular and mine so flabby, and debating whether to have frozen peas or tinned green beans and thinking that this was all very pleasant and relaxing but hardly hot flush sort of stuff, then - two odd things happened!

First there was the unmistakable click, scratch, jingle of Norman's key in the lock a whole half an hour early, and second, something very peculiar began to happen to my body.

At first it was just a hot heart-beating rush of panic, that there he was downstairs in the hall, and here I was, sprawled across the bed, half-dressed, gripping something undeniably phallic. But then I realised that another, unfamiliar heat was flooding other bits of me, and I was throbbing in an incredible set of spasms that were making me feel all at once both helpless and incredibly high and powerful.

Just as I was gasping from the shock of this assault of strange and delicious sensations, I heard his foot on the stairs and somehow I got off the bed and flung myself out of the bedroom and into the bathroom and turned on the taps and then leant weakly against the mirror grinning wildly.

'I had one,' I informed the toothbrushes in wonder. 'I bloody well had one.'

Norman was puzzled and not altogether pleased to find me getting into the bath at this thoroughly unexpected time of day. He grunted irritably at my cheerful explanations of post-gardening sweatiness and went heavily downstairs to await his dinner.

Later I phoned Carla in ecstatic whispers to share my good news. She was touchingly delighted and proud.

But I couldn't do it again. I tried everything. I went right back to chapter one, spent hours fantasising about a wide variety of tall, handsome, famous men (and even a few short balding ones who worked in the High Street) smothered my self from head to foot in sensuality-enhancing oils and creams and read my way through three volumes of women's sexual fantasies that Carla said would blow my mind.

One or two of them made me wish I'd eaten a lighter lunch but none of them produced the faintest ripple of orgasm.

Until one afternoon, I lay there, belligerently determined not to move from the bed until I had forced my body to ecstasy when once again Norman's key was heard turning in the lock.

And as I glared wildly at the clock, wondering where on earth the last three hours had gone and how the hell I hadn't noticed their departure, the most exquisite feeling began pulsating through my body with an intensity that took my breath away.

And as I groaned a most peculiar groan that sounded nothing like me and certainly bore no resemblance to the magnificent wails I'd produced in my youth at an attempt at persuading fumbling boyfriends that the earth had moved, the penny finally dropped and I realised I had discovered my own secret.

After that it was easy. A bit of a warm-up ten minutes before Norman was due home and then, oh, the agony and the ecstasy of hearing his feet slap their way up the path and the indescribable delight that wracked my body as I heard him come in.

Norman got used to my six o'clock bath ritual and no longer seemed surprised to find me flurrying about in a dressing gown when he came upstairs to change.

As the weeks passed I grew more daring, how close could he get to the bedroom door before I moved? Before I leapt to my feet, threw the vibrator into the bedside cupboard, tightened my dressing gown cord and stood beaming as Norman entered the room.

I was now a multi-orgasmic woman. My record was three heart-stopping ones between first hearing the scrape of his shoe on the pavement outside the front gate, and the creak of the landing floorboard as he came towards the bedroom. Carla was deeply impressed.

'He's going to catch you at it,' she said in awe. 'Then what will you do?'

I was rather more concerned about what Norman would do! There was a whole chapter in the book about the threatening nature of sex toys to the average male; a series of sobering testimonies from women whose husbands, lovers and boyfriends had smashed their vibrators to smithereens and removed themselves to the shed at the bottom of the garden to have a penis-crisis for three days.

This, I felt, was not really Norman's style, not being a man given to displays of emotion of any kind, but still a frisson of alarm sent my blood pounding as I took ever-increasing risks until I was shuddering in abandon right up to the moment when the door of the bedroom began to open. What would he say if he found out? The thought filled me with a mixture of shame and wicked delight. And I could not stop.

Of course he did find out. One day he burst through the front door like an elephant possessed and came pounding up the stairs, flinging open the bedroom door and appearing at the foot of the bed when I was mid-writhe and could not do a thing to hide from him what I was doing.

This did not stop him shrieking: 'What are you doing?' as if there could be some doubt, but I was so convinced that actually I was having a heart attack that I could not summon the wherewithal to reply. I just stared in mute horror at his crimson face and wondered wildly - as I looked at the feverish workings of his jaw - if he was going to kill me.

Then I realised he was trying to undo his trousers.

I think there we will draw a polite bed sheet over the rest of the evening. I may be bold enough to discover hitherto uncharted territories of my own sexuality with a battery-operated tool and a self-help book but, as I said to Carla, I'm still a prude at heart and not about to share the details of my marital intimacies with anyone.

Suffice to say that the Lancashire Hotpot dried right out and Norman went very happily for fish and chips.

And, far from smashing my vibrator, he found it a place of its very own in the hallowed cupboard where he keeps his electric razor and toenail clippers. He took the *You-too-can-have-one* book with him to read on the train and ever since then, well, things have changed around here.

I asked him to indulge me the other night. I said: 'Norman, borrow your brother's wife's Ford Escort and come with me.' And we drove it right to the very rooftop of the multi-story in the middle of town and looked at the stars. Then I silently thanked Carla for the most precious of gifts and ordered Norman out of his clothes.

I thanked Carla out loud the next day - on the quiet - in the corner of the coffee morning.

But I didn't bother to mention my success to the others. I don't suppose they would have congratulated *me* either!

Biographies

Carolyn Steele Agosta's short stories and essays have been published in various literary magazines, ezines and broadcast on BBC Radio 4. 'After the Wink' was originally published online at *Conversely*. Carolyn lives in North Carolina and is currently working on her second novel. www.CarolynAgosta.com

Robert Barnard was recently announced as the winner of the 2003 CWA Cartier Diamond Dagger Award for a lifetime of achievement in crime writing. He regards Agatha Christie as his ideal crime writer and has published an appreciation of her work, A TALENT TO DECEIVE, as well as books on Dickens, a history of English literature and nearly thirty mysteries. His most recent novel, THE MISTRESS OF ALDERLEY is published in hardcover and paperback by Allison and Busby and features one of his detective creations, Charlie Peace.

Lynne Barrett-Lee was born in Brixton, London in 1959, is married to a consultant oncologist and has three children. Her short stories and articles have been published in the top women's magazines for many years and her first novel, JULIA GETS A LIFE, came out in 2000. This was followed a year later by VIRTUAL STRANGERS, and she now enjoys the luxury of being able to write full-time. ONE DAY SOME DAY was published by Black Swan in January 2003.

Tina Brown started to take more interest in writing when one of her short stories was selected as a winning entry in a Woman's Day/Mills and Boon Romantic Fiction Competition. She lives in Australia, two hours south of Sydney.

Lesley Cookman has been a freelance writer and editor for over twenty years. Her work has appeared in an eclectic variety of magazines, books and on stage. She recently commuted to Wales in pursuit of an MA in Creative Writing, she teaches creative writing and occasionally dons an anorak and lectures on pantomime.
www.lesleycookman.co.uk

Hazel Cushion. Founder of Accent Press Ltd. Her work has been published in various international newspapers and magazines, on the BBC website and in SINS, AN ANTHOLOGY. Having completed an MA in Creative Writing Hazel choose to combine her writing and charity experience and created the 'Sexy Shorts' range of charity books. www.accentpress.co.uk

Sue Dukes originally qualified as an English teacher, but presently works in I.T. She has had many short stories, nine genre novels and one business book published. She is a short story and novel-writing tutor for the London School of Journalism, the Writers' News, and the Open College of the Arts correspondence courses. She runs Storytracks which offers ghost-writing, editing, and typescript analysis services. www.storytracks.net and www.chrisdukes.com.

Katie Fforde has had nine novels published and is currently writing her tenth. Most of her books are based loosely or otherwise on her own life which is chaotic and fairly frivolous. It involves nearly adult children and animals as well as a long-suffering husband. PARADISE FIELDS was published by Century in June 2003.
www.katiefforde.com

Liza Granville has been writing for about 10 years and has been published in many national women's magazines. She has an MA in Creative Writing from Plymouth University, and is currently researching for a PhD in Creative and Critical Writing at the University of East Anglia. Her novel CURING THE PIG - a feminist fairy tale - is being published by Flame Books on October 1st.

Jeanette Groark lives in Reading, Berkshire with her husband and two children. She is a former prizewinner in Woman and Home magazine's annual short story competition. She has always been fascinated by social history and is currently working on a novel set in the Georgian period.

Bill Harris lives in Ramsgate in Kent. Under his pen name of Katie May, he has been widely published in the women's magazine market. As Bill, he writes short fiction and non-fiction and has had stories and monologues performed. In 2002, his short film, PARADISE, was premiered at the Kent International Film Festival. He is currently working on a European travel project, developing guide scripts for a leading tour company.

Rosie Harris is the pseudynom of Marion Harris who writes both fiction and nonfiction. Born in Cardiff, she grew up there and in the West Country and spent some years on Merseyside before moving to Buckinghamshiire. Now, as Rosie Harris, she writes sagas based on Cardiff and Merseyside in the 20's 30's. ONE STEP FORWARD is published by Arrow in October 2003 and LOOKING FOR LOVE, published by Heinemann in December 2003.

Jan Jones has had short stories published in a variety of women's magazines. She is currently working on her second Regency novel, though she also enjoys writing contemporary romantic comedy, young adult fantasy and children's stories. She was recently extremely grateful to Addenbrooke's Hospital Breast Unit for diagnosing a lump as a cyst and aspirating it there and then. Jan lives in Cambridgeshire with her husband, two teenage children and two teenage cats.

Christina Jones has been writing all her life, having her first short story published when she was 14. The only child of a school teacher and a circus clown, Christina still regularly contributes short stories and articles to national magazines and newspapers, and has won several awards for her short fiction. She has been a best-selling novelist for the last six years. After years of travelling, Christina now lives in Oxfordshire with her husband Rob and thirteen rescued cats. Her latest novel, HUBBLE BUBBLE, will be published by Piatkus in April 2004.
www.christinajones.co.uk

Bernardine Kennedy achieved her ambition of writing

for a living after a varied working life that included careers as an Air Hostess and a Social Worker. She cut her teeth on general features and travel articles for popular magazines and newspapers before moving onto fiction. Her latest novel, CHAIN OF DECEPTION was published by Headline in August, with her fourth, TAKEN, due out in January 2004.

www.bernardinekennedy.com

Sara MacDonald lives and writes in a cottage by the sea in West Cornwall. She has settled there after many years of travelling and living abroad. She has two sons. Her latest novel, SEA MUSIC, was published by Harper Collins in April 2003.

Jo Mazelis, was born in Swansea in 1956. Her stories have appeared in a number of magazines and anthologies and have been broadcast on Radio 4. She was one of the winners in the Rhys Davis Competition in both 1995 and 1999. Her collection of short stories, DIVING GIRLS was published by Parthian Books in 2002.

Linda Mitchelmore, Devon born and bred, began writing with a view to publication about six years ago, as a way of communication when her hearing began to deteriorate to the point where it became non-existent. She has now had stories published in all the weekly women's interest and has been shortlisted in and won numerous competitions.

Sue Moorcroft writes fiction for the weekly magazine market and has sold nearly ninety stories in five countries. She has just joined the panel of tutors at Writers' News

Home Study Division. In 2002 she was the RNA Katie Fforde Bursary Award winner.
www.suemoorcroft.tripod.com

Biddy Nelson has published over thirty stories in the-women's weekly magazine market, including *My Weekly* and *Fiction Feast*. Her next goal is to hit the forty mark while she works on her novel.

Caroline Praed has had short stories published in magazines such as *Bella* and *best*, and is currently completing a commissioned non-fiction book on education for children with autism. A member of the Romantic Novelists Association, in 2003 she won the Katie Fforde Bursary.

Sarah Salway's first novel SOMETHING BEGINNING WITH will be published in 2004 in the UK by Bloomsbury Publishing. She lives in Kent where she teaches creative writing. Her short story collection is available from www.eastoftheweb.com

David Wass, who hails from Bournemouth, has had a number of short stories published in women's magazines, on the internet, and has written two one-act plays, one of which has been performed by the KCA Players in Bournemouth whilst the other is scheduled to be produced at the end of 2003 by the Alfaz English Theatre group on the Spanish Costa Blanca where he temporarily resides.

Pam Weaver began her writing career in the late eighties after half a lifetime working with deprived children. Her short stories have been published in most of the popular women's magazines and on Radio 4. A member of West Sussex Writers' Club, Pam was made a lifetime honorary member for her services to the club in 1999. Pam now has ambitions to break into radio drama.

Jane Wenham-Jones lives in Broadstairs, Kent where she walks by the sea and dreams of fame. Her short stories and articles have been published in a variety of women's magazines and national newspapers and she writes a humorous column for her local paper. Her first novel RAISING THE ROOF was based on her experiences in the Buy-to-Let market and her second, PERFECT ALIBIS, has led to appearances on TV and radio to talk about infidelity.
Both books are published in paperback by Bantam.

Sophie Weston writes romances for Harlequin Mills and Boon; very long narrative poems about knights standing in the butter for godchildren; science fiction for anyone who will listen. Like Vladimir Brusillov, her influences are Tolstoy and P G Wodehouse. She has only written one, deeply private, short story before. And never published any. www.sophie-weston.com

Liz Young started writing after a variety of jobs that included cabin crewing for an airline, working for the Sultan's Armed Forces in Oman, and EFL teaching. She has two daughters and lives with her husband in Surrey. A GIRL'S BEST FRIEND will be published by Arrow in November 2003 and the film rights of her first book, ASKING FOR TROUBLE, have been sold.

If you have enjoyed this anthology, look out for **SEXY SHORTS FOR SUMMER** available Spring 2004.
For further information on events and publication dates, visit our website: www.sexyshorts.info

A word from Breast Cancer Campaign

Breast cancer is the most common form of cancer in the United Kingdom, it affects one woman in nine. But statistics cannot describe the impact of the disease on those women who are affected by it, nor on the friends and family who support them through it.

We look at the one woman in nine as someone's mother, someone's sister or someone's wife, and we believe that research is the only way forward if we are to prevent so many people from developing and dying from breast cancer.

Breast Cancer Campaign funds research which looks at improving diagnosis and treatment of breast cancer, better understanding how it develops and ultimately either curing the disease or preventing it. In the same way that breast cancer is not one disease, there will not be one cure. Breast Cancer Campaign's jigsaw piece logo symbolises the missing pieces of the puzzle that is the cure for breast cancer. Each research project is another piece of the puzzle that will offer all women with breast cancer effective diagnosis and treatment and eventually help us prevent the disease. That's why the Charity is currently supporting 43 research projects, worth over £3.8 million in 20 cities across the UK and over the past eight years has awarded

72 grants, with a total value of nearly £5 million to universities, medical schools/teaching hospitals and research institutes across the UK.

A donation of £1 is being made to Breast Cancer Campaign for every copy of 'Sexy Shorts' that is purchased. Breast Cancer Campaign is entirely reliant on voluntary donations to continue its vital work.

For further information or to make a donation, please contact:

Breast Cancer Campaign,
Clifton Centre,
110 Clifton Street,
London EC2A 4HT
Tel: 020 7749 3700
Fax: 020 7749 3701
www.breastcancercampaign.org

Registered Charity Number 299758